A Brief History
of Montmaray

A Brief History of Montmaray

Michelle Cooper

Alfred A. Knopf
New York

THIS IS A BORZOI BOOK PUBLISHED BY ALFRED A. KNOPF

Visit us on the Web! www.randomhouse.com/teens

Educators and librarians, for a variety of teaching tools, visit us at www.randomhouse.com/teachers

Library of Congress Cataloging-in-Publication Data
Cooper, Michelle.
A brief history of Montmaray / Michelle Cooper. — 1st American ed.
p. cm.
Summary: On her sixteenth birthday in 1936, Sophia begins a diary of life in a fictional island country off the coast of Spain, where she is among the last descendants of an impoverished royal family trying to hold their nation together on the eve of the second World War.
ISBN 978-0-375-85864-2 (trade) — ISBN 978-0-375-95864-9 (lib. bdg.) — ISBN 978-0-375-89359-9 (e-book)
[1. Family life—Europe—Fiction. 2. Princesses—Fiction. 3. Islands—Fiction. 4. Europe—History—1918-1945—Fiction. 5. Diaries—Fiction.] I. Title.
PZ7.C78748Bri 2009
[Fic]—dc22
2008049800

The text of this book is set in 10.5-point Goudy.

Printed in the United States of America
October 2009
10 9 8 7 6 5 4 3 2 1

First American Edition

This is the journal of
Sophia Margaret Elizabeth Jane Clementine FitzOsborne,
begun this twenty-third day of October 1936,

on the occasion of her sixteenth birthday.

23rd October 1936

Dear Sophie,

Happy birthday to my favorite little sister! I've been trying to recollect the day you were born so I can gush about it
in an appropriately sentimental fashion, but I'm afraid it's
all a blank. I must have been too busy pulling Veronica's hair
or smearing stewed apple over my smock to notice you popping into existence. I do remember Henry's arrival ten years
ago, and if you were anything like her, you were a most un-
attractive baby wrinkled, red-faced, loud, and rather
smelly. Lucky for all of us that you've improved somewhat
with age.

Now, did the presents arrive safely? I had to go all the
way to Knightsbridge for the journal, and then I got deten-
tion for sneaking off from Games, so I hope you appreciate
it. You can use it to write down your thoughts. You must
have plenty of them at the moment, given Aunt Charlotte's
letter—I assume you've read it by now. Are you thrilled?

3

Terrified? Well, it's all your fault for turning sixteen—you gave Aunt Charlotte quite a shock when she realized how old you'd suddenly become. She had to sit down and have an extra-large sherry to recover.

As for me, this new school is almost as ghastly as the old one. I suppose I'd been hoping Rupert would come too when I was thrown out of Eton, but his parents keep saying no, worse luck. The House Masters have finally sorted out dormitories, and now I share with three boys. Two are in the Rugby First XV, ugh. The other has noxious feet and learns the bagpipes, so is nearly as bad. I have already had two detentions, one for missing Games on Saturday and one for not doing Latin prep. The Latin prep wasn't my fault. I didn't know there was any prep because the Latin Master told us about it in Latin and I didn't understand a word he said.

Remember, I am in MarchHare House, so please make sure you put that on the address when you write, otherwise the letters might get lost. It's a good House to be in because it inevitably comes last in the House Cup, so no one cares much when I lose House points. The other good thing about MarchHare is that we can climb out the top-story windows onto the roof and look into the hospital next door, which is very educational. Also, sometimes the nurses come out onto a balcony to smoke, and they throw us a cigarette if we beg nicely.

It's almost lights-out, so I'd better finish. Tell Veronica

to come and live in my trunk so she can secretly do my Latin
prep for me. She could write my History essay as well, it is
on the Restoration. And ask her to bring Carlos with her so
he can eat the bagpipes.

Love from your wonderful brother,
Toby

As usual, Toby's letter was coded in Kernetin, which Toby and
my cousin Veronica and I invented years ago so we could write
notes to each other without the grown-ups being able to read
them. Kernetin is based on Cornish and Latin, with some Greek
letters and random meaningless squiggles thrown in to be extra
confusing. Also, it is boustrophedonic (I adore that word and
try to say it as often as possible, but unfortunately it hasn't many
everyday uses). "Boustrophedonic" means you read one line left
to right, then the next right to left. Veronica can translate Kernetin straight off the page into English, but I find it easier to
write it out, so there it is, my first entry in my new journal. It has
a hundred blank pages thick as parchment, and a morocco bind-
ing, and is *almost* too lovely to write in.

I did get some superb birthday presents this year. Veronica
gave me a pen with my initials on it. From my little sister, Henry,
came a new *Pride and Prejudice*, because I dropped my old one in
the bath and it hasn't been the same since. (Henry, who wishes
she'd been born a boy, looked quite disappointed when I opened
the journal from Toby—she'd probably told him to get me one of
those pocketknives with attached magnifying glass, screwdriver,

and fish-scaler, hoping that I'd then lend it to her.) The villagers presented me with a honey-spice cake, a lavender pillow, and a beautiful comb carved out of driftwood. Uncle John doesn't even know what year it is, let alone the date, so I never expect so much as a "Happy birthday" from him, but Rebecca, our house-keeper, gave me the day off from washing up the breakfast dishes. Even Carlos, our Portuguese water dog, managed a birthday card, signed with an inky paw-print (now I understand why Henry was being so secretive yesterday and how the bathtub ended up with all those black streaks).

And then there was Aunt Charlotte! I opened her letter long after breakfast was over because I couldn't imagine her approving of anything as indulgent as birthdays, but *that* turned out to be the most exciting part of the whole morning. I won't copy it all out, most of it being her usual scoldings about our idle, extravagant lives here on Montmaray, and do we think she's made of money, and so on. But here is the important part:

> . . . *and now that you are sixteen, Sophia, I am reminded yet again of the sad burden I have been forced to bear since my youngest brother and his wife were so cruelly torn from this world, God rest their souls. My only comfort is knowing how grateful Robert and Jane would be if they could see all that I have done for you children.*
>
> *However, my responsibilities are not yet complete, and your mother in particular, Sophia, would have wanted you to be given the same social opportunities she had. As for*

Veronica, it is not her fault that her feckless mother is who-knows-where and quite unable to make appropriate arrangements regarding a matrimonial match. I feel it is my duty, then, to sponsor your debuts into Society. We cannot postpone this event much longer, in light of your advancing ages.

I expect early in the new year would be the best time for both of you to travel to England. I leave it to Veronica to write to Mr. Grenville regarding steamer passage and railway tickets. In the meantime, I shall begin perusing the Almanach de Gotha for eligible prospects . . .

I took a moment to savor that glorious phrase "your debuts into Society," then raced off to the library tower, at the far end of the courtyard, in search of Veronica. She had locked the little black cat out and it was crying with rage on the doorstep. The door was barred from the inside, too, not just closed. I had to hammer at it for ages before she peered out.

"Oh, sorry," she said, opening the door wider. "I thought it was Henry being annoying again. No, you *can't* come in," she told the cat, but it had already shot past my legs and launched itself at Veronica. "Oh, for heaven's sake," she huffed, but the cat only curled its claws into her skirt and wailed harder. (All the castle cats are a bit mad; I'm not sure why. The ones down in the village seem quite normal.)

I thrust the letter at Veronica, threw myself upon the shredded-looking chaise longue, and glanced around while I waited for her to read it. Behind me were the tower stairs, winding their way up through five stories of books, most of which are bound in royal blue and stamped with the FitzOsborne crest. Veronica's domain, on the ground floor, is a large, square room that could be handsome if it tried. However, Veronica would rather it be serviceable, and so the desk is an old wooden door set on trestles; the papers on it are weighed down with stones; the walls that aren't hidden behind bookshelves are papered with navigation charts and genealogy lists; and everything reeks of tansy, which smolders in a little clay pot to ward off insects.

"Well?" I burst out as she refolded the letter with her usual precision and prepared to hand it back to me. "We can make our debuts next Season, can't we? Do say yes!"

"Why are you asking me?" Veronica plucked the cat off her skirt and deposited the wild-eyed creature next to me; it had stopped yowling by then. It immediately began sharpening its claws on the armrest. "Aunt Charlotte's the one who'd do the presenting at Court. I can't remember all the rules, but she was married to a British subject, so I'm sure that's all right."

"Yes, yes, she was presented after her wedding, but—"

"We'll find the money for dresses and shoes and things somehow, if that's what you're worried about," said Veronica. She hesitated, gnawing at her bottom lip. "We could always sell the King James Bible . . ."

"Veronica, no!" I said at once. Veronica may be an avowed atheist, but that Bible is her pride and joy. It's a first edition, first printing, said to have been owned by King James himself, and it's been in our family for more than three hundred years. "Absolutely not."

She smiled at me crookedly. "Well, I don't think we have anything else of value left to sell."

I shook my head. "The whole thing needn't be too expensive, and Aunt Charlotte will pay for it, she'll have to. I'll get Toby to ask her—she dotes on him."

"She ought to regard it as an investment," said Veronica wryly. "Once you've made your debut, you'll be invited to all those parties, where you'll meet a very rich banker and marry him and restore the FitzOsborne family fortune."

"As though any man would even glance at me with *you* in the room," I scoffed.

"Me?" said Veronica. "I'm not going."

"What?" I said, jumping to my feet.

"Well, someone needs to stay here to look after Henry and make sure Father doesn't go on a rampage," Veronica said. Then she caught sight of my face. "Now, Sophie. You surely didn't think *I'd* want to spend an evening curtseying to some foreign king, then having to make polite conversation at endless parties."

"But I can't do it by myself!" I cried. "I wouldn't even consider going to England without you!"

"Don't be silly, you'd be fine," she said. "Anyway, Toby will be there."

And so will Simon Chester, said a little voice in my head, but I brushed it away. "Veronica, I couldn't possibly—"

"Well, I'm not leaving Montmaray," she said. It's nearly impossible to shift Veronica once she's made up her mind. That didn't stop me trying, though.

"You'll have to leave at some stage," I pointed out. "How else will you get married?"

"Why would I need to?" she said. "Toby is the heir to the Montmaravian throne, he can have lots of children to carry on the family name. And you'll marry someone rich." She smiled. "It's a pity girls can't inherit in our family. 'Queen Veronica' has quite a nice ring to it, don't you think? But one can't argue with tradition. Oh well, Henry and I shall be spinsters, then. I'll be the dry, bookish sort and Henry will be the mad, adventuring sort."

"I'm being serious!" I protested. "What if you fall in love?"

"I won't," she said. "I'll just have lots of affairs with good-looking young men." Then she laughed at the expression on my face.

It's all very well for Veronica to joke about falling in love. She doesn't have the slightest idea how miserable it can make one feel, especially when the object of one's affection barely knows one exists. And even if he did realize I existed, even if he returned some of my feelings, it would be utterly, utterly impossible . . .

"Anyway, what did Toby have to say?" asked Veronica. I fished around in my pocket for his letter, then sat back down and frowned at the stone floor, trying to gather my thoughts into some sort of coherent argument. I knew that moving Veronica closer to my point of view would require all my mental resources, and then some. But I got distracted, as I tend to do, and started thinking about the herringbone pattern in which the stones were set and whether herrings really did have their bones arranged in that particular manner.

Then Rebecca started shrieking for Veronica and I went to see what she wanted, because poor Veronica gets so little time to work on her *Brief History* as it is. But it turned out that the upstairs loo had flooded again, and Veronica's the only one who can fix it. By the time we'd mopped up and washed the towels and hung them on the line, it was luncheon. And then the kitchen garden needed weeding, and one of the hens got her leg stuck in a loose bit of the cucumber frames, and one thing led to another, and before I knew it, the day was over.

And now here I am, sitting up in bed, scribbling away in my new journal by the light of the half-moon, Henry having borrowed my candle to visit the downstairs loo (she claims the upstairs one is too pink). It would be an ideal time to set down my thoughts about Aunt Charlotte's letter, but they are in such a muddle. On the one hand, it is, as Toby said, utterly thrilling. Oh, I can just picture the perfect debutante dress—chiffon of palest blue, with layer upon layer of floating skirt. Lovely new shoes with high heels, and silk stockings, and long white gloves. A necklace studded with sapphires, matching earrings, and— most gorgeous of all—a glittering diamond tiara . . .

Although I expect all the FitzOsborne jewels have been sold by now. And if Aunt Charlotte, as Princess Royal, firstborn daughter of the late King, has any of her own to lend us, Veronica ought to get first pick; she's the eldest. A tiara would look ridiculous on me anyway, with my colorless, frizzy hair (Toby and Henry got the blond curls, lucky things) and my bumpy nose (Toby accidentally threw a croquet mallet at me when I was three).

Besides, Veronica has refused to go—and I can't even contemplate the idea of being separated from her. We've shared a room ever since I was born. We're closer than even sisters could be. And then, the thought of leaving Montmaray is so horrible . . .

And yet how can we possibly ignore Aunt Charlotte's orders? We have to do as she says; she's the only proper grown-up left to look after us, even if she is all the way over there in England. Officially, the head of our household is Uncle John, who is Aunt Charlotte's brother and Veronica's father (and the King of Montmaray), but he's rather distracted on his good days, and downright alarming on his bad ones (though we do our best to keep *that* quiet). Besides, Aunt Charlotte's the only one with any money—she married an elderly coal magnate named Sir Arthur Marlowe, who promptly died and left her a fortune—so we rely on her to pay for Toby's schooling and just about everything else. I've never met her, but based on her letters and Toby's reports, I can't imagine anyone actually saying no to her. Except Veronica, of course.

It's at moments such as these that I almost wish I were religious—then I could pray for guidance, leaving the decision in heavenly hands. But even though I'm fond of many bits of the Bible—the Garden of Eden, baby Moses in the bulrushes, the Nativity—I find it hard to believe that a real God is behind them. Isn't it enough that they're beautiful stories? Besides, religious people can be so unpleasant. Rebecca this morning, for example, screaming that Henry was the spawn of the Devil and swiping at her with the rolling pin, just because Henry chalked a hopscotch grid on the chapel's flagstones. One can't blame Henry—those flagstones are exactly the right size, and there's lots of room now the pews are gone (we used up the last of them two winters ago when we ran out of firewood during a tremendous storm). The rest of us were just relieved Henry had found a way to use up some of that excess energy of hers.

And speaking of Henry, where on earth is she with my candle? She's been gone half an hour. Either she's fallen down the loo and drowned, or she's gone fishing with her friend Jimmy from the village. It really is *too* bad of her. Why can't she use her own candle if she's going to go wandering across the island in the middle of the night? She'd better not drop the candlestick holder—it's the last silver one we own. (I'm not concerned about Henry; *she's* pretty much indestructible. She fell off a cliff once and didn't do anything but scrape her elbow a bit.) She always runs wild once Toby leaves for school each year—not that she's much better-behaved when he's here at Montmaray. Here is my New Year's resolution, then, ten months late—I resolve to be firmer with Henry.

And now the moon has shrunk behind a cloud and it really is much too dark to see. I'm going to lie under the blanket and have a good think, and if I think anything particularly profound, I'll have to write it down tomorrow.

24th October 1936

I did have several thoughts last night after I put my book away, but they were pathetic rather than profound. They were, I must admit, mostly about Simon Chester, Rebecca's son. My thoughts have been wandering relentlessly in his direction ever since his last visit, at the start of summer. He is not exactly a visitor, having lived at Montmaray for all those years before he went off to London. However, that was so long ago that I can't help imagining how he must see us now. Not that he *does* see me. And no wonder he barely notices I exist—I'm so dull, compared to the others. Veronica is clever (even Simon acknowledges that, and the two of them loathe each other). Toby is charming, funny, and handsome. Henry is like a Force of Nature. I am neither pretty nor strong-willed nor particularly talented at anything, which doesn't usually bother me except when Simon is here. He makes me feel so dissatisfied with myself! Except I have no idea how to go about improving the situation, so I just berate myself silently, which makes it worse, like picking at a scab.

(Note: Whenever I feel like this, I must pretend to be Veronica and say firmly to myself, *Who on earth cares what Simon Chester thinks, anyway?* Then think very hard about some other subject.)

All right.

Lovely weather we've been having lately.

Oh, it's no good. I might as well write it down—it's not as though anyone else is going to read this (I've found an excellent hiding place for my book). I'm not sure that it's *love*, exactly—what I feel for Simon. Perhaps it's just a peculiar and embarrassing type of curiosity. During his last visit, for example, I found myself staring at his strong fingers curled around the salt-cellar and admiring the precision of the comb furrows in his shiny hair. It could simply be that he's the only young man I know who is not related to me, but it's all very awkward. For one thing, Veronica would be horrified if she found out, and it's awful not being able to speak with her about something important. Usually we talk about absolutely everything. Not that Simon's really important—I mean, it's not as though I'm planning to *marry* him. But I'll have to marry someone, at some stage, and if I'm this inept at being charming and interesting around Simon, then my prospects of attracting anyone better are fairly dim.

Heavens, what a snob I sound! But it's not my fault I'm a princess (albeit one from an impoverished and inconsequential island kingdom that is miles from anywhere). *I* can't help all the rules and regulations that govern those born into our noble and ancient family. And I can't exactly tell Aunt Charlotte, "Sorry,

I'm unable to accept the proposal of Erich Ludwig-Wilhelm, that young Habsburg you've managed to unearth—you see, I've fallen in love with the housekeeper's son."

Oh, change the subject, Sophia!

All right, I will look out the gatehouse window and contemplate the view. Yes, that's better. Unlike me, it is very beautiful, especially at this time of year. I can only imagine how mysterious and menacing the island must seem to strangers. An enormous black rock looming out of the ocean, its jagged peaks circled by seabirds and wisps of cloud. Towering cliffs with caves gashed into their faces. A narrow, windswept plateau at one end. The grim memorial cross at South Head, dozens of dead men's names etched into the stone under a single date. Abandoned cottages scattered along the edge of a dark, deep pool, their roof slates long blown away and great gaping holes where the doors and windows were. And then there is the castle, stark and forbidding, cut off from the rest of the island by a perilous chasm.

But when one has lived on Montmaray all one's life, when one's family has lived here for centuries, it is simply *home*. That long stretch of rock spread thinly with grass, for instance—we call it the Green, and it's where we build our Midsummer bonfire each year. The Great Pool is for summer picnics and swimming races. The line of rocks past the old cottages is where we gather mussels; the cove at the base of the most imposing cliff is the best place to sink lobster pots. Wild strawberries spring up around the base of the memorial cross each summer, sheltering under the rosemary bushes. The hill is spread with sweet-smelling briar and whispering grasses, with bright patches of asters and heartsease and Bartholomew's treasure. Then, either side of the hill, there is the beautiful indigo sea, rolling on and on and up into the sky. As for the sky itself—well, *infinity*, that's the only way I can describe it. Nothing interrupts it. Toby says that in London, there are places where one looks up and can only see a tiny square of sky, and it's hardly ever blue. No wonder the people in city streets always look so grim in photographs. No wonder *I* feel grim at the thought of ever having to leave the island . . .

And now I can see Veronica, striding through the tall purple grass and looking the very opposite of grim. She has her canvas satchel strapped across her front and a bundle of driftwood for the stove under one arm. She's probably on her way back from visiting George in the village. We call it the village because of all the cottages, but really, only one family lives there now. Well, two—the Smiths and the Spensers—but they're all related. The Smiths are Jimmy, who is a bit older than Henry, and his widowed mother, Alice. The Spenser family is Mary, Alice's sister, and George, Jimmy's great-great-uncle.

No one knows how old George is, but he claims to remember the wedding of Queen Victoria of England (which, personally, I have my doubts about—it would make him nearly a hundred). But it's certainly true that he knows more about Montmaray than anyone else alive, which is one of the reasons Veronica loves spending time with him. Another is that she can practice her Cornish with him, as he's the only one left on the island who speaks it fluently. She writes down everything he says, in Cornish or in English, and then adds it to the mountain of paper in the library that will eventually become *A Brief History of Montmaray*. She has been hammering away at this for the past three years and says she's barely made a dent in it. It's very intellectual—she read me out a bit yesterday on the Portuguese-Montmaravian Alliance of 1809 and I barely understood a word.

Normally Henry would be down at the village, too, but I think she went back to bed after breakfast (she *did* go out fishing last night, the horrible child). Henry is meant to do three hours of lessons every morning now that Toby is back at school, but she's managed to avoid them so far. Not that Veronica or I have pushed *too* hard for lessons to resume, because we're the ones who are supposed to teach her. When we were her age, we had a governess and tutors; but there was more money then, and besides, there was Toby to consider (it would have been quite embarrassing if he'd turned up at Eton unable to read). After Toby went away to school, Veronica and I mostly taught ourselves from books in the library. Veronica, of course, proved to be much better at developing her mind than I was. (One could argue that this was because she had a better mind to begin with. However, one could also argue that I've squandered countless hours reading romantic novels, planning my future trousseau, and daydreaming about Simon, hours that could have been far better employed learning French grammar or reading Plato.)

Aunt Charlotte did continue to dispatch tutors to us at irregular intervals for a while, but they didn't tend to last long.

Often it turned out their agency had neglected to mention that we live on a small island in the middle of the Bay of Biscay, and they didn't cope very well when they ran out of cigarettes or face powder and realized that the nearest shop was two hundred miles away.

Or worse, we were sent the sort of girl who thought that living in a castle would be madly poetic, who pictured herself drifting along the wall-walk in a flowing gown whilst reciting Keats, or trailing her fingertips in the moat as swans glided by. We don't have a moat, just a rickety drawbridge that connects the castle to the rest of the island. There *is* water beneath the drawbridge, at the bottom of the Chasm, but it contains sharks rather than swans. Furthermore, climbing the ladder to the top of the curtain wall while wearing a flowing gown would look very undignified, especially in howling gales and torrential rain, which is our usual weather for a great deal of the year. Even when one of these girls managed to last more than a fortnight in the absence of hot baths and electric lights, *something* always happened—Henry would accidentally-on-purpose lock her in the Blue Room with the ghost, or Uncle John would tip his soup over her, or Veronica would catch her mixing up her ablative and her accusative during Latin translation and be very scathing. It always ended in tears, and the tears were rarely ours.

Anyway, I decided that this morning was not the time to confront Henry on the issue of lessons. So much for my resolution to be firmer, but I'm never at my best first thing in the morning and I was feeling especially wobbly today because I had that dream again last night. Perhaps I should have written "nightmare." I don't know whether it is or not—I see the same thing each time, and sometimes I feel quite calm about it and other times I wake up gasping and trembling and longing to shake Veronica awake for a dose of her logical comfort.

Last night was somewhere in between. As always, I was alone in a small boat, rocking back and forth with the slap of the waves, my fingernails digging into the damp wood. The sky was black and silver, but there was no wind, no lightning, nothing truly threatening—and yet the back of my neck began to prickle with dread. I knew that whatever I did, I mustn't look down into the water, but I couldn't help myself and there it was. That *thing*. Long and white and unraveling, just beyond my reach, drifting slowly towards the ocean floor.

I never manage to figure out what it is. Sometimes I'm almost certain it's a fragment of sail wrapped round a sinking mast. Other times I think it's a dying sunfish. Or a shark. Last night, I could have sworn a part of it moved sluggishly against the current, as though it were trying to signal to me.

But then I woke up, shivering.

And now Veronica is marching across the drawbridge, which makes me shiver all over again. I always step very warily, taking care not to look down through the gaps where the slats have rotted away (it's not heights I mind, so much as depths). Peering further out the gatehouse window, I can make out the green-and-white swell of the sea below her, deceptively calm today. "The spent deep feigns her rest," as Kipling would say. It makes me picture all the torn-apart ships and picked-clean skeletons shifting about beneath the waves, victims of Montmaray's treacherous rocks. Oh, all those poor dead sailors, eels slithering through their staring eye sockets . . .

What's that noise?! Oh. It's probably just some of Toby's pigeons nesting in the chimney. It *couldn't* be ghosts; ghosts don't make cooing noises, and besides, I don't think anyone ever died up here. (Note: Ask Veronica about this.) I wouldn't really mind if there was a ghost, so long as it was friendly—the one in the Blue Room is. Anyway, a ghost would keep Rebecca away. She's fearfully superstitious; it's one of her many faults.

Well, whatever the mysterious sound is, it's not very good at repelling Rebecca after all, because she's just shouted up the ladder that she needs me to go down to the village for the milk. Isn't that supposed to be Henry's job? Bother. Will write more later . . .

No idea what the date is, 1936

Rebecca has been in a lather of cleaning all week. She usually gets the villagers up to help, but I think she's had another row with Alice, so there was No Escape for me. It is very annoying; I haven't had five seconds to myself to think about Aunt Charlotte's plan, so I still have no idea how I can convince Veronica to go to England—or even if I really want to leave Montmaray. Also, now I reek of scouring powder and ache in muscles that I didn't know existed. However, I have *just* enough energy to sit up in bed and write a page or two. Veronica has generously donated her candle (mine is less than a stub, and we are down to only five for the whole castle). Handing it over, she told me how wonderful it was to see a FitzOsborne taking the trouble to write a detailed account of life on Montmaray and how historians in two hundred years' time would praise my name. I don't think she was *entirely* joking, so I haven't had the heart to explain that my journal is subjective and rambling and will be completely useless to historians, especially as I can't even remember the date

(I think it may be November by now, but can't be bothered to get up and look at the calendar).

Poor Veronica—it's a source of enormous frustration to her and her *Brief History* that most of our ancestors seem to have been either illiterate or wild fantasists. Take, for example, Edward de Quincy FitzOsborne, the family's only writer of note. His most famous work is an epic poem that describes how Bartholomew FitzOsborne (then merely a baron) was forced to flee his Cornish estate in 1542, sailed south, tangled with a sea monster for a day and a night, defeated it valiantly, and then washed up on the shore of an uninhabited island halfway between France and Spain. This he declared his new kingdom, which he called Montmaray.

In fact, no large ship has ever washed up in one piece on Montmaray—the rocks and the currents are too dangerous. Most likely Bartholomew was shipwrecked as he made his way to Spain, but managed to salvage enough to survive until he could send some men off for supplies. Edward also completely avoids the question of what Bartholomew did in the first place to so enrage his King, Henry the Eighth, that he was forced to flee. (Although Veronica has pointed out that Catherine Howard, Henry's then wife, was beheaded that same year for adultery, which may not be a complete coincidence.) Furthermore, Montmaray—mangled Latin for "Mountain of the Sea"—was not named until nearly forty years later. Possibly there was some initial dispute over whether Bartholomew was truly entitled to call himself a king. I believe the usual method is to lead an army into bloody battle

and emerge the victor, having slaughtered anyone who might dis-
agree with one's claims to loyalty. Still, it wasn't as though there
were any people here to conquer—just a lot of puffins and lob-
sters. At any rate, they must have sorted it out, because Queen
Elizabeth referred to Bartholomew's son as "King John" when she
thanked him for helping her defeat the Spanish Armada. We
have the letter in the library, not that anyone can read much of
it except the "Elizabeth R" at the end (penmanship wasn't her
strong point).

Also, George did tell Veronica that he once saw a giant
squid while he was fishing off South Head as a boy. He said it
wrapped its tentacles around their gig, then seemed to realize
that long wooden boats are not at all tasty and vanished in a
cloud of black ink. So perhaps there is some truth to the sea
monster story after all. And even if there isn't, it does make a
nice tapestry over there on the far wall of our bedroom, beside
the wardrobe. The sea monster is picked out in silver thread and
is devouring one of the sailors headfirst. The other sailors are
lined up glumly along the deck of the ship, awaiting their turn.
Bartholomew himself is clinging to a mast and brandishing his
longsword—the very sword that Rebecca made me polish earlier
this week. It is named Benedict and hangs in the Great Hall over
the chimneypiece. In those days, swords were always christened,
because they were in the shape of a cross and therefore holy. Isn't
that interesting? Sometimes I quite understand why Veronica
spends all her spare time interrogating George about ancient
customs and poring over crumbling bits of parchment. She also

told me that after Bartholomew died, his son stuck the sword up on the wall of the Great Hall and declared: "Benedict will protect the House of FitzOsborne, now and for eternity!"

Except he said it in French, which is what all noblemen spoke in those days, or possibly in Latin, so it must have sounded even more impressive. In any case, this has been translated to mean that we need to keep it razor-sharp at all times, no matter how many nicked fingers I end up with whenever I take it down for polishing.

I also asked Veronica tonight whether anyone had ever died in the gatehouse. She said the nearest she could recall was when one of King Stephen's sentries got drunk on shipwreck brandy and fell through the murder hole, breaking his leg.

"But did he die?" I asked.

"Well, I'm sure he did eventually die of *something*," said Veronica. "Everyone does in the end, you know."

The murder hole is a square cut into the gatehouse floor and covered with a trapdoor. It was built so castle defenders could pour hot sand on enemies who managed to make it across the drawbridge. Apparently hot sand can get inside a suit of armor better than anything and is absolutely agonizing, so I'm glad no enemies ever got that far. Imagine how malevolent their ghosts would be. Anyway, the pigeon theory is now looking much stronger than the ghost theory, regarding the mysterious noises coming from the gatehouse chimney. Homing pigeons were one of Toby's seven-day enthusiasms last year. He and Henry built a loft—more of a pigeon palace, actually—but a few of the birds escaped. Henry looks after the remaining half a dozen, and makes me include detailed reports on their well-being whenever I write letters to Toby.

However, I'm neglecting today's most important event—the Basque captain's cargo ship stopped by. Henry, Jimmy, and I rowed out in the *Queen Clementine*, our little rowboat, and traded a bucket of Montmaray mussels (Captain Zuleta is inexplicably fond of the horrid, beardy things) for proper food, namely:

1. Two pineapples

2. A tin of cheddar crackers

3. A box of Turkish delight, tied up with pink and gold ribbon.

He also gave us some newspapers that he indicated he'd found lying around the ship—he knows what little news we get of the outside world. He really does seem a very nice man, even if I can barely understand a word he says.

We gave Alice one of the pineapples and half the crackers (it was only fair; Jimmy had gathered most of the mussels). I do love visiting Alice—I wish *she'd* been the one, rather than Rebecca, to come up to the castle to take care of us after my parents were killed. Alice is soft and sweet-natured instead of bony and sharp-tongued; also, she can cook. Today her cottage smelled of thyme and shallots and sweet peppers and codfish, all bubbling away over the fire. One of her cats was crouched beneath the rocking chair, dabbing at a hermit crab with a curious paw, and the other was washing itself on the hearthrug. Sitting down in a puddle of sunlight at the table, I felt a bit like purring myself, it was so warm and cozy (although it's probably not at all cozy in the middle of a storm—I bet her roof leaks even worse than ours).

"Well now," said Alice after she'd finished exclaiming over the pineapples (neither of us had a clue what to do with them, but I promised to ask Veronica and report back). "And how are things up at the castle, Your Highness?"

I keep asking Alice not to call me that—it's ridiculous when there are now as many Royal Highnesses on the island as there are subjects—but she's very old-fashioned and it's no use. So I helped her shell a basin of peas and told her what had been happening, which was not much. (Henry had dropped a jar of honeycomb and the tabby cat rolled in it and glued itself to the pantry floor; the hens had somehow got into the chapel.)

On the way back, we passed Mary, who was weeding the vegetable garden, and George, who was sitting on his doorstep, mending a fishing net. George looked rather disappointed to see us without Veronica. He's fond of Henry and polite to me, but Veronica's the one he adores. I'm not sure whether it's because she's the only one who'll sit for hours listening to his stories, or because she's the King's daughter. George was manservant to our grandfather when he was King, so George is even more old-fashioned than Alice when it comes to royalty. Dear old George! He's gaunt and leathery-looking, pickled in salt water and rum, but still agile and sharp-witted. And *so* knowledgeable about the rocks and the currents and the fish and so on—Henry and Jimmy are quite in awe of him.

Speaking of Henry, she made a great ceremony of presenting the Turkish delight to Veronica when we reached the castle. Veronica didn't go out to meet the ship this time because she was cleaning out Vulcan, our ill-tempered stove. Henry claimed the Basque captain had sent along the sweets as "a totem of his affection."

"Do you mean a token?" asked Veronica, pushing her hair off her forehead and leaving a smudge of charcoal. "A token is a symbol or a sign, whereas a totem is an animal used in primitive cultures to represent a particular—"

"Yes, one of those," cried Henry gleefully. "'Cause he's in *love* with you!"

It's true that we always seem to get a better trade for the mussels when Veronica goes out in the rowboat, and it doesn't surprise me that men would be attracted to her. After all, her mother was a Celebrated Beauty (according to an old *Tatler* I found, which had a whole page about Isabella's engagement in it) and Veronica looks more and more like Isabella each day. Except that Veronica doesn't always bother about brushing her hair or that sort of thing, because she generally has more important matters on her mind.

Anyway, she was far more delighted by the newspapers than the sweets—Veronica likes facts, especially fresh ones. (Oh, there's an idea—could Veronica be lured to England by the promise of unlimited supplies of newspapers?) Actually, it's a pity

Veronica didn't go out in the boat today—she could have asked the Basque captain for candles or some paraffin for the lamps, as she's the only one of us who speaks Spanish. Still, the supply ship is due next week, so we will just have to do without until then. In the meantime, I suppose I should confine my writing to daylight hours. And give Veronica her candle back.

2nd November 1936

This morning, I came downstairs in my threadbare nightgown in search of my hairbrush (Henry had borrowed it when I'd not been awake enough to object) and found Simon Chester sitting at the kitchen table.

"Simon!" I gasped. "What . . . how . . . ?" Then I remembered that I'd outgrown my nightgown bodice some months back and hurriedly crossed my arms, meanwhile turning an unflattering shade of scarlet (I could even feel my elbows blushing). I wish I didn't blush so easily. Veronica never blushes. This is because she has Poise, something I sadly lack.

"Good morning, Sophia," said Simon, glancing up with his usual half smile. (I've yet to figure out whether this is because he's never *wholly* happy or because he's worried about displaying his slightly uneven teeth.) He politely ignored my embarrassment and began to explain how he'd got a ride on a steamship headed for Lisbon.

Halfway through his account, Veronica walked in with the

egg basket. "And I don't suppose you thought to bring any candles with you," she said, as though they were continuing an argument, which they probably were.

"No," said Simon, glaring at her. Veronica gave him a withering look in return and stalked over to the sink.

"But does Rebecca know you're here?" I asked.

"Oh, yes," he said. "She's just gone in there." He nodded towards Uncle John's room, glanced at Veronica's rigid back, then lowered his voice. "And how *is* His Majesty?" Simon asked me.

"The same," I said as Veronica smashed an egg with unnecessary force against the rim of the mixing bowl. (Veronica maintains that her father's odd behavior is pure self-indulgence and attention-seeking, and that Rebecca just encourages him.) Simon nodded slowly.

"Well, I brought some papers that need his signature," he said. Simon works as a clerk for Mr. Grenville, our family's solicitor. "And Toby needs more pocket money. The account's almost empty. I'm afraid the Princess Royal . . ." But he didn't need to explain to us that Aunt Charlotte had paid for the bare essentials this term, and nothing else.

"How much?" asked Veronica, turning.

"Twenty-five pounds should do for the term," he said. "With some left over for next." Toby tries to be as thrifty as he can, but there are all sorts of things outside school fees to pay for—sweets and postage stamps and bootlaces and so on. Although he does spend most of it on presents for us, I must admit.

"I want to see the accounts," Veronica said, swinging the cast-iron frying pan down from its hook in a rather threatening manner.

"Of course," said Simon, and they glared at each other a bit more.

Meanwhile, I was wishing I could tidy my hair (it must have looked a complete fright), but my hairbrush, lying on the draining board, was matted with our dog Carlos's black curls. So I switched to thinking about what we could sell next. All the good china and crystal went a long time ago, along with the small, valuable bits of French furniture and the coin collection and the Ming vases. Despite the various antiques cluttering the Great Hall, I couldn't think of anything that a stranger, or even a Fitz-Osborne, would pay good money for. But then I remembered Great-aunt Elizabeth's Russian suitor.

"What about the egg?" I wondered aloud. Veronica frowned down at her mixing bowl. "The Fabergé egg," I added quickly.

"Oh, yes," said Veronica. "I'd forgotten about that."

"What *are* you talking about?" said Simon.

So I took Simon into the Great Hall to show him, snatching up Rebecca's shawl to wrap around my top half as we passed her chair. I have to say that the Great Hall is probably my least favorite part of the castle. The portraits all seem to glare, and there is simultaneously too much cold empty space and too much clutter, most of it ugly. There are moth-eaten bear rugs, five enormous clocks (none of which work properly), an elephant's foot bristling with walking sticks and broken umbrellas, dozens of uncomfortable chairs, a Steinway grand badly in need of tuning, and a vast collection of battle-stained halberds and maces (and I don't care what Veronica says, it's *blood*, not rust, on that dented mace over the chapel door).

It's such a chore keeping the place tidy, too. Rebecca has been making us tackle it bit by bit over the past week, and yesterday we had to do the flagstones. Henry sat on a rag and tried to get Carlos to pull her up and down on the section of floor she was waxing, but Carlos got overexcited and ran into the suit of armor. After we put it back together again, we found we had a bit left over, but Henry hid it inside the piano before Rebecca could find out. Not that it would be any of Rebecca's business if we decided to toss the entire thing off South Head at high tide, but she does get rather worked up about certain family possessions—generally souvenirs of that time, long past, when we were rich and powerful. One would think Rebecca was a FitzOsborne herself, the way she fusses about the family heritage.

Anyway, I knew exactly where the egg was—in the big glass-fronted cabinet, tucked away behind Montmaray's only Olympic medal (fencing, Paris, 1900) and an old silver hurling ball engraved with the words GUARE WHEAG YU GUARE TEAG ("Gentle play is handsome play," according to George, who can remember the hurling matches that used to be held each Shrove Tuesday, Castle versus Village, and were anything but gentle). I opened the cabinet, plucked out the egg, and held it up for Simon's inspection. It was the size and shape of a hen's egg, but enameled red, green, and blue, studded with a swirling pattern of tiny rubies and emeralds.

"Great-aunt Elizabeth always thought it was rather vulgar," I told Simon. I flicked the catch at the side and the top swung open, revealing a hollow lined with blue velvet. "There used to be a miniature portrait of her in here, on a little gold easel, but I don't know where it's got to. What do you think it's worth?"

Simon peered at it, sunlight glinting off the gems and streaking his black hair gaudy colors. His eyelashes, as long and thick as Veronica's, were a terrible distraction. "Who did you say gave it to her?" he asked.

I shook my head. "Some Russian nobleman. Veronica will know."

"If he were one of the Romanovs, it might be worth more," he said. "The Bolsheviks sold some Imperial eggs a few years ago and the Americans paid a couple of hundred pounds each."

"Really? A couple of hundred *pounds*?" I said, looking at the egg with new respect even though I couldn't help agreeing with Great-aunt Elizabeth's opinion. Imagine all the dresses and shoes and things that two hundred pounds could buy! Then the loudest and ugliest of the clocks started to toll and kept on going till thirteen o'clock. "It's a pity you can't take one of *them* to sell," I sighed. I put the egg back on its gold stand for the time being and two of the other clocks started up. "Or all of them," I added. Then Henry yelled that breakfast was ready and we went back to the kitchen.

Simon must find us terribly primitive after living in London for so long. He rides an underground train to his office, and his landlady has an electrical machine for making toast. Watching him eat scrambled eggs with one of the bent forks, I was painfully aware that our windowpane, broken last Christmas, still hadn't been mended, and that one of the cats had been sick on the doorstep again.

Not that Simon gave any indication that he disapproved, or had even noticed. Although this may have been because he was too busy dealing with Rebecca's questioning. Was his landlady giving him meat at every meal? He was so pale, was he sure he wasn't anemic? Had he been taking his tonic? Was his room well aired and his mattress turned weekly? And on and on until Veronica couldn't bear to hear another word and asked for the latest news on the war in Spain. The newspapers the Basque captain had given us had turned out to be mostly in Portuguese, and Veronica was still trying to decipher them. At any rate, Simon said, how could anyone expect Portuguese newspapers to tell the unvarnished truth when everyone knew that Salazar supported Franco? Then he went on to inform us that Madrid was under attack, the Nationalists had closed Spain's border with France, and the Basques had established an autonomous government in the north.

This meant almost nothing to me, but Veronica started chewing on her lip.

"There's an international committee been set up in London to discuss the situation," he added. "No one wants it turning into another Great War. And if there's a non-intervention agreement signed, as there will be, then I believe . . ." He cleared his throat. "*I* believe that Montmaray should be part of it."

Veronica's expression went from thoughtful to scathing in an instant.

"As one of Spain's closest neighbors," Simon continued, squaring his shoulders but unable to prevent a faint (and, in my opinion, rather attractive) flush creeping into his cheeks, "if any nation has an interest in avoiding an international conflict, then surely Montmaray—"

"And how exactly is Montmaray going to contribute to this international effort?" Veronica asked. "Send George out in the rowboat to stop German submarines from smuggling arms to Franco? For that matter, whom do you propose to send to these diplomatic meetings in London?"

Simon shifted in his seat. "Well, Toby is heir to the throne . . ."

My brother Toby is the dearest person in the world, but I'm certain he has even less of an idea about Spanish politics than I do.

"With you as his advisor, I suppose," scoffed Veronica.

"And why not?" said Rebecca indignantly, turning from the stove. "Henry, run and fetch some of that blackberry jam Simon likes from the pantry, and mind you don't let the jar slip this time." Henry dropped her napkin in her egg and dashed out, not wanting to miss any more of the argument than she could help. "And anyhow," said Rebecca, setting a fresh pile of egg and chives in front of Simon, "there's only *one* who can decide on matters of state."

Simon half smiled at Veronica. "And it isn't you," he said as his mother gave Uncle John's closed door a reverent look.

"And it isn't you, either," said Veronica in an equally sweet tone, and I got the impression that I was witnessing the opening round of yet another of their epic battles, one that would probably still be in progress long after the dust had settled on the Spanish war. I resolved to ask Veronica to explain the whole Spanish situation to me as soon as possible, so I could sit through at least one meal while Simon was here without feeling a complete idiot.

I managed to catch up with her in the library after luncheon.

"We're going to have to do something about Simon Chester," Veronica announced before I'd even settled myself on the chaise longue.

"Er . . . what?" I said, feeling a little thrill of pleasure at the very sound of his name—even though I knew Veronica would have nothing good to say about him. "I mean, why?"

"Because," she said, "he has Ambitions." She began pacing the floor and waited for me to ask what she meant, which I did at once. "It was a mistake to allow him that job in the first place," she said over one shoulder. "A few months of carrying files between offices and he fancies himself capable of taking over diplomatic duties for Montmaray! How he ever managed to talk my father into letting him . . . All *Rebecca's* influence, of course . . ."

Watching her was making me dizzy, so I concentrated on poking some of the horsehair stuffing back into the chaise longue.

"But it's too late now," Veronica said. She whirled around. "What's important is that we keep a careful eye on him. And the accounts."

"Are you saying that Simon is . . . taking money from us?" I said, trying to keep up.

"Perhaps not," Veronica admitted. "I'm not sure he wants money, as such. No, no—he wants to be *important*." Her lip curled. "He wants to join committees and dine with Cabinet ministers and be interviewed by newspapermen, *that* sort of thing."

Which all sounded terribly boring to me, and it wasn't as though any of us could do it instead. Veronica and I are girls, Toby is still at school, and Uncle John is out of the question, even if he *is* King. As far as I was concerned, Simon was welcome to it, and I said so.

"But he's not a FitzOsborne!" cried Veronica. "He doesn't have the best interests of Montmaray at heart, the way we do. He doesn't even live here! And that's another thing. He has *far* too much influence over Toby. It'll be even worse now that Toby is at school in London—he's barely two miles from Simon Chester's doorstep. Who knows what Simon's capable of talking poor Toby into? And you know how sweet and trusting Toby is . . ."

I wasn't so sure about that. I think Toby might be far

stronger-willed than he appears. For example, look at how he managed to get himself thrown out of Eton. He'd hated everything about it (except Rupert Stanley-Ross, his best friend from their very first day), but Aunt Charlotte was determined Toby should stay. All the FitzOsborne men had gone there; he would be breaking a tradition that had lasted hundreds of years; he ought to think of all the important social connections he would make . . . But Toby had his way in the end. He generally does; it's just that he's so charming about it that no one minds or even notices. Also, it seems perfectly natural to me that Toby would look up to Simon a bit, Simon being five years older and rather charming himself.

But I can't expect Veronica to be swayed on this particular subject, especially not by someone as useless at arguing as me. I had also hoped I might be able to bring up the topic of our going to England, but I couldn't think of any convincing arguments for that, either. All I could come up with was that moving there would enable her to keep a closer eye on Simon. Except that they're both happiest when they're as far away from each other as possible. So instead, I asked Veronica to explain the Spanish situation to me, and while I succeeded in getting her off the dangerous topic of Simon, I'm not sure I actually understood much of what she said. Perhaps writing it down will make it clearer.

Firstly, the things I already knew. I know the King of Spain, Alfonso the Thirteenth, was forced into exile a few years ago. I remember having a discussion about it with Daniel, our tutor at the time, who said that the Spanish people had blamed the King when they lost the Moroccan war. He also said the King had done some terrible things—executed people who didn't agree with him, for example—and that when the Spanish people finally had the chance to vote in democratic elections in 1931, they voted for a Republic and King Alfonso was forced to leave and Good Riddance to Bad Rubbish. That's what Daniel said (Daniel may have been a tiny bit *Communist*, now that I think back on it).

What Daniel didn't realize is that Veronica is related to King Alfonso through her mother (I think Alfonso and Isabella are second cousins or something). Poor Daniel was very embarrassed when he realized. But Veronica didn't mind, partly because Daniel was so nice, but mostly because she despised anything to do with her mother, who had left a few years earlier and not bothered to send us so much as a postcard. Anyway, once King Alfonso was out of the way, the Spanish government made lots of liberal reforms, allowing divorce and letting women vote and that sort of thing, which made some people upset.

That was the bit I already knew. What happened earlier this year is that there were more elections and the Popular Front won narrowly. The Popular Front, according to Veronica, is mostly Communists and Socialists, but there are also some Basque separatists from the north, who of course are not Spanish at all and have a language of their own (I know this because of the Basque captain, as well as all the Basque fishermen we see around here).

This new Popular Front government made certain people— the military, the Fascist Party, people who supported the

King—rather unhappy, so a couple of months ago, General Franco started his rebellion against the government. And this is where I started to get lost. Apparently the Germans and the Italians are helping Franco, because they are all Fascists and hate the Communists. The Russians are helping the Popular Front government, because they are Communists and hate the Fascists. The Basques have set up their own separate government in the north. And Britain and France don't want anyone but the Spanish to be involved in the conflict, because it might lead to another Great War. And now I have an enormous headache from trying to make sense of all this. There is more, but I will have to write it down later. First I have to go and make some betony tea for my poor head.

3rd November 1936

I didn't have time to finish all I wanted to say yesterday, but will try to do so now. It's been a very unsettling morning, though. A keening wind blew up before dawn, rattling windows and slamming doors and startling me out of *that* dream (which had just started to turn nightmarish, so it was a relief to be awake, however early it was). Then Henry came into the kitchen before breakfast and announced that the hens were behaving very strangely.

"Running round in circles. And the speckled one is missing. Do you think the others *attacked* her?"

"Full moon last night," said Rebecca lugubriously before disappearing upstairs with another jug of hot water.

Veronica snorted. "What does she think they are, werechickens?"

"I could only find one egg," said Henry. "And I looked everywhere."

"It's probably just the change in the weather," I said. "You know they always go a bit funny at this time of year."

"What's the bay look like?" Veronica asked Henry.

"Frothy," said Henry. "Like God's been at it with a giant eggbeater."

"Bother," said Veronica, because we were expecting the supply ship. Henry went up on the roof with the telescope to watch for it, and I went outside to see if I could find any more eggs and to have a bit of a think. I couldn't go back upstairs to think, because Simon was in the bathroom, which leads off the bedroom Veronica and I share, and the door doesn't close properly. Simon was shaving, which is another unsettling thing—nobody here shaves, usually, although Henry probably wishes she could. Toby doesn't really need to, and Uncle John has a phobia about sharp objects and blood, so he has an enormous beard instead.

On my way to the henhouse, I discovered Spartacus, our big red-and-white rooster, flapping his wings and crowing triumphantly. He had cornered the tabby cat, which was cowering against the wall of the woodshed (perhaps that's why all our cats are a bit mad; they have been driven that way by Spartacus). I told him off, but he didn't even bother to listen, just strutted unrepentantly towards the henhouse.

The henhouse and the pigeon loft are built in what used to be the armory, along one of the curtain walls. The Montmaray garrison lived in it while the castle was being built and so it is quite roomy and comfortable, even though there are only arrow loops for windows and the roof has fallen in at one end. As Henry had reported, the hens (and half a dozen of Toby's pigeons) were in an agitated state. They crowded around me in a ruffled feathery heap; then, realizing I wasn't about to give them a second breakfast, flapped off to their perches to sulk.

"What *have* you lot been up to?" I asked the fluffy white hen, who often snuggles up for a pat, but she only goggled at me and scuttled away. They'd clearly been out exploring yesterday, laying eggs in inconvenient and dangerous places along the cliffs—it's all Spartacus's fault; he leads them on. Which suddenly reminded me of that day last week when we'd found half of them in the chapel. I'd assumed at the time that Rebecca had left the chapel door open (she spends hours on her knees in front of that altar, muttering away). But now I wondered if the hens had managed to find one of the old secret tunnels. The tunnels are so old and secret that nobody, not even George, is entirely sure where they begin or end. Veronica says they definitely exist, though; she found references to them on some old maps in the library. The tunnels lead from beneath the chapel to the curtain walls or beyond, and were built to allow the castle dwellers to escape if the castle was invaded and All Was Lost. But not even Henry is prepared to spend days poking around the crypt to find a tunnel entrance, what with the damp, the dark, the unsteady piles of bones, the rats, and so on (ugh, the very *thought* of going down there makes me nearly sick). Assuming, of course, that any tunnels still exist, that they didn't all cave in centuries ago. Although perhaps there is one with hen-sized access . . . Anyway, I had a look around the henhouse, but didn't find anything except a smallish egg under a pile of straw, and I don't think it was very fresh.

After breakfast, Veronica went up on the roof with our little wireless, hoping to pick up a signal from Spain. The reception is never very good, but sometimes, if the Pyrenees are cloudless and the wind is blowing in just the right direction and all the important parts of the Spanish transmitters are functioning correctly, it's not *too* bad. She had no luck today, though—perhaps it's all the fighting going on there. Or else the batteries are dying. Heaven knows how we'll ever manage to recharge them, or afford to buy new ones.

Meanwhile, I tidied the bedrooms and Simon disappeared into Uncle John's room for a chat. Uncle John tolerates Simon, for some reason—it must be because Simon is Rebecca's son. Rebecca is the only one Uncle John will normally have anything to do with. He ignores the rest of us—except on the odd occasion when he doesn't, which is worse.

Last night, for example, Rebecca made Veronica knock on his door and ask what he wanted on his supper tray, and the moment he caught sight of Veronica, he had one of his fits. This time, he hurled his chamber pot at her. Fortunately, he missed (even more fortunately, Henry had just emptied it); unfortunately, it hit the long looking glass. Then Rebecca rushed in and shouted at Veronica for upsetting him, and Veronica shouted back, and Henry ran in to see what was going on and stepped on Carlos's tail, making him yelp. So what with Rebecca moaning on and on about how we'd have seven years of bad luck now and Simon and Veronica snapping at each other, it was a thoroughly miserable evening.

But never mind about that; I need to finish what I was writing yesterday about Spain. Except now I have only a lot of unanswered questions. For example, what is the difference between a Socialist and a Communist? What exactly is Fascism? But the biggest question is: Which side are *we* supposed to support? The side of our cousin Alfonso and the Monarchists? But from what Veronica said, even if General Franco wins, King Alfonso will not be allowed to return to power. And in any case, how could anyone support Franco, a person whose forces massacred all those civilians in Badajoz?

And yet—the other side are Communists! And they murdered the Russian royal family, all those poor Romanov children shot dead (and we are related to *them*, too, distantly, which is why Great-aunt Elizabeth was being courted by that Russian nobleman in the first place). Of course, some of the Russian people did have reason to be unhappy with the Tsar. Not all monarchs are wise, kind, and just. Sometimes they make mistakes, I know *that*.

How could I not, when each time I catch sight of the stone cross at South Head, I'm reminded of all those young Montmaravian men who were slaughtered in the Great War? Was it necessary, politically? Did their sacrifice achieve anything worthwhile? Veronica might be able to attempt a response to that question, but I can't. All I know is that it happened in 1917, when Uncle John had just become King and was, perhaps, overeager to prove himself worthy of the title. At any rate, he decided to give some of his fellow Old Etonians a hand in their war and volunteered a battalion of Montmaray men, with himself as their commanding officer. The men—all fishermen, none of whom had even seen a rifle before their basic training—lasted only two days at the Western Front. Not that rifle expertise would have helped them much—the trenches they were defending were shelled by German aeroplanes. Only six of them survived, all but one wounded badly. And apparently Uncle John was never quite the same after that.

But to return to the current war, the one in Spain—most of the people of Spain wanted their King to leave, and they did vote the Communists into government. It makes choosing sides very complicated. I don't suppose my opinion counts either way. It's not as though it can really affect us, here in Montmaray. And yet watching Simon and Veronica argue so passionately about the war last night made me feel I should care about it, too.

And there it is, what I wanted to have a think about. You see, I couldn't help feeling just the tiniest bit *envious* yesterday as I observed the energy Simon devotes to his dislike of Veronica. All those flashing looks of his, those explosive sighs, those barely reined-in gestures! All those fervent words tumbling from his lips! It's especially galling when I compare this to the few "conversations" I had with Simon yesterday, the most thrilling of which was as follows:

Simon: Could you please pass the salt?

Sophia (reaches out, knocks over saltcellar): Oh dear . . .

(Rebecca shrieks, flings spilled salt over left shoulder.)

Sophia: Sorry.

Simon (in the kindly tones one would use when addressing a small child or an idiot): Never mind.

So I can't say I blame him in the slightest for preferring to argue politics with Veronica than to talk with me. In fact, I didn't even attempt to follow their debate last night. Instead, I gave in to Henry's pleading and read her two chapters of *Johnny Hercules and the Diamond of Azoo-Beeza*. This is a dreadful book that Toby sent her, full of man-eating pythons and marauding tribesmen and skeletons with tattered maps clenched between their teeth. Veronica refused to have anything to do with it, hoping this would encourage Henry to learn to read by herself. I also suspect that if Veronica had picked it up, the historical and geographical inaccuracies would have driven her to distraction by the end of the first page. Veronica doesn't really see the point of fiction. When I asked her what she'd thought of *Pride and Prejudice*, she only wondered aloud how anyone could have written a novel set in the first part of the nineteenth century without once mentioning Napoleon.

Oh! I have just had another thought!

What if Simon has fallen in *love* with Veronica? And, rather like Mr. Darcy regarding Miss Elizabeth Bennet, hasn't yet recognized his true feelings for her? Although Veronica's more like Mr. Darcy than Simon is. And actually, Simon's brow is a bit Rochester-ish. Or even Heathcliff-ian. Well, perhaps Simon has realized how hopeless and doomed his love is (she a princess, he the mere son of a housekeeper) and has decided to mask it with a display of passionate hatred.

Oh, *Sophia*. Change the subject.

So—I am currently sitting at the kitchen table, waiting for the others to return. They've taken the gig out to meet the supply ship and Rebecca went because Simon did, so I am left to look after Uncle John. Fortunately, he's asleep. I'm hoping he stays that way for a bit longer. I need all the peace and quiet I can get in here. Outside, the wind is whipping the royal standard above the gatehouse into a frenzy and sawing the kitchen shutters back and forth (the latch has snapped off again), and an ominous rattle has started up in Vulcan's flue. I can hear the Blue Room ghost moaning and shuffling around upstairs, too. I've just finished ironing the only dress that still fits me, an apron, and some pillow slips. I did ask Veronica if she wanted me to do her blouses while she was gone, but she looked at me as though I'd offered to wash some toast—she can't understand why I bother with ironing when there's no one here who cares what we look like

Heavens, I nearly *died* of shock just then! An enormous crash sounded from Uncle John's room! I whirled around just as the bolt rattled and shot back. Then the door creaked open an inch and a bloodshot eye appeared.

"Where's Rebecca?" demanded the eye. Or rather, the mouth below the eye, except I couldn't see it, what with all the grimy, tangled hair in the way.

"Oh, she's . . . she's just gone out to meet the supply ship," I managed when I was able to breathe again. "Can I get you something?"

The eye blinked. The door wavered on its hinges.

"Why don't you sit down?" I said. "And I'll make you a cup of tea." I stood up, but he just shook his great shaggy head at me. His beard straggles halfway down his chest now. Even his eyebrows have grown feral—it's a wonder he can see at all from beneath them.

"Where's *Rebecca?*" he said again.

"She won't be long," I assured him untruthfully (they'd only been gone twenty minutes) as I put the kettle on. We'd finished the last of the Basque captain's crackers the night before, but I found some bread left over from breakfast and pushed it through the gap at Uncle John, feeling like a zookeeper feeding a caged mountain bear. He gnawed at it while the water boiled. I snatched the kettle off Vulcan at the first faint hint of a whistle for fear the sound would set him off, but he didn't seem to hear it. He just stood there, wedged against the doorframe, his one visible eye staring at the sooty kitchen ceiling.

"I was married," he declared suddenly.

"Yes, I know," I said, pouring boiled water into the teapot and sloshing it around. He still hadn't sat down, and it was making me nervous.

Then his eye narrowed on me. "You're Robert's girl," he said.

"That's right," I said carefully.

But all he said was, "Robert had three children, not just

two." Then he refused his tea and slammed the door shut. I kept thinking of Hamlet and "There is method in his madness," but I can't see that there is much method in it for Uncle John. Unless his method is to make Rebecca feel so sorry for him that she waits on him hand and foot, but she would do that anyway—she reveres him. Also, I'm not entirely certain he's *mad*. I think it's just that he prefers to stay in bed (I sometimes feel that way myself, especially in winter) and that he has a lot of thinking to do and sometimes this leaks out into talking to himself. After all, I talk to myself all the time—this journal is nothing *but* talking to myself. And the awful things he must have seen and heard during the war would make *anyone* dislike sudden loud noises and the sight of blood. Not that Veronica has much sympathy for this point of view. Still, I suppose if he wants Veronica's compassion, he should stop shouting and throwing things at her. She always seems to get the worst of it when he's in a rage. I suppose it's because she looks so much like her mother.

But I can hear voices now—the others are back! I had better go and help with the packages.

Carlos is a hero. One of the bags went overboard when they were loading the gig, but he leapt into the sea and dragged it back. Veronica was worried that there may have been some letters lost, but I'm not too concerned. The only letters we really care about are from Toby, and we've just had one from him. At any rate, the two big hams were saved, as well as the flour and the candles—six dozen of them! So we gave Carlos the best spot in front of Vulcan to dry out and scratched behind his ears the way he likes, all of which he accepted solemnly as his proper due. At the moment he is lying on the hearthrug looking very noble, despite Henry and Jimmy being draped all over him. It's mainly his furrowed brow, I think, and his penetrating black gaze. The Portuguese water dog is such a *majestic* breed. We've had them here at Montmaray for hundreds of years, although Carlos is the only one left now, George's poor old Missy having died two winters ago. Portuguese water dogs were supposedly carried on the Spanish Armada. Then, when the battle was lost and the ships were scuttling home, the dogs were tossed overboard with the mules and the horses, and the dogs managed to swim here. Or else they were brought here by Portuguese fishermen. Although I prefer the Armada story; it's more dramatic.

Anyway, now we are all slumped around the table, recovering from an enormous luncheon. All the villagers stayed except for George, who always makes excuses (I think Uncle John's brooding presence behind the door intimidates him). We had ham with a honey glaze, boiled potatoes with parsley, a salad made from nasturtium leaves and spinach, and afterwards, oranges and walnuts. I am now so full of good food and so unwilling to move that I think any of Aunt Charlotte's reproaches about our idle, extravagant lives would be quite, quite justified.

It is much later, and Veronica has just finished giving Henry her spelling lesson (I did all the washing up instead and think I got the better end of the deal). Henry was in a very bad mood because firstly, Jimmy went back to the village to mess around with fishing nets and she wasn't allowed to go with him, and secondly, Rebecca called her Henrietta all through luncheon. Veronica had to promise a Gory Story to get Henry to pay any attention at all, and even then, Henry spelled "city" with an *s* and "cake" with the *k* in the wrong place and no *e*. Her reading is almost as bad. And she doesn't even care. She says George can't read and he knows everything anyone would ever need to know, so why should she have to learn? She then recites a list of FitzOsbornes who lived perfectly happy lives despite being unable to spell their own names, beginning with our great-grandmother, who signed the marriage register with an X. Veronica now regrets having told Henry this fact.

It's hard to believe Henry and Veronica are cousins, they're so different. Veronica begged and begged for us to be allowed to go to boarding school, just for a year or two, when Toby started at Eton. It did no good, though. There wasn't enough money, of course, but Aunt Charlotte also has a horror of overeducated females. The way she told it, the English counties are littered with aging spinsters who accidentally displayed a spark of intelligence at a debutante dance and were banished forever from civilized society.

But now Veronica is telling Henry the promised Gory Story. It is about Robert FitzOsborne at the Battle of Hastings (not my father, obviously, but the much earlier Robert FitzOsborne). Heads are getting chopped off with battle-axes, arrows are taking people's eyes out, and horses are coughing up bloody froth, then falling down dead right on top of the Saxons. Henry is loving it.

"And after the battle," Veronica continues, "as one of William of Normandy's most favored knights, Robert Fitz-Osborne was given a hundred men and sent south to cross the Tamar, and there he built a castle . . ."

This is my favorite part. I watch men scurry like ants, quarrying flat the solid rock, cleaving the rock into vast blocks, hauling barrels of sand and lime up onto the mound. At night, the work continues by the light of burning rushes. The round walls of the keep rise ten feet high, twenty, thirty. Not for the Fitz-Osbornes a flimsy wooden motte-and-bailey castle, but a proper stone keep, right from the beginning.

"Just like the Tower of London," says Henry proudly.

"Only because there was a great deal more stone than timber in Cornwall," Veronica says, never one to let a good story get in the way of the facts. "And the castle was really quite small. A couple of rooms, a chapel—"

"And battlements," Henry says. "And they hid behind them and rained down arrows, while their enemies catapulted dead horses over the top. SPLAT!"

I think I'll go and finish this in the gatehouse.

Much, much later and nothing got written in the gatehouse after all. I noticed at once that the grit on the windowsill had been swept away and the basket attached to the pulley system was missing. Leaning out the window, I saw the basket balanced on a shelf of rock that vanishes at high tide. Beside it is a shallow cave where driftwood tends to collect in great piles—something to do with the ocean currents and the shape of the Chasm, I believe. It's very convenient; it saves our having to go all the way to the cove for firewood.

Simon was down there, hacking away at what looked like the remains of a wooden crate. He swung the ax with neither grace nor skill (Henry could have done a better job), but there was something compelling about the determined set of his back and the sturdy plant of his feet upon the rock. He'd taken off his jacket and rolled up the sleeves of his blue shirt. I could see his forearms, see the muscles shifting under the London-pale skin. And all at once I was thrown into a rather embarrassing memory (and thank heavens Veronica is too honorable to read this journal without my permission) of the time I came across Toby and Simon bathing in the Great Pool. Not that I saw very much of Simon—he had his back to me and was thigh-deep in water—but still . . .

Isn't it odd that something I barely registered at the time could have lurked in the shadows of my mind all those years? And then suddenly emerge with such force that as I sagged against the windowsill, I could actually *smell* the weedy pond water, feel the damp grass crushed under my feet and the sun burning into the back of my neck, hear Toby giggling as he sent a spray of water towards Simon. And then, just as my face heated up and I decided I really oughtn't to be gawking out the gatehouse window at Simon, he turned to toss a chunk of wood into the basket and caught sight of me hanging half out the window with my face pink and my hair upside down. He tilted his head and gave me his half smile.

"Oh, hello!" I cried breathlessly. "Er, just . . . just wondering if you want me to pull up the basket yet!"

He looked at the basket and its meager contents.

"Or I could come down and help!" I said. "I'll help load the wood, it's much quicker with two people!"

I must have sounded an absolute fool. When flustered, I talk and talk instead of staying sensibly silent. But he was too polite to object, and I realized I'd been hoping for just such an excuse to spend time alone with him. So I climbed down the ladder to the courtyard and then descended the two dozen rusty iron spikes hammered into the Chasm wall below the drawbridge. It's safer than it appears, but I was wearing my best (my only) dress, which I'd changed into once I realized everyone was staying for luncheon. I tied the hem in a knot on one side so it didn't billow too much, but I probably showed far more leg than is decent. Not that Simon appeared to notice. Of course, for all I know, fashionable young ladies in London are wearing hemlines up around their *knees* this season. At least worrying about my dress stopped me thinking about the sheer drop to the waves below—there's only a finite amount of worrying a person can do at any one time, as Veronica once pointed out to me. It was helpful to realize this, because there are so *many* things that terrify me—deep water, the dark, rats, blood, spiders, any kind of bones except fish bones, bees, enclosed spaces, and albino rabbits, just for a start.

Up close, Simon chopped wood even more badly than was apparent from above (he must be terribly out of practice), but I wasn't quite foolish enough to offer to take over. Instead, I busied myself gathering up bits of wood, scraping off the seaweed and barnacles before tossing them in the basket, while trying not to trip over any of Henry's rubbish (she and Jimmy have been building a raft in the cave) or drop anything on Simon's jacket (which was folded on a rock with his rather nice gold watch sitting on top).

I couldn't think of anything fascinating to say, so I concentrated on trying to decide whether Simon really is handsome or not. His face is all planes and sharp angles, with thick brows and deep, dark eyes. I noticed he had quite a lot of blue-black stubble along his jaw, even though he'd shaved only hours before. He's taken to slicking his hair back with some sort of oil, too. It doesn't suit him; it makes him look severe and much older, although I suppose that could be the effect he's aiming for. He certainly hasn't any of Toby's golden-haired, blue-eyed good looks, but Toby is a completely different type of boy. Perhaps that's it—that Toby is a boy and Simon is a man. *A man of the world*, I thought with a lovely shiver.

Then it occurred to me that Simon might have some advice regarding my dilemma. At any rate, it would be something to talk about. The silence was becoming awkward—for me, at least.

"Um," I said. "Simon. Has . . . has Toby said anything to you about Veronica and me going to England?"

"Not to attend school, I presume," he said, tossing a chunk of wood in the basket.

"No, to be presented at Court. It's Aunt Charlotte's idea. And after that—well, you know . . ."

"Society awaits," he said dryly. He straightened and gave me an appraising look. I could feel myself starting to blush—again. "Well then, that's very exciting news for you, Sophia. And, of course, for *Her Highness*."

I'd asked him to call me by my first name years ago, but I can't imagine Veronica ever extending him that courtesy. He does manage to infuse her royal title with such disdain that it turns the words meaningless. Mind you, she never calls him anything but Simon Chester, usually spat out as though they're swearwords.

"Yes, but the thing is," I continued, "Veronica refuses to leave Montmaray. She doesn't have the slightest interest in Society. And I can't possibly go without her. So I wondered if—well, if *you* might . . ." I trailed off, giving him a pleading look.

"Are you suggesting she'd listen to me?" He almost laughed, then caught himself.

"Well, no, but you could give me some ideas about how to persuade her," I said. "I mean, I haven't been to England. What might make Veronica want to visit?"

"Why do you want to go?"

I thought about it for a moment. I wasn't entirely sure I *did* want to leave Montmaray, but there were certainly some things beckoning me towards England. "Dress shops. Parties. The cinema. But *that's* not going to help. She's so much more . . . I mean, she's an intellectual."

He narrowed his eyes, and I was reminded of the lessons the four of us—Toby, Simon, Veronica, and I—had shared before Toby went away to school. Veronica had always been clever, but Simon had focused so intensely, worked so doggedly, that he nearly always matched her in the tasks our tutors set us. It might seem nothing much to boast about, given that she's five years his junior, but then he'd lived in the village, with hardly any access to books, until he was twelve. For him to have achieved as much as he had was evidence, I thought, of his innate intelligence. At any rate, I was sure he could solve any problem I might care to throw at him—provided I could persuade him it was in his interest to solve it.

"Aunt Charlotte would be *so* grateful if you could help me convince Veronica," I said, putting on what I hoped was a winning expression. "There's going to be an awful battle otherwise—you know how stubborn they both are."

I could see that my pathetic attempt at scheming amused him. Still, if he was half as ambitious as Veronica claimed, he'd want to get on Aunt Charlotte's good side. And regardless of anything else, at least he was *looking* at me for once.

"Very well," he said, leaning on his ax. "I'll give you some reasons why *Her Highness* might want to leave Montmaray for England. And in return, you'll convince her that Montmaray needs to take part in those non-intervention talks regarding Spain."

"But, but . . . ," I spluttered, "I don't know anything about . . . and anyway, she doesn't—"

"I'm aware she doesn't trust me," he said evenly. "But she ought to. I care about the same things she does. We *all* want the best for Montmaray."

Had he been eavesdropping on Veronica and me in the library the day before? I was instantly ashamed of myself for having such an awful, suspicious thought. Meanwhile, Simon kept talking—about how Montmaray needed to regain its rightful place in Europe, about politics and diplomacy and the important role Montmaray played all those centuries ago during the War of the Spanish Succession, and then later, when Napoleon invaded the Peninsula . . .

Well, to be honest, I can't remember his exact words, even though I was listening very hard to his voice (so deep and rich— a bit like treacle, if treacle were a sound) and watching his eyes lighten and darken, and his brows rise and narrow, and his hands wave around in elegant patterns.

". . . a united front with Toby, don't you agree?"

I blinked. What was I supposed to be agreeing to? "Yes?" I ventured.

He sighed, and I felt ashamed all over again.

"So you'll talk to her," he said with studied patience. "About the need for Montmaray to take part in these talks in London? She'll listen to you."

"I . . . All right," I said.

"Excellent," he said. "Now, as for your problem. What might

appeal to Her Highness? The British Museum. Westminster Abbey. Debate in the Houses of Parliament. Exhibitions at the Royal Academy. The Tower of London. St. Paul's Cathedral. Libraries. Bookshops. Speakers' Corner in Hyde Park. Dozens of daily newspapers. Radios that actually work and regular news broadcasts, in English."

Of course, I could have figured most of that out by myself.

"Mind you," he added, "if she's determined to stay here, then let her. It shouldn't stop *you* from going wherever you please."

"She's not stopping me!" I said. "I just . . . We do everything together and—"

"You pay far too much attention to her opinions and not enough to your own," he said, taking up the ax again.

I gaped at him. "Well!" I said, because he was so *wrong* I couldn't think of anything else to say. Of course I pay attention to Veronica's opinion! That doesn't mean I don't have opinions of my own, just that hers are interesting and well thought out and . . .

Anyway, why *shouldn't* she be the most important person in my life? I don't have a mother or a sister (I can't really count Henry), or neighbors my own age or school friends. Thank heavens I *do* have Veronica. I can't picture my life without her—truly I can't, because every significant memory of my life features her. I remember her hitting Toby after he threw the croquet mallet at me. I remember her sneaking into the Blue Room to read to me from *The Magic Fish Bone* when I was quarantined with measles and going mad from itching and boredom. I remember curling up in her bed each night for weeks on end after Mother and Father were killed—it was the only way I could get to sleep. She's part of all the big memories—and all the little ones, too. She was the one who taught me how to tie my bootlaces, how to extract bee stings, how to light Vulcan without setting my eyebrows on fire. But how could I explain all this to Simon? And anyway, he'd already turned his attention back to the woodpile.

Oh, it's just habit, his dislike of Veronica—he probably can't help himself saying unfair things. He simply doesn't know her as I do. I'm just going to ignore what he said.

Except I gave my word that I'd speak to Veronica about that non-intervention thing . . .

Bother.

4th November 1936

My attempt to discuss the Spanish situation with Veronica this morning was as unsuccessful as I'd feared. In fact, I didn't even manage to get my first, carefully rehearsed sentence out. It was my fault—I interrupted her as she was going over the accounts.

"Are they *very* bad?" I asked. "I mean, worse than usual?"

I peered over her shoulder at the columns of numbers, but they might as well have been Ancient Greek to me—no, Ancient Greek I would've had more chance of understanding, thanks to all that practice decoding Kernetin.

"Ten *pounds*," groaned Veronica, tapping her pencil on one of the red squiggles. "Why on earth would Toby have needed ten pounds before term had even started?"

"Didn't his friend Rupert invite him to their country house then?" I wondered aloud. "Train fares? New shoes? Tips for the servants?"

Veronica started massaging her temples with her fingertips.

"Never mind," I said. "We'll sell the Fabergé egg. Simon thought he might get a couple of hundred pounds for it."

"Oh, *Simon Chester* thought! Why hasn't he left yet, anyway? He's got his precious papers signed now. He could have gone back on the supply ship."

"But it was headed for Santander," I pointed out.

"He's up to something," she said, scowling at the accounts. "He and Rebecca."

"I thought you said he wasn't interested in money," I protested. "Besides, we haven't got any."

"And *why* don't we have any?" said Veronica, giving me a dark and meaningful look. Then she snatched all the papers up and went off to the library, muttering something under her breath about Uriah Heep.

It was this that made another nasty, suspicious thought pop into my mind. I suddenly remembered Simon's watch, sitting on his folded-up jacket. I'd never seen him wearing a watch before, and it had looked so new and shiny. How had he been able to afford it on a clerk's wages? Not that I have any idea how much a watch costs (or how much a clerk earns). It probably wasn't real gold anyway—I expect it was brass or something. No doubt handed down from his father and he's always worn it, and I haven't noticed it before because it's only been recently that I've paid much attention to him.

But why did it look so new?

Oh, but I *know* Simon would never take money from us. Especially as he understands far better than me how little we have. It hasn't always been that way. In fact, at one stage the FitzOsbornes were very, very rich. For the record (I'm trying to be more ordered and objective about my writing, the way Veronica is, using proper footnotes and everything), this is how our family made its fortune:

1. Salvaging the cargo of ships wrecked off Montmaray (a lucrative business, given the perilous Montmaray coastline and the continuing refusal of Montmaray kings to construct a lighthouse or any other kind of warning system).[1]

2. Piracy (possibly).[2]

3. Smuggling rum and brandy into England (possibly).[3]

4. Selling salt to the English whenever they were at war with France and their regular suppliers were cut off.[4]

5. Whaling and fishing.[5]

6. Making anyone else who wanted to catch whales or fish in Montmaray waters pay license fees.[6]

7. Marrying coal magnates, etc.[7]

8. Buying and selling shares in the stock market.[8]

[1] *The Wreck of the* Zenobia *and Other Tales of the Treacherous Seas* by S. E. Morpurgo (1899).
[2] Ibid.
[3] Ibid.
[4] See abandoned salt ponds, east coast of Montmaray.
[5] See records of conversations with Mr. George Spenser kept by HRH Princess Veronica of Montmaray.
[6] See records held by Mr. L. P. Grenville, solicitor, London.
[7] Ibid.
[8] Ibid.

And this is how our family lost its fortune:

1. Invention of steamships and modern navigation equipment, which greatly decreased the frequency of shipwrecks.[9]

2. Scarcity of whales in Bay of Biscay due to overenthusiastic whalers; also, development of the petroleum industry, which decreased the demand for whale products.[10]

3. Spending a lot of money on rifles, cannons, military uniforms, etc. (the Great War, 1914–1918).[11]

And, most importantly,

4. The Stock Market Crash, 1929.[12]

I don't think I'll do footnotes anymore; it took me half an hour to look up those ones. Also, reading back over this, I realize I make it sound as though we are poor. Which of course we aren't, not the way that orphans in Dickens are poor. Well, I suppose we are orphans (at least Toby, Henry, and I are, and Veronica might as well be for all the use her parents are), but it's not as though we're starving, or wearing rags, or forced to pick pockets or worse on the streets. Not that there are any streets in Montmaray. (As I wrote that last bit, Henry wandered through the kitchen wearing an ancient jersey of Toby's that is more holes than wool, but that's because she idolizes Toby, not because she is a Dickensian beggar child.)

Money, then—it would be nice to have more so Veronica

<hr>

[9] *Modern Shipping* by F. R. Martin (1911).
[10] *The Wonderful Whale* by Miss Z. Flagg (1929).
[11] See records held by Mr. L. P. Grenville, solicitor, London.
[12] Ibid.

doesn't have to worry so much about it all the time, but we have enough at the moment, as long as Aunt Charlotte keeps paying Toby's school fees. Although I must say, I think it's quite unfair the way interest works at the bank—that the more money one has, the more one earns. The bank ought to give more to people *without* much money in their savings accounts; they'd appreciate it far more than rich people. And I've just had another thought! I wonder if there's anything valuable left in the Solar that Simon could sell? Just a moment . . .

Well, no, as it turns out, unless one counts two very tarnished silver photograph frames, a broken music box, and a moth-ravaged hat, all of which I found under the bed. I must say it's rather creepy in here—not in a lovely, shivery way, as it is inside the Blue Room when the ghost strokes her fingers down one's neck and whistles in one's ear, but in a sad, dusty, and abandoned way. Still, at least it's quieter than the gatehouse (Henry and Jimmy are having sword fights along the top of the curtain wall) and the edge of the bedframe is quite comfortable now that I've padded it with the folded-up dust sheet.

I suppose I'd better describe where I am. If one were to climb the tower stairs from the kitchen and emerge at one end of the gallery, one would see . . . actually, one wouldn't see much of anything, because the walls and floor and ceiling are black granite, two feet thick at the narrowest bits, and there are no windows in the gallery and hardly ever any oil to spare for the lamps hanging on the walls. The blackness swallows up the light of a candle, so if all the doors are closed, one has to grope along the wall, counting steps.

But let's suppose one had a good strong torch. Then one would see, on the right, the door to the large bedroom Veronica and I share. Our room connects to the bathroom, which connects to the Solar (where I am currently sitting and in which Montmaravian kings and queens have slept for hundreds of years, until Uncle John started refusing to come upstairs). On the left side of the gallery, across from Veronica's and my room, is Rebecca's room, which connects to Henry's room, which connects to the nursery. Next to that is the Blue Room, and then Toby's room, which connects to the Gold Room, where my parents used to sleep. Most of the gold has flaked off its walls now, but Rebecca usually puts guests in there (on the rare occasion we have any), on account of the Blue Room being haunted.

As for the Solar, it used to be quite grand when Isabella lived here. She was constantly redecorating it according to the latest craze (which Uncle John used as an excuse to move downstairs, although I suspect it was really that they couldn't spend ten minutes together by then without having a screaming row). She never got rid of the old stuff, so the room ended up a fascinating, exotic muddle, with an antique kimono draped across one wall, Persian rugs, a Tutankhamen-inspired frieze, bed-curtains made out of Indian silk, Parisian etchings propped on the chimney-piece, and a pair of Art Deco figurines holding up glass spheres. Even now, stripped of its decorations, the Solar is impressive— the largest room in the castle, apart from the Great Hall. There are two big mullioned windows fitted with window seats, an enormous fireplace, and a dais for the four-poster bed. Most of the furniture is gone now, but the bed is still here because no one could work out how to take it apart and it's too big to fit through any of the doors.

I have propped the silver-framed photographs I found beside me so I can look at them as I write. One is clearly of Toby and Veronica, their christening gowns trailing over the lap of someone wearing a long, shiny skirt. (Isabella? My mother? Her face is blurred and shadowed.) Toby is gnawing at his fist and Veronica is either grinning or grimacing—it's hard to tell. The only way I can distinguish them is that the little bit of hair Veronica has is scraped into a wisp and secured with an enormous bow. Along the bottom of the photograph, someone has written, *The twins, 1919.* (And I can just hear Veronica exclaiming, "What if some poor future historian reads it and thinks we actually *were* twins? When in fact we were born *six weeks apart*! And are *cousins*, not siblings!")

The other photograph is of a vaguely Moorish mansion with a fountain in front. I've never seen it before. Is it somewhere Isabella lived? Her family home? Does Veronica know it's here? Peering closer, I see that what I'd imagined was flowering vine creeping up the walls is in fact mold. Ugh. It's underneath the glass, too—it may be too late to save the photograph, but I'll take it back to our room anyway, along with the other one. I don't think Veronica will mind, even if the house does turn out to be Isabella's. I don't think Veronica cares anymore.

Looking around at the blank walls and dusty flagstones of the Solar, remembering how it used to be, makes me wonder again at how little Isabella took with her. I was only eight when she departed, but I recall sitting on her favorite rose-patterned rug afterwards and thinking that surely she could have rolled *that* up and strapped it to her suitcase. But she left in such a hurry. There'd been an argument between her and Uncle John, the sort involving shouting and smashed china (these had become depressingly ordinary). What was out of the ordinary this time was Isabella's storming upstairs to toss some clothes into her little alligator suitcase. She'd caught sight of a ship making its slow way past the island.

"Enough!" she screamed, loud enough for the entire castle to hear. I remember standing in the bathroom in my striped pajamas, shivering violently, while Veronica patted my shoulder, saying, "Never mind, Sophie, never mind." Toby, peering through a crack in the bathroom door, watched Isabella stalk out of her room in a swirl of calf-length mink, suitcase handle clenched in one hand. He was the last one to see her.

We were all certain that she would come back, or at least send for her things once she was settled in her new place. But she never did. We waited and waited, and we never heard a thing. And after a while, Veronica stopped going up on the roof with the telescope to scan the sea for ships. The fox fur Henry had taken to play with lost its Isabella scent, and then its glass eyes and chunks of its fur. Uncle John sank even further into his misanthropic gloom and refused to leave his downstairs burrow, so

Rebecca and the villagers moved most of the Solar furniture into the other rooms and threw dust sheets over the enormous bed. Isabella's remaining possessions scattered throughout the castle, and beyond. We sold the most valuable of her trinkets to pay for a new water pump in the village. We used bits of her old woolen bathrobe to block a drafty gap in the bathroom wall. Her white crêpe de Chine skirt came in handy for bandages when Jimmy broke his wrist. Mind you, most of Isabella's clothes got burnt up in the stove one night. We never did find out whether that was Uncle John or Rebecca.

"I expect it's just that she's still settling into the new place," Toby whispered consolingly one evening to Veronica and me. We were all huddled under the covers of her bed (Henry was there, too, but asleep). It was nearly summer by then, but Uncle John was on one of his rampages downstairs, so we'd decided we were better off invisible under a blanket. "It must take such a long time to buy carpets and furniture and all that," Toby added. "I expect she's awfully busy."

"She probably wants it to be all nice before she asks you to visit," I told Veronica. "You could take some of her things in your trunk when you go. The little things—the jade elephant and—"

"No," said Veronica firmly. "She doesn't care about any of this anymore. About any of *us*." Then she turned over on her side, and Toby and I looked at each other and silently vowed not to mention Isabella again, at least not in Veronica's presence. And as the months passed, this became easier and easier.

We exhausted the subject of where Isabella might be (I thought Spain; Toby said Paris) and what she might be doing (being a mannequin for Schiaparelli, decorating rich people's houses, learning to fly an aeroplane). We were too young then to understand what I now can guess—that back in the big world, where she belonged, she'd found another lover. Perhaps he'd even been one of her former suitors (I imagine she'd had plenty of those), someone who'd waited patiently for her all those years. And when she'd protested that really, she was *married* now, he'd pointed out that she deserved better than life on an isolated island, in a crumbling castle full of someone else's children (this was a year or two after my parents died, and although Toby and I were fairly well behaved, Henry was a toddler by then and given to throwing monstrous tantrums). Perhaps he was rich—perhaps he'd promised her exquisite gowns and diamond necklaces and pink champagne. Or perhaps he was good-hearted but poor, charming but middle-class, and she'd never really stopped loving him, despite his unaristocratic origins. So she took the hand he held out and he whisked her off to some exotic place, Argentina or Mexico or Barbados, where she strolled through admiring crowds in one of her beautiful swirling dresses, a bright flower tucked behind her ear.

At least I assume that's what she did. Toby kept an ear out for any mention of her after he went away to school, but he didn't hear a word. The one time he asked Aunt Charlotte, she snapped that she hadn't the faintest idea where "that woman" was, but if Isabella had any decency, she'd continue to stay away from polite Society. This attitude seems to have been shared by Isabella's own aristocratic family. They weren't thrilled when she married a non-Catholic and had her child christened in Montmaray's chapel instead of Seville Cathedral, but they were even less thrilled when she abandoned both husband and child. We haven't heard from any of them in years. I suppose that could be the result of all the recent upheavals in Spain, although I suspect it's simply that when they disapprove of something, they do it passionately and wholeheartedly. Just like Isabella.

It's odd, actually, how vivid my recollections of Isabella are, when my own mother is such a blur to me. I was six when she died. I know that she was named Jane; that she was the only child of an impoverished viscount; that she played the piano, wore spectacles, and enjoyed the poetry of Wordsworth. But this is secondhand information, gathered from the personal possessions she left behind. I *ought* to remember more. After all, I can recall other, earlier events quite clearly: the croquet mallet incident; Nanny Mackinnon forcing me into a scratchy pink frock for Henry's christening; George rowing us out past South Head one spring morning to see the milky blue swirls of a plankton bloom spreading across the bay. And I can recall my father—blond and handsome, always laughing, everyone's favorite. But as for my mother, I have no idea what her smile was like (she looks shy or solemn in photographs, even her wedding portrait) or what scent she wore, or even the exact color of her eyes. I don't know whether she wrote poems or was frightened of the dark or missed her parents (they had both died by her twenty-first birthday). I haven't had any success asking the others about her, either. Toby just changes the subject, and Veronica is uncharacteristically vague. A few weeks ago, for instance, I was struggling with a handful of hairpins that would *not* stay in and I asked her whether Mother's hair had been the same.

"Oh, it was sort of . . . wavy," Veronica said. "Or wait— perhaps she put curlers in it at night? I think it was brown—no, more a darkish blond. She kept it short, I recall, although it may just have been that she tucked it up under her hats . . ."

Even Alice and Mary, while agreeing that my mother was "lovely," are frustratingly short on details. I think it's simply that Isabella was so beautiful and vivacious, so utterly dazzling, that my mother faded into the background.

I *do* take after her, then.

Much later, written in bed (hooray for candles). I stayed in the Solar for an hour this afternoon, then returned to our bedroom in a glum mood. Veronica was sitting on her bed, reading, having just washed her hair—it splashed like black ink down her back. I offered to brush it for her.

"Thanks," she said, smiling over her shoulder at me. "Oh, what's that you've got?"

The photographs did not spark much reaction. She shook her head at the label under the "twins" and said she had no idea about the house. Then she went back to her reading. I drew the brush through and through her thick, glossy waves, trying not to sigh with envy.

"I ought to ask you to cut it off," she remarked, turning a page. "Although I suppose it's easier to tie it back when it's this length."

"How can you even *think* of cutting it?" I exclaimed. "It's so beautiful!"

"But isn't long hair terribly unfashionable?" she teased.

"I wouldn't know," I grumbled, looking down at my skirt (the hem has been let down so many times that it seems to have horizontal pleats). "Especially as—Veronica, what's that you're *reading?*" Because I'd just glanced over her shoulder and seen the most horrific photographs—of people who'd been *tortured*, it looked like.

She flipped it over to show me the cover, which was even worse—a maniac dressed in a blood-soaked apron, waving a cleaver. *"The Brown Book of the Hitler Terror,"* I read. "What is it? And where did you find it?"

"It's about the Nazi government in Germany," she said calmly. "Communist propaganda, of course, put out by the Left Book Club. Nevertheless, there are some rather interesting sections. You see, it puts forward a theory about the burning of the Reichstag—"

I squeezed my eyes shut. I was certain I was going to have nightmares about those awful pictures.

"—and if even a tenth of it is true, it raises some serious questions about the British policy of . . . Oh, I'm sorry, this must be boring you."

"No, no," I said, suddenly spotting an opening. "You mean, about Britain not wanting to get involved in the Spanish war?"

"Exactly!" she said, clearly too fascinated by the subject to stop and wonder about my puzzling level of interest. "I mean, obviously the Nazis are assisting Franco. And a significant number of British politicians support the principles of Fascism, if only because they believe Fascism is the true enemy of Communism. On the other hand, how can they be seen to support a military coup against the democratically elected Spanish government? Hence their policy of non-intervention. Best to do nothing at all, you see." She sighed heavily. "There was a time when Montmaray played a vital role in Britain's diplomatic relations with Spain. In 1710, for example, we hosted secret talks between Henry St. John and the Marquis de Torcy regarding who should rule Spain. They may not have agreed to meet otherwise, but this was the perfect location—midway between the two countries, a neutral island with impregnable defenses—and both sides were thoroughly sick of the fighting by then. Why, if it hadn't been for the Montmaray peace talks, there might not have *been* a Treaty of Utrecht . . ."

"Anyway," I said hastily, because Veronica was getting that faraway look she gets whenever she starts theorizing about history. "Don't you think Montmaray should be doing something *now*? Taking part in these non-intervention talks, for example? Shouldn't we have some sort of diplomatic presence in London?"

"Toby, you mean?" she said quizzically.

"Er, yes," I said. "Toby. Yes."

Veronica looked thoughtful. "Well, it would be *wonderful* if Toby started to take more of an interest in . . . Oh, not now, of course, he has his studies to concentrate on, but in a year or two . . ."

"I expect he'd need a lot of help from you," I said. "I don't think he has much of a clue at the moment, but if *you* were there . . ."

"There?" said Veronica, her gaze suddenly sharpening. "In England, you mean?"

"Well . . ." But there was no point equivocating; Veronica's too clever and knows me too well. I put down the hairbrush and slid onto the rug so I could peer into her face. "Oh, Veronica, wouldn't you love to visit London? Imagine, all that history! Westminster Abbey, the Tower of London, the Houses of Parliament, all those libraries and museums and newspapers and, and . . ."

"I can't," she said. "You know I can't. Someone needs to stay here to look after things. What about Henry? And Father? And making sure Rebecca actually does some work instead of sitting by Father's bedside all day? Besides, there's the *Brief History*—"

"But wouldn't there be all sorts of information—about Queen Elizabeth and the Armada, for example, or Henry St. John in 1710—that you could only find in England?"

Veronica looked almost wistful at that, but she shook her head. "Aunt Charlotte won't pay for me to go over there and spend all my time digging through archives," she pointed out. "I'd be hopeless at what she *does* want—being decorative and charming—and I've no interest in finding a husband. Really, Sophie, it makes more sense that she should spend all her money on you. And you know you'd love all that dressing up and—"

"Not without *you* there!" I burst out. I stared down at my suddenly blurry skirt and blinked furiously for a moment. "Wouldn't you . . . wouldn't you miss me a bit if I wasn't here with you?" I whispered.

"Oh, Sophie!" she cried, grasping my shoulders. "Of *course* I would! I'd miss you terribly! But I'd be happy that you were getting the chance to do all the things you enjoy. And we could write lots of letters. Remember when you were in quarantine with measles and we had to write each other letters instead of being able to talk to each other? Your letters were always so entertaining you had Toby and me in fits. Even when there really wasn't much new to write about, you were so clever and funny."

"No, I wasn't," I mumbled. "*You're* the writer in this family, not me."

"Stop that," she said firmly, tipping my chin up. "What about that diary of yours? I saw you yesterday, scribbling away with the most intense look on your face—"

I felt myself starting to blush—that had probably been when I was writing about Simon.

"—and I think it's a wonderful idea that you're writing about Montmaray now, all your observations and memories and thoughts, before you go off and have lovely new experiences in England."

Is *that* what I'm doing? Recording my last months here for posterity? Perhaps I am. Not that I'm certain I want to leave, but . . .

"Veronica!" I said. "Wait, what about Aunt Charlotte? She expects *both* of us to go to England."

"Oh, don't worry about that," said Veronica airily, closing her book and standing up. Of course, this is the same person who ignored my quarantine to read aloud to me when I complained in my letters about being bored—and she didn't get much more than a few spots and a runny nose, either, despite the grown-ups' dire predictions. Normal rules don't apply to Veronica. I watched with great affection and not a little awe as she piled her hair on top of her head with a couple of pins and wandered off, saying something over her shoulder about having a chat with George before dinner.

I don't think she'll go to England. I don't think I can make her; I don't think anyone can make her. And I can't stand up to Aunt Charlotte by myself. And I *do* want to go to England, I do, except the very idea of leaving Veronica and Henry and Carlos and everything else at Montmaray fills me with such a sense of panic—how would I possibly cope in a strange place, all alone?

I must say, it's a very good thing that I have this journal as an outlet for all my moaning and whinging.

After all the angst of the afternoon, it was a profound relief to have a pleasant evening. Veronica and Simon had a brief but polite conversation about the French government over dinner, and I managed not to spill anything or otherwise embarrass myself. Rebecca was unusually talkative as well. She got out her darning while Veronica and I washed the dishes and delivered her version of a bedtime story, which consisted largely of warnings to Simon: that he ought to make sure his barber burns any hair he cuts off, lest birds fly away with it and weave it into their nests and cause Simon to suffer horrendous headaches; that if—God forbid, touch wood, spit thrice—Simon was to grow a wart, he should rub meat into it and bury the meat until it rotted away, whereupon his wart would disappear; and that Simon must take care to block his ears with sealing wax when sailing back past Land's End, because to hear the bells of wrecked ships was terrible luck.

When Rebecca is in such a mood, Henry can occasionally nudge her into other, more entertaining tales, of Piskies and Spriggans and Knockers. Not tonight, though. So Henry had to make do with my version of one of her favorites, the story of Bolster the Giant, whose doomed love for Saint Agnes led to his gory death at Chapel Porth, where the sea still boils blood-red.

Then Veronica was prodded into recounting the slightly more factual tale of Queen Matilda's brave stand against the Moroccan pirates in 1631, when King Stephen was away in England. After she heard that pirates were approaching South Head, she strapped the sword Benedict to her waist and led the castle battalion down to the village, where she waited on the edge of the wharf, her ebony hair streaming behind her in the sea breeze, her noble chin held high. (Veronica didn't mention the bits about the hair and the chin; they are my own invention. I always picture Queen Matilda as a cross between Joan of Arc and Veronica.) Queen Matilda triumphed, of course. A storm blew up and the pirate ship ran into the rocks and sank, which was attributed to a combination of Queen Matilda's determination and Benedict's mystical powers. One would think that the

FitzOsbornes might have reconsidered the edict against women inheriting the throne after that, especially as Matilda and Stephen had three feisty daughters. But no; Edward, the youngest in the family, was crowned King when Stephen died.

Then Henry wanted to hear more from Veronica—about how King John the First had fired upon the Spanish Armada and how King John the Fifth used the very same cannon to threaten Napoleon—but Veronica said someone else should have a turn, and everyone looked at Simon. Simon said he didn't have any thrilling tales of old to relate, but went on to do some wickedly funny impersonations of his landlady, the British Prime Minister, and a very rude London bus driver he'd once encountered. Veronica was laughing by the end; even Rebecca was smiling. Oh, I do love it when everyone gets along in this family!

Although I will probably have dreadful nightmares tonight. Those Nazi photographs seem burnt into my memory. Where *did* Veronica get that book, anyway?

And now I've jinxed myself by writing about something horrible last thing before I go to sleep! Quick, think of lovely, happy things, Sophia. Think of . . . think of . . .

Why is it that the only image that comes to mind is Simon's slow half smile?

Simon left after dawn this morning, a thick letter for Toby tucked into his jacket and the Fabergé egg rolled up inside a spare pair of socks. George and Rebecca rowed him out to the ship, a Portuguese steamer on its way north. (There are quite a few ships that will take passengers—we put a flag up above the gatehouse to signal them and eventually one stops.) The castle feels quiet and empty, which is odd because Simon is not a particularly loud or large person. One wouldn't think he would leave such a gap.

Rebecca is now sunk in gloom. Today she is wearing her black dress, and her graying hair is scraped back so severely that her cheekbones look sharp enough to cut. It's hard to believe that she was once thought a very handsome woman, but apparently it's true. Mary told me. She said that Rebecca could've had any of the village men, but none of them were good enough for her. Eventually they all married or went away from the island and the only one left was Phillip Chester, who was fifteen years older and a widower, so she had to marry him. I'm sure there's more to this story, but Alice came in at that point, scolded Mary for gossiping, and sent her out to check the lobster pots, and I never heard anything else on the topic after that.

Phillip was killed a few years later in the Great War, so I should feel sorry for Rebecca and be nicer to her, but it is very difficult. She's so horrid to Veronica, for a start—worse than she is to anyone else. She orders the rest of us around and swipes at Henry, but it's Veronica who ends up with the worst tasks when Rebecca supervises the cleaning or when we're out in the kitchen garden. And she's always stabbing away at Veronica with her knifelike tongue, taking aim at anything she thinks might be a soft spot, from Veronica's habit of gnawing at her bottom lip to Veronica's runaway mother (as if that's Veronica's fault!). Then, when this fails to get a reaction, Rebecca resorts to muttering under her breath about how Veronica is plain, clumsy, or (most ridiculous of all) lazy.

For I realized afresh this morning that Veronica runs this place. Rebecca is officially the housekeeper, but she's too busy fawning over Uncle John to do much more than supervise the cleaning and take care of some of the cooking. It's Veronica who keeps track of the bills and handles the correspondence with our solicitor; Veronica who orders the supplies and remembers the villagers' birthdays and fixes the plumbing. Even the animals seem to recognize her as head of the household—the little black cat is constantly presenting her with choice specimens of freshly killed prey, to everyone's disgust. Veronica's only a year and a bit older than me, too—it makes me uncomfortable when I think of how little I do in comparison. And even then, it's usually what I've been *asked* to do—figuring out what needs to be done, that's the difficult, grown-up job.

So today I shooed Veronica away from chores after breakfast and sent her straight to the library to work on her *Brief History*. I tidied the upstairs bedrooms and did the washing and hung it on the line. I made Henry help. We even managed a mathematics lesson at the same time, calculating the quantities of soap shavings and pegs needed.

Then I attempted to make a spinach-and-cheese pie for luncheon while Henry sat at the kitchen table. She propped the old atlas against the teapot and we played Guess Which Is Closer. I tried to be practical ("Which is closer—London or Paris?"), but Henry always goes for the most bizarre names she can find ("Which is closer—Timbuktu or Vladivostok?"). I suppose at least it gives her some reading practice. The answers, by the way, are that Montmaray is closer to London than to Paris but only by thirty miles, and that Timbuktu is closer to us than Vladivostok is by about half a globe. It always amazes me, the size of Russia—I mean, the Union of Soviet Socialist Republics or whatever they're calling themselves this year. It is absolutely enormous. If the Tsar had lived for a thousand years, he couldn't have visited all his subjects. And not knowing the individual people he ruled over, it would be so much easier to be unfair to them. (Not that I'm turning into a Communist or anything.)

Sadly, my pie wasn't very successful—the crust got burnt on

one side when Vulcan flared up and there was too much salt in that last batch of cheese (I shall have to find a tactful way to inform Mary, who is a bit too fond of experimenting with her cheese-making). Also, isn't housework *unrewarding*? One spends all that time stirring sheets around in the boiler and feeding them through the wringer and pegging them on the line and taking them down and folding them, knowing one will have to do the same thing all over again in a fortnight. Dusting and sweeping are even worse—it seemed I'd just finished one room when a breeze blew in and I turned round to find everything covered in salt and sand again.

After luncheon, I took up the scarf I've been knitting for George—I'm determined to finish it by Christmas, although it's not looking hopeful. Two months of work and it's barely a foot long, because I keep having to unpick rows. Either I find myself winding the wool so tightly that I can barely prize the loops off the needles or else I gallop along and drop stitches all over the place.

A short while later, I gave up, stuck the needles back into the snarl of wool, and came up here to the gatehouse to brood about Simon. It really is rather dull now he's gone. Although I must say, remembering my encounters with him is far more enjoyable than the actual encounters, possibly because I do an awful lot of editing. In my memories, my clothes are new and they fit perfectly, despite my somehow having grown bigger in the bust and longer in the legs. My hair is always a shiny, sweet-smelling gold and it never slips free of its pins. I never trip over pigeons in the courtyard, I never catch my sleeve on that loose nail on the kitchen door latch, and I'm never at a loss for words.

I wonder when he'll be back. No—I don't. I don't care in the slightest. I hope it won't be for months and months, by which time I will have grown sensible and sane and will have trained myself out of blushing . . .

What *is* that noise?

Heavens, will write more later!

It's late and I can barely keep my eyes open, but I feel I must set down at least a little of this afternoon's events (especially after what Veronica said about my journal-writing). Today has been like something out of a Brontë novel—strangers having staggered across the hostile moors to collapse upon our doorstep, begging for shelter and the means to repair their conveyance. Except it wasn't moors but ocean, and they didn't exactly beg for shelter, and they're not truly strangers. But their arrival was certainly dramatic. Let me see if I can recall it in order, the way a proper chronicler would.

I was in the gatehouse, curled up in a very dim patch of afternoon sunlight and daydreaming about Simon, when I first heard the faint buzzing. A bee, I thought, glancing around warily, or a wasp, but I couldn't see anything. Just as I was about to start panicking in earnest, I realized what it was. I scrambled to my feet and rushed to the window just in time to see an aeroplane swoop overhead, its wings dipping as though in salute. I stared upwards, astonished. We see aeroplanes occasionally (even an airship, once), but never so close. I tried to determine whether it was in distress—not that I could have done anything to help if it had been—but as I watched, the wings straightened and the aeroplane flew on across the island. Henry and Jimmy burst out of the kitchen and raced over the drawbridge after it, Carlos barking at their heels. Veronica leaned out the library tower, book in hand, and Rebecca did the same out a bedroom window, only without the book. The aeroplane soared towards South Head, then suddenly banked in a sharp curve. The buzzing became a spluttering. The aeroplane seemed to hesitate in midair, as if contemplating the view. Then it turned its nose down at the ground and plummeted, engine screaming.

"It's headed for the Green!" shouted Veronica, dashing into the courtyard. "Come on!"

I was already sliding down the ladder, and together we ran across the drawbridge and up the hill. The Green is more than a mile distant, almost at the end of the island. By the time Veronica and I reached it, I was panting and overheated and had a dreadful stitch in my side. But the aeroplane was apparently unharmed. It had come to rest at the near end of the Green, sitting back on its haunches, nose pointing at the sky. Henry and Jimmy were already clambering in and out of the cockpit and having a shouted conversation with one of the pilots, while the other knelt beneath the propeller, fending off the friendly attentions of Carlos.

"Are you all right?" I gasped. The person talking to Henry turned, halfway through peeling off a leather helmet, and I was surprised to see that it was a woman, a very pretty one with arched eyebrows and scarlet lips.

"Oh, my dears!" she cried. But before she could say anything else, Henry hurled herself to the ground and rushed over to us.

"This is Rupert's sister!" shouted Henry. "Toby's school friend Rupert! This is Julia! And her fiancé! And they're on their way to Madrid!"

Veronica then introduced us all properly, ordered Jimmy out of the aeroplane, and grabbed hold of Henry, who looked ready to combust with excitement. The man under the propeller stood up and bowed politely, but was too oil-smeared to shake hands.

"This is Anthony," said Julia, waving a beautifully manicured hand at him. "We're so *dreadfully* sorry for dropping in unannounced like this, but with that dratted engine—Ant was getting *quite* fed up with it, weren't you, darling?—and even if we'd turned round and managed to make it to Brest in one piece, who *knows* how the gendarme would have reacted, some of them are terribly Fascist. But Toby has told us so much about Montmaray and there you were, *right* below us, with this lovely flat landing strip . . ."

All this was said very rapidly as Julia unwound her scarf, shrugged out of her brown leather jacket, and retrieved a carpetbag from the cockpit.

"You're most welcome," said Veronica. "We're very pleased to have the opportunity to return your hospitality, after your family's great kindness to Toby over the years." She managed to seem the very image of regal graciousness, despite her torn trousers (a very old pair of Toby's) and the smear of ink along her cheek.

At that point, Alice, Mary, and George appeared, puffing a bit after a rapid climb from the village, and there were more introductions all round. Anthony pointed out bits of the engine to George, who nodded knowledgeably, then took Anthony off to the village to look for something to replace the split what's-its-name. George said he had the very thing, left over from when they installed the new water pump. Alice and Mary rounded up Jimmy and followed them, promising to walk Anthony up to the castle before nightfall. Then the rest of us headed off towards the castle ourselves, Julia still talking nonstop, apparently drawing breath through her ears.

"Absolutely *wonderful* views from here, exactly as Toby described, and what are all those—oh, *cottages*, yes, I do see that now! Heavens, there must have been hundreds of people living here at one stage—and *look* at that magnificent castle! How *unfair*, we just have an Elizabethan pile falling to bits—and, my dears, the *taxes*, you've no idea. Oh, a *drawbridge*, how divine . . ."

Veronica explained that Montmaray was, strictly speaking, a fortified house rather than a true castle, having been built in the sixteenth century rather than in medieval times. She also pointed out where Napoleon's cannons had shot an enormous hole in our curtain wall in response to King John the Fifth's threats. No one has ever got round to repairing it (as we walked past, another few bits of wall crumbled into the ocean), nor to rebuilding the East Wing, which burnt down in Edward de Quincy FitzOsborne's time ("the Crimson Conflagration," as he termed it, inspired yet another of his epic poems).

None of this deterred Julia. She exclaimed over everything with delight, from the royal standard flapping above the gatehouse ("What a heavenly shade of blue!") to the hens trailing after Spartacus ("I *adore* hens, especially those little fluffy ones, and look at the colors on that one . . . Oh, it's a pigeon—good Lord, is it one of Rupert's? I expect he's got Toby involved in all that pigeon fancying now . . .").

The only time the flow of chatter ceased was when we entered the kitchen. By unlucky coincidence, Uncle John had just emerged from one of his rare baths. He was wearing his usual tattered robe (the ermine trimming black where it trailed upon the floor), and his hair hung around his face in wet ropes. Catching sight of us, he jerked back in alarm. Henry and I looked at Veronica. She took a deep breath and gestured at our visitor.

"May I," she said, "present the Honorable Julia Stanley-Ross—"

He growled and twitched and stumbled backwards into his room, slamming the door shut.

Julia blinked.

Veronica looked at the door. "His Majesty King John the Seventh of Montmaray," she said.

"Veronica's father," added Henry helpfully. Julia's knees wobbled, as though they couldn't decide whether or not to curtsey.

"Won't you sit down?" I said quickly, pulling out a kitchen

chair. I suppose visitors should really be entertained in the Great Hall, but it's so gloomy. And in any case, Julia had already recovered and was exclaiming a bit too loudly over the rustic charms of Vulcan and our scrubbed oak table.

Rebecca clomped downstairs at that moment, no doubt having been up on the roof with the telescope. She looked dourer than ever when we told her we would have visitors for the night—she was probably thinking of the sad state of our linens. I asked her to organize tea and urged Henry to show Julia around the Great Hall so that Veronica and I could sneak upstairs and figure out what to do about beds. Fortunately, I'd washed Simon's sheets and all the towels that morning.

"The Gold Room," said Veronica, leading the way.

"But we can't put Julia *and* Anthony in here," I protested as Veronica shoved open the door, showering us both with flakes of gilt.

"They're engaged, aren't they?" said Veronica.

"There's only one bed!"

"So?" said Veronica, but she relented when I gave her a scandalized look. "Fine. Julia can have this one and Anthony can go in . . . in Toby's room."

"The roof leaks," I pointed out. "Right over the bed, that's why he spent the holidays in the nursery."

"Perhaps we could move a dresser into the Solar and put someone in there."

"No mattress, remember? Unless we haul Toby's all the way down the gallery." We both winced at the thought.

"The nursery, then, but do we have enough sheets for two extra beds?"

In the end, we decided my sheets were the cleanest. Veronica made up the Gold Room bed with them and Toby's pillow, while I readied the nursery, where Simon had slept. However, when we showed Julia her room, our careful plans collapsed. Dropping her carpetbag with an exaggerated yawn, she threw herself across the bed and promptly disappeared in a cloud of dust and feathers.

"Julia!" we shrieked.

We each took an arm and heaved her out of the sunken mattress. Examining the bed slats, Veronica discovered that two had completely rotted through and most of the others were suspect. Carlos, determined to be helpful, squeezed himself next to Veronica and thrust his nose into the mattress.

"There's the Blue Room," said Henry.

"Which doesn't contain a bed," said Veronica over Carlos's tremendous sneezes.

"And is haunted," I pointed out.

Henry nodded at Julia's raised eyebrow. "Oh, yes, the ghost is awfully fearsome if you're not a FitzOsborne. But you can have my room, Julia, I'll go in with Veronica and Sophie."

Veronica gave her a dubious look (Henry's room is full of cuttlefish shells, shark jaws, barnacle-encrusted driftwood, fish skeletons, broken lobster pots, and old bird eggs, none of which smell very nice), but in the end, it seemed the best solution. Then we left Julia to change for dinner after giving her our only spare towel and demonstrating how to unstop the loo if it looked as though it was about to overflow.

I bet they don't have to worry about that sort of thing at Buckingham Palace.

Luckily, dinner went well. To start, we had cold lobster (Alice brought a pair of them with her when she and Jimmy walked Anthony back up to the castle, bless her) and spinach salad. Then there was fish pie. It was a bit gluey, but Rebecca opened a dusty bottle of wine she'd found in the cellar and kept Julia's and Anthony's glasses full, so I don't think they noticed. Afterwards, there were two types of cheese, both Mary's, but the lavender one turned out to be rather good. We probably should have had soup to start with, but there wasn't anything to put in it except spinach or fish. In any case, Julia said the lobster was better than the Savoy's.

Anthony nodded forcefully every time Julia said anything, but was otherwise quiet during dinner—too busy eating, perhaps. He is not very pleasant to behold, poor man. He has a lot of freckles and a mustache that looks as though a furry caterpillar has fallen asleep on his upper lip. (Simon appears increasingly handsome, now that I have someone with whom to compare him.)

After dinner, Anthony and Veronica discussed the Spanish situation—or rather, Veronica asked him a lot of questions and he did his best to keep up with her. Anthony explained that he'd tried to volunteer his services to the Republican cause in August when the war began, but the London recruiters weren't very encouraging—he wasn't a proper member of the Communist

Party or the trade union movement, and he didn't have any military training. He thought this was rather unsporting of them. Then his mother somehow found out and made him promise not to take part in any fighting.

"So I had to give her my word," said Anthony, frowning at the tablecloth.

"Ant's the only son and heir," said Julia, patting his arm.

"But it's just so, so . . . unfair!" he burst out. "Now that blasted Prime Minister of ours has banned British businesses from selling weapons to the Spanish government, and you know Hitler and Mussolini are giving those Fascist rebels all the help they can!"

"Well, rumor has it the Soviet Union is doing its utmost to aid the other side," said Veronica. "Anyway, what about the Non-Intervention Committee in London? Have they reached any decision yet?"

"I don't think so. But wait—Julia, didn't your uncle say something about that?"

Julia winked at us. "He's rather high up in some top-secret government department."

"He thinks they'll probably want everyone to keep out of the whole thing," Anthony said.

"Yes, the name Non-Intervention Committee does rather hint at that," said Veronica dryly. "But anyway, Anthony, if you're supposed to keep away from the fighting, what are you doing flying to Madrid? Isn't it surrounded by the Fascists?"

"Well, yes. They say it's getting a *bit* hairy, but the International Brigades are putting up a good defense! So I thought I might just drop by and . . . well, see what I could do. Offer to take mail back to England, maybe write down some observations for the newspapers, that sort of thing—"

"To be frank, we weren't sure we'd get quite as far as Madrid," interrupted Julia. "Perhaps the northern bit of Spain, if we were lucky."

"We *would* have got to Madrid," said Anthony, giving Julia a look, "if that dratted engine hadn't packed it in."

I sat there thinking that Julia must be terribly brave— imagine agreeing to go anywhere *near* a battle zone! I mentioned this, which started off a discussion about women going to war. Apparently one of the first British volunteers to die in this Spanish conflict had been a woman—an artist who'd been working in Barcelona. She'd been part of a unit trying to blow up a Fascist munitions train. Anthony seemed personally offended by this—that they'd let her in to fight and not him, when everyone *knew* women were physically weaker and always went to pieces in a crisis.

"Do they?" said Julia doubtfully. "Always go to pieces if there's a crisis, I mean."

"I certainly would," I said.

"I wouldn't!" cried Henry, popping out from the shadows of the stairwell.

"I thought you were supposed to be in bed," said Veronica.

"I was, but I couldn't sleep, your bed is all lumpy," said Henry. "It's full of *books*."

Veronica took her back upstairs again, probably to avoid an

argument with Anthony. Faulty logic ("Women always go to pieces in a crisis") annoys her no end. And I suppose even the "physically weaker" assertion could be the subject of debate— after all, it's women, not men, who have babies. If all women were as frail as men seem to believe, the human race would have died out millennia ago. I found myself wondering whether most of the men at debutante parties would be like Anthony, and whether I'd want to get engaged to such a man. But it turns out his mother is an American oil heiress (which must come in handy when buying aeroplanes and such) and his father is an earl. I think this is why Julia's parents haven't objected to her engagement, even if Anthony *is* a bit of a Communist . . .

7th November 1936

I fell asleep over my journal last night and awoke to find ink smeared over both my face and the page. Fortunately, there were no sheets left on my bed to get ruined—just the blanket, which is dark blue anyway.

I'm snatching a few minutes here in the gatehouse before I go down to help Veronica with luncheon. Anthony had hoped to leave this morning, but storm clouds are skidding past to gather in an ominous clump near the horizon. I don't expect they'll get away now until tomorrow.

It is lovely having new people around to talk to, but rather exhausting having to keep the bathroom clean and make proper meals all the time. I have a sinking feeling when I think about tonight's dinner—I fear we'll have to sacrifice one of the hens (we can't keep having fish all the time). If we do, I think it ought to be the beady-eyed yellow one that keeps pecking at my ankles. It's spent too much time with Spartacus, I can tell. We'll get Rebecca to do the bit with the ax, and I'll make sure I'm a safe distance away this time. Last Christmas, I fainted at the sight of all the blood. (I don't mind my own blood; it's other blood that bothers me—which is not really very logical when I think about it.)

I'd better go—Veronica's alone in the kitchen, as Rebecca's devoting all her time to Uncle John at the moment. He is very agitated by the strange voices and refuses to leave his bed. I wonder if we can get away with serving omelets for luncheon. Perhaps if we put lots of herbs and cheese and spinach in and call them *omelettes de Montmaray* . . .

It is evening now, the washing up is all done and I am sitting in the kitchen. I have annexed the stove end of the table so I can take advantage of the firelight (I'm writing mostly in Kernetin, so it doesn't matter if Julia or Anthony peeks). Julia and Henry are playing Squid, a card game of Toby's invention, down the other end of the table, and Anthony and Veronica are in the middle, having a debate about Communism. Anthony is not much of a match for her (he's rubbish at arguing compared to Simon), but whenever Veronica bests him at a point, she argues on his side for a bit to make him feel better. He is looking rather confused at the moment.

"Of course," Veronica is saying, "one only needs to look at the Soviet Union to see Marx's predictions unfolding. The workers have certainly seized control of the means of production there."

"Yes!" says Anthony. "Exactly! It's . . . it's an inevitable conflict between the workers and the middle class! Just as Marx said would happen. All over Europe!"

"And yet, not quite *all* over Europe, surely? Not here in Montmaray." Veronica paused. "Of course, we don't actually have a middle class. Oh, wait, yes we do—we have Simon Chester."

"That's Rebecca's son," Henry says, glancing up from her enormous pile of cards. (She's probably cheating, but Julia looks more amused than annoyed.)

"I think we're more feudal here, really," Veronica continues. "Except we don't have very many subjects anymore. But one thing does confuse me—if the Spanish workers' triumph over capitalism is so inevitable, Anthony, why do *you* need to help them out?"

"Er," says Anthony.

"And yet," Veronica says thoughtfully, staring up at the ceiling, "didn't Marx also predict that government would wither away when the workers were finally in control of the means of production? And there's certainly nothing withering away about Stalin's government, is there? It makes one wonder what else Marx got wrong . . ."

Anthony looks towards Julia helplessly, but she just gives him a fond smile, then goes back to studying her cards.

I had a nice long chat with Julia today while I was getting dinner ready. (She did offer to help, but is not very experienced at vegetable peeling, it turns out—I think they must have rather a lot of servants.) She told me all about her presentation at

Court two years ago—she seemed to assume that Veronica and I would be doing the same next Season. Julia wore a gold-and-cream brocade dress with her mother's wedding veil as a train, a headdress of three ostrich feathers and Alençon lace held in place by diamond clips, long white kid gloves with pearl buttons, and shoes with two-inch gold heels. The dress *alone* cost thirty-two guineas. As she said, imagine how many Spanish refugees that would feed and shelter! Of course, she hadn't even met Anthony at that stage. And there weren't any Spanish refugees then anyway.

I did enjoy hearing about the coming-out parties, despite my guilty twinges over all the conspicuous consumption (as Anthony—or Marx—would say) All the flowers and fairy lights and champagne and ices and beautiful dresses! I almost felt I was there.

"And there are *never* enough men for dance partners—you should have heard my mother frantically telephoning round the day before my dance. 'I need a man! No, men! Lots of them, as many as you can find!' Now, if only *your* brother had been a few years older! What a triumph that would have been for her! *So* handsome, and heir to the throne—he already has half my friends and all my cousins in love with him. Toby is going to be *devastating* when he finishes school."

"He *is* rather good-looking, isn't he?" I said, a bit embarrassed. I don't know why I felt I had to be modest, though—it wasn't *my* looks we were talking about. Except it does seem a bit silly to be discussing good looks in a boy, when they're so irrelevant. It's not as though Toby needs them to catch a husband. You'd think God, or whoever, could have saved up just a tiny bit of Toby's beauty to pass on to me.

"Darling!" said Julia. "You have no idea, he'll be like King Leopold of the Belgians, only more so, debutantes swooning all over the place. Did you hear about that tragic accident last year, his poor wife dead and they say he was driving! And *speaking* of royalty . . ."

Then she related a lot of terrible scandal about Britain's new King and a married American woman who seems to be his mistress. I was worried Veronica would come in and overhear and realize how utterly frivolous I am. Not that she would say anything. And if she did, I could always argue that there's a fine line between gossip and history when one's talking about kings.

Julia also asked me if I was in love with anyone. It turned out she was just making conversation (what peculiar conversations English girls must have with each other!), but for a second I was terrified she'd seen something in my face that had given away my secret—although what that something could have been, I've no idea. In novels, women in love tend to become even more beautiful or else wither away to a shadow. Neither of these things seems to be happening to me, which is further proof that I am *not* in love with Simon, which is a profound relief.

I considered asking Julia for some general advice on the subject of love, but I was worried I would get muddled and she might end up thinking I was asking about the Facts of

Life, which could prove embarrassing. For me more than her, probably—she is so very Modern, with her red lipstick and permanent-waved hair and aeroplane-flying. I wonder if she and Anthony have done It . . . but I don't think she is quite *that* Modern. They'll probably wait until they're married. I certainly would, if I were engaged to Anthony. I'd want to put It off as long as possible.

I already know how It works, of course—Toby told Veronica and me years ago. I was so revolted that I immediately added "men" to my list of Horrifying Things to Be Avoided, but Veronica dug out an old medical textbook and discovered Toby hadn't been entirely accurate. He'd got the information thirdhand anyway, from someone at school. Since then, I've read a few Modern novels (one of them, left behind by a governess of ours, was particularly informative, even if I didn't understand all the French) and it sounds like It could be rather nice. With the right man, of course, and after one was properly married.

Unfortunately, all this talk of It has conjured up images of Simon, and now I cannot get them out of my head. I can't help wondering how many girls he's kissed. I can imagine Simon taking kissing as seriously as he does everything else. He would frown slightly, his dark eyes focused on the girl's lips. He'd curl his fingers into her hair and stroke one thumb across her cheek and bend down to capture my . . . *her* lips. It would probably be quite scratchy unless he'd recently shaved—yes, best to concentrate on the unpleasant aspects of it. His hair would be stiff with hair oil, too—although it does smell lovely, of cloves and oranges, and at least *he* doesn't have a horrible mustache . . .

Now Veronica is looking at me oddly because she caught me running my fingertips along my bottom lip. Oh dear.

I think I had better go to bed.

14th November 1936

Since Julia and Anthony left, I've spent most of my time curled up in the Blue Room, reading Walter de la Mare and sighing a lot. The weather is doing its best to match my mood—mist and showers, interspersed with icy squalls. It's affecting everyone, even Veronica. Yesterday, she and Henry had an enormous row in the kitchen—I could hear the shouting all the way up in the Blue Room. Ten minutes later, Henry burst in, ranting about how mean and unfair Veronica was, and how Veronica only cared about people if they'd been dead hundreds of years. I gathered Veronica had accused Henry of taking a piece of paper from her *Brief History* notes and then drawing on the back of it.

"She never even listened to me!" Henry shouted. "She's always blaming me, I'm *always* the escape goat!"

"The . . . what?" I said. "You mean 'scapegoat'?"

"That's what I said!" Henry stomped around the room a bit more. "Anyway, I *needed* that paper. I'm drawing up some very important plans for Jimmy's and my raft. It's going to have a mast, and a special diving bell off the side so we can collect all the sunken treasure at the bottom of the Chasm. Maybe even *two* masts!"

Then I went downstairs to find the shouting had set off Uncle John, who was stalking around the kitchen and raving about Isabella, with Rebecca nodding and urging him on whenever he seemed to falter. It's like living in Bedlam here, sometimes. If it hadn't been pouring, I would have gone off to the village to spend the rest of the afternoon with Alice.

However, today dawned a little brighter—and we had letters delivered. There was a fat package from Toby, a thin one from our solicitor, and a little brown-paper parcel that Veronica immediately hid in the sewing basket. It must be from the solicitor as well, although I don't know why she'd bother hiding it. Unless it's some sort of surprise for someone—no, the next birthday is Veronica's, and that's three months away. Wait, could *Simon* have secretly sent Veronica something?

One would think that all this cold, wet weather would have doused any lingering sparks of romanticism in me. Clearly not.

Anyway, here is Toby's letter, translated:

Dear Everyone,

Rupert just told me all about Julia's visit! She was most impressed with the castle—yes, yes, Veronica, fortified house, I know—and found Rebecca and Uncle J terrifyingly Gothic. Julia's rather fun, isn't she? None of us can work out how she ended up engaged to Ant, who could bore for

England. But perhaps girls go for men who are Political; is that true, Veronica? Ant's certainly that—last time I saw him, at Rupert's brother's engagement party, he was droning on about the evils of Capitalism, all the while stuffing himself with plover eggs (which were scrumptious, I must admit). I hope you put him in my room and he got dripped on when it rained—he adores it when he gets a chance to experience how the Poor live.

Speaking of parties, Aunt Charlotte made me spend the midterm holiday with her, which would have been dire except for two things. Firstly, I took Simon with me (he had papers and things for her to sign, anyway), and secondly, Lord Bosworth had a three-day shooting party and invited us for dinner on Saturday. Thank heavens he didn't think to invite me to the shoot. I wish I could say it's because I feel sorry for those poor pheasants, but it's really that I'm afraid I'll blast my foot off, or worse.

I suppose you want to know what we ate and who was there. Well, there were five courses—caviar, grilled sole with salad, beef with mushroom sauce and potatoes, cheese soufflé, and a pudding of sponge cake with angelica syrup and whipped cream—also, champagne and three sorts of wine, and then port. By the end, I felt like the snake that swallowed the bison in that book of Henry's. I just sat there, digesting, certain I wouldn't be able to move for another six months, while all around me the men lit up their smelly cigars and talked over the top of one another. It was all about politics, of course, and if it hadn't been for my enormous stomach being in the way, I would have ducked under the tablecloth, crawled towards the door, and tried to make my escape.

The politics was even worse than usual because the German Ambassador, von Ribbentrop, was there—oh, I heard the most amusing bit of gossip about him from Julia! It seems he was only a Ribbentrop, not a von, but he managed to persuade some elderly female von Ribbentrop that he was actually related to her, and he had her adopt him so he could take on her aristocratic name. Isn't that a scream? Especially as all the girls call him von Ribbensnob—you should have heard him at dinner, he's worse than Lady Bosworth.

As for who else was there—Rupert's eldest brother and his wife (who is Lady B's niece); a young American widow called Mrs. Hooper, dripping with diamonds (she even had them on the ankle straps of her shoes); one of the Mitford girls (forget her name, but not one of the madly Fascist ones, thank heavens, there was more than enough politics already); two Earls; and a French Duke. I rather think I was invited to see if I'd "do" for Lord and Lady B's youngest daughter, who looks and sounds almost exactly like a horse. At first I wondered if Lady B mistakenly thought we had money, but no, turns out she's just gaga about royalty, even unimportant ones like us. Needless to say, I tried to be as charmless as possible around the daughter. (And don't tut, Soph, I wasn't cruel. To mollify you, please find enclosed two Tatlers and *a* Country Life, *which I stole from Aunt C's drawing room.)*

Now I am back at school, which is as horrid as ever. I have failed two Latin tests, History is a mystifying blur of dates and names, and we are doing Titus Andronicus in English. Also, the Music Master is in love with me, so I have to keep dashing into broom cupboards to avoid him in the corridors. By the way, an accident happened with my room-mate's bagpipes; I can't imagine how it occurred, but they are unplayable. The entire school is prostrate with grief.

Must go, lights-out in a minute. Do write back lots and lots, you know how much I miss you all.

Love from,

Toby

Then there were notes for each of us, even Carlos—that's supposed to encourage Henry to practice her reading aloud. Carlos's and Henry's were in English, of course. Veronica's mostly consisted of a copy of a letter that Simon had drafted and Toby had signed regarding Montmaray's policy of non-intervention in the Spanish conflict, which had been sent to the British Foreign Office. Veronica read it aloud to us and I understood just enough to be impressed by Simon's clever phrasing. Veronica said it was meaningless diplomatic drivel and that Simon had better not have used the Royal Seal, but that perhaps it would remind someone somewhere in that government that Montmaray was once an influential presence in European politics.

Then she went off to the library. Lucky she did before I translated my note; otherwise she would have wondered what I was
squeaking about and asked to read it. It said:

Dear Soph,

 *I didn't dare put this in the letter because I knew V
would have a fit, but Simon came to dinner at Lord B's. I
pretended he was some sort of cousin of ours and a diplomat
besides (well, he is, sort of). Aunt C didn't realize until it
was too late, and then it didn't matter because Simon was so
charming and clever. Truly. Lady B's daughter, the horsy
one, was quite taken with him.*

 *Then we played a game after dinner, where you say a
line of verse and everyone has to guess where it's from. I was
completely stupid at it—all I could think of to recite was
"The Lady of Shalott"—but Simon quoted Edward de
Quincy's "Voyage of King Bartholomew," which had everyone stumped (even me—I'd forgotten just how awful
Edward's verse could be).*

 *And then Simon started telling all sorts of Montmaray
stories—pirate raids and sunken treasure and the Armada
and Napoleon and so on—and the girls were mad for it,
which of course drew von Ribbensnob over like a bee to
honey (he has wandering hands, just in case you ever have
the misfortune to meet him; the girls were all giving him a
wide berth). Then he and Simon had a long fireside chat
about history and politics. I didn't understand a word, but*

*von R was most impressed, I could tell. Isn't it splendid for
Simon? He is wasted in that clerk's position. If only he spoke
German . . .*

*Also, I must tell you that Julia thought you were very
pretty. She said you had beautiful eyes and the sweetest expression. I know you won't believe a word of it, but it's true.
So there. Just wait till you come over here and acquire some
nice dresses; you'll outshine all the debutantes. And yes, of
course I'll convince Aunt C to buy you lots of lovely things;
did you really need to ask? Is V still being stubborn, or have
you talked her round by now? Regardless, make sure she
writes to Grenville about the traveling arrangements—or I
could get Simon to do it. Let me know. But do get on with it.*

I'm not sure which I found more thrilling—the thought of
Simon in evening dress, impressing everyone with his clever-
ness, or the image of myself in a glorious, glittering gown, walking into a dinner party on (I might as well admit it here) Simon's
arm. Drawing gasps of admiration. "Who is that elegant couple?"
Et cetera.

Yes, utterly pathetic, I know. Anyway, it's a sharp reminder
that I need to stop being such a jellyfish and determine once and
for all what I'm doing—staying here with Veronica or leaving.
But any decision-making will have to wait till tomorrow—I'm
going to bed now. My throat feels as though I've swallowed a
handful of sand. I do hope I'm not getting a cold . . .

16th November 1936

The weather is miserable and so am I. My nose is clogged, my head aches, and I can't stop coughing. I've been trying to read, but have to keep breaking off to grope for a handkerchief, and then I lose my place—and besides, my eyeballs hurt whenever I move them. I thought writing might be better, but it's no good, either. I can't help wondering if this is God's punishment for me fancying myself in love with Simon. And now I'm sounding like Rebecca—I really must be feverish. Going to try to sleep now, although every time I drift off, I dream I'm drowning in a deep, dark sea . . .

Veronica just came in to bring me hyssop tea and the news. Henry is coughing now, and so is Rebecca—although they're attempting to outdo each other in protestations of wellness, Henry because apparently it's *girlish* to be confined to bed and Rebecca because she believes His Majesty would starve to death if she wasn't up and about to look after him. There has been no communication to or from the village today, most unusual for us, but that's probably a good thing, as we don't want to spread this whatever-it-is to them. Imagine if George became ill—he's not getting any younger, and this incessant coughing is so wearying. Veronica points out, however, that we probably caught it from the men who brought our mail, one of whom she remembers coughing and spluttering all over our parcels, in which case we've all been exposed to it.

I've just read back over this and cannot believe I actually wrote the inane phrase "not getting any younger." I do hope my brain hasn't been permanently affected by this flu . . .

18th November 1936

I write this sitting by Henry's bed. Her face is flushed and damp, and her limbs keep jerking the blankets crooked, but at least she's sleeping now. Awake, she is a most uncooperative patient. She fusses when I try to get her to sip some hyssop tea, refuses spoonfuls of broth, and pushes my hand away fretfully when I sponge her forehead. Veronica, the only one to have escaped the contagion, is worried enough to have raised the "Doctor Required" signal flag over the gatehouse. Not that many ships are likely to see it—there's a storm bearing down on us from the north and another from the west. Any captain worth his salt would be steering well clear of us. There have been hardly any ships around lately, anyway—I think it's to do with the Spanish war. But as I keep telling myself, what could a doctor do that we aren't already doing?

Veronica has just taken a pot of chicken soup (she promised me it wasn't the white fluffy hen) and a jam roly-poly down to the village in case any of them are ill. Meanwhile, my voice has disappeared almost entirely after reading Henry three chapters of *Treasure Island* (using appropriately terrifying tones for Black Dog and old Pew). It's the only way to keep her in bed. At least her fever seems to have broken, thank heavens. Going downstairs now to brew some hot lemon and honey for my throat . . .

Veronica is back and says Alice, Jimmy, and George are all coughing, but George is by far the worst affected. He wouldn't let her visit him—he was afraid she'd catch it, even though Veronica shouted through his door that we have been coughing all over her for days and she feels fine. Mary reported he looks dreadful, gray and withered, with his chest sunken in. Veronica has left the doctor's flag up over the gatehouse, but the weather is terrible, there are no ships on the horizon, and in any case, George despises doctors. He maintains that sea air, brandy, and comfrey ointment cure just about every ailment known to man and that "bone saw-ers" just make matters worse.

Oh, Henry's awake again—back to the Admiral Benbow Inn and marauding buccaneers . . .

23rd November 1936

Veronica went down to the village early this morning and Mary was waiting for her on George's doorstep; she said he'd been asking for Veronica all night. Veronica didn't tell me what he said to her—it couldn't have been much, he was so ill—then Jimmy came in, coughing himself, to sit with his great-great-uncle, and ten minutes later, George took his last breath. Neither Veronica nor I can bear to tell Henry just yet. I can't quite believe it myself. Imagining Montmaray without George is just so . . .

Well, I've had a good long cry, and although my nose is all clogged up again, I feel a bit better. I am madly praying to a God I'm not sure I believe in that George is now floating on a tranquil sea with a good supply of fresh pilchards for bait, a set of unknotted lines, and lots of cloud cover so the fish can't see any shadows. That's a lovely picture. I will try to keep it firmly in my mind now as I write to Toby and tell him. Veronica has gone back down to the village to help Mary pack up George's things and clean the cottage.

It is still raining, but slow and steady now. The gale has eased to a stiff breeze. Every now and then, the clouds tear themselves apart and silver shows through. It's the closest I've seen to sunlight in days.

25th November 1936

Today we buried George and something very strange happened. I have told and told myself that I was just being fanciful, but I know I wasn't. It really happened, and I don't see how it could have. But I'm determined to write it all down—that might help me figure it out.

All right. Today we buried George. There's no room for a cemetery on the island (and it's difficult to dig six feet down into solid granite), so all the villagers are buried at sea. I wouldn't want it for myself, but George loved the sea—at least, he respected it and was grateful to it, and I suppose that's pretty close to love. Veronica, Henry, and I walked down to the village after breakfast—rather slowly, as Henry was still coughing and even I felt a bit wobbly after all those days in bed (Rebecca stayed back to look after Uncle John). Alice and Mary were still sewing George inside his sailcloth shroud when we arrived. They'd dressed him in his good trousers and a clean blue shirt, and tied something heavy to his feet to stop him floating. I think it was that broken bit of anchor he used as a doorstop. After they were finished, we carried him to the gig—he weighed hardly anything—and then set off towards South Head in the thickening rain.

It was the most wretched boat trip I've ever taken. The wind scooped up armfuls of icy water and tossed it in our faces, meanwhile whipping our hair around so hard that we could barely see. Alice, Mary, Jimmy, and I handled the oars. Henry was coughing harder than ever, although she insisted she was fine—and indeed, she looked ten times better than Veronica, who was as white as the shroud. Veronica has always been close to George, but I was surprised at how badly she was letting her grief show. It isn't like her at all; she's always been the most stoic of us. And George was nearly a hundred years old, after all. He'd had a full life, a good one; he'd been loved by his family; he'd died quietly, without much pain, watched over by his great-great-nephew. If one has to die, there are far worse deaths than his.

But I didn't say any of that to Veronica, of course.

We were well past the rocks, out on the dark blue water, when Alice and Mary finally stopped rowing. They looked at Veronica expectantly.

"Here, then, Your Highness?" Alice called over the moaning of the wind. Veronica said nothing. I'd expected her to take the lead in the ceremony—I certainly hadn't a clue what we were supposed to do, other than toss the body overboard—but she merely huddled in the prow, staring at the thrashing sea. Alice and Mary turned their enquiring looks on me. We were all aware that I was a very poor second choice of leader, but I nodded.

"There's usually a prayer first," Mary whispered. "Shall we?"

I nodded again, and she and Alice recited the Lord's Prayer, Jimmy joining in halfway through after a prod in the ribs from his mother. I mouthed along, but couldn't help wondering what George would have thought of it. The only time I'd ever heard him mention God was once when he'd stepped on a fishhook. I'd never seen him go anywhere near the chapel or say grace at meals or spend Sundays doing anything other than what he usually did. If he'd believed in any god, it would have been Neptune or Poseidon, not the God of the Anglican Book of Common Prayer.

"Amen," said Alice, Mary, and Jimmy.

I was fairly sure that something from the Bible came next— "I am the resurrection, and the life" or "Ashes to ashes, dust to dust" or "O death, where is thy sting?"—but I couldn't remember what, exactly. Clearly, neither could anyone else. After an awkward pause, Alice and Mary hoisted up the bundle, one at each end. The gig rocked wildly for a moment as we all struggled to retain our balance. Veronica's arm shot out to steady Henry and I felt my shoulders slump in relief—*now* she had come back to herself, now she would take over. But she still said nothing, and suddenly George's body was overboard, slipping into the sea with barely a splash.

"Someone ought to say something now," Henry said hoarsely between coughs. "Something . . . special."

I glanced at Veronica. Her hand was still clenched around

Henry's upper arm, but her face was hidden behind her hair, which the wind had wrenched out of its pins. Everyone but Veronica seemed to be looking at me.

So I stood up, not quite knowing what I would say. I opened my mouth and suddenly it was full of words—Shakespeare's, not my own, but I thought George might approve, since he'd battled so many storms at sea.

"Full fathom five, thy father lies," I said. "Of his bones are coral made, those are pearls that were his eyes—nothing of him that doth fade, but doth suffer a sea-change, into something rich and strange. Sea-nymphs hourly ring his knell . . ."

My voice was barely audible, even to me, over the wind and the waves.

"Hark!" I said, louder. "Now I hear them! Ding-dong, bell!"

Henry tilted her head, as though listening for underwater chimes. Alice reached out for Jimmy and laid a broad hand on his back, nodding at me all the while.

"That were lovely, Your Highness," said Mary. Veronica looked up and gave me a surprised, pleased half smile, bringing Simon to mind, and I was still basking in the general approval when an enormous wave crashed over the prow. In all the shouting and confusion, one of the oars slid overboard.

"I'll get it," I yelled, because I was closest. I leaned over the side. The oar bucked in the gray-blue froth, brushing my fingertips.

"Let me, Your Highness," cried Alice, but I'd already curled my hand around the paddle and was dragging it closer.

That was when it happened.

I looked down into the water, still clutching the oar, and suddenly everything went dark. And I *know* I often get a bit faint when I hang my head upside down for a long time, but this was different—I could see, but the noise and the cold seemed far away and I wasn't even sure if I was still breathing. I felt as though I were in a dream. Then a long white shape drifted under the boat, under my outstretched arm, and I nearly screamed because I realized I *was* inside a dream, *that* dream, except this time it was all real.

Of course, the shape was George's body, not yet sunk in the turbulent water. I knew that. The bundle moved restlessly, the bit of anchor tied to his feet not quite heavy enough to drag his body under. I could see where the stitching of the canvas had started to come undone. Thick, dark hair poked out of the top, washing around in the swirling current . . . except George hadn't had any hair; he'd been bald ever since I could remember. I was shivering by then, trying to pull my arm back, but it seemed frozen solid. The waves tossed the bundle up and down, to and fro. All at once, the head flopped out of the cloth, its face lolling to one side, and that was when I saw it clearly.

It was Isabella.

I stared into her dead eyes for an infinite second—and then I was being yanked back into the gig and someone was shouting and I felt a jersey being pulled over my head. The wool smelled of Veronica, of soap and tea and ink.

"Sorry," I gasped. "Just . . . felt a bit faint."

Henry unclenched my fingers from the oar and Veronica insisted on rowing back in my stead. The rain had turned to a downpour by then, and I was cold and wet and bone-tired. Shock, I suppose.

Well, I'm not in shock now, eight hours later, sitting up in bed with a blanket round my shoulders and a hot brick at my feet, and I'm certain it was Isabella's face. It wasn't even how I imagine she must look now, but how she looked years ago, before she left. The face I saw was Veronica's face, only with a sharper nose, darker eyes, more of a peak where her hair was pulled away from her forehead. Yes, it was Isabella; I *know* it was.

And now— now I understand that it's been Isabella all along, that *she* has been the thing in my dreams. But what does it mean? It doesn't make any sense. Firstly, Isabella isn't dead, and secondly, if she did, by chance, die sometime in the past eight years without anyone informing us, she certainly wasn't buried at sea off South Head—we'd know if she had been. Unless it's some sort of prophecy—except she looked so young. Isabella was always very diligent about her lotions and facial massages and so on, but she'd be nearly forty now, and the face didn't look that old.

If this vision (for want of a better word) involved anyone but Isabella, I'd tell Veronica about it—she'd soon talk me back into common sense. Although perhaps not—not in the mood she's in right now. She's barely said a word these past few days.

Also, while I remember—another odd thing happened. I came into our bedroom the day George died, and Veronica was sitting on her bed with her back to the door, holding a long piece of shiny cloth. Now, I am familiar with every single garment that each of us owns (there are not that many of them, and I've pretty much taken over doing all the laundry now), and this didn't belong to either of us, or to anyone else in the castle. It was too glossy, too richly colored. Veronica jumped up and disappeared into the bathroom as soon as she heard me, and when she came back, rubbing her towel over her face, there was no sign of the cloth. I didn't like to ask, but because I have Isabella on my mind, all I can think now is that it was one of *her* dresses. I can almost see Isabella striding along in it, the fabric swirling around her long legs. Veronica must have kept it all this time—but why? Where could she have hidden it (we do share a room), and why would it be any comfort to her now in her grief over George, given her poor opinion of her mother?

I have had more than enough of mysteries for one day. I am wary of falling asleep and dreaming, so I'm going to sit up all night (or as much of it as I can manage) and reread *Northanger Abbey*. If any book is able to make dark mysteries seem ridiculous, it's that one.

15th December 1936

Poor journal, I've been neglecting you. But I haven't felt like writing and nothing much has happened. However, I *have* finally made up my mind to go to England. I haven't actually told any one this yet, but there it is, written down in ink. Now I'll have to go through with it.

You see, I've resolved to become Sensible. It's futile, me trying to set myself against Aunt Charlotte, against family tradition and social custom—and that's what I'd be doing if I attempted to stay here. It's all very well for Veronica, but I'm not her. *I'm* not strong-willed or clever. I *want* to go to dances and dinner parties and the theater and meet eligible young men and fall in love and marry and have children. Well, I don't particularly want to have children (not if they're going to turn out like Henry), but the other things sound lovely. I'll just have to learn to cope with being in a terrifying new situation so far away from home.

Now that I've turned Sensible, I've also resolved to restrain my natural tendency towards being fanciful. So I've told myself firmly that whatever I thought I saw at George's funeral was merely my overactive imagination—the result of reading too many Gothic novels, probably. And whenever I'm in the Blue Room and feel invisible fingers trailing down the back of my neck, I will remind myself that it's merely a draft, as Veronica says.

It's fortunate I have all my resolutions to occupy me, because Veronica is not a very cheery companion at the moment. She's never been like Rebecca or Henry, who let the whole world know they're in a black mood by stomping around, lashing out, and shouting. Nor is she like me—I sit in corners and sulk. No, she simply seems . . . absent. Yesterday, for example, Rebecca launched into a monologue about Simon's immense intelligence and natural leadership abilities (I can't remember what started her off), but Veronica didn't so much as raise an eyebrow after Rebecca returned to Uncle John's room.

"Is Simon going to become something important, then?" said Henry. "Is he going to be a solicitor like Mr. Grenville? Or a . . . a commodore? No, that's the navy, isn't it? What's that gentleman called who used to live in Montmaray House in London and have meetings with their Prime Minister?"

"Ambassador?" I offered.

"Yes, that's it," said Henry. "Is Simon going to be an ambassador for Montmaray? Veronica, *is* he?"

"No, he's not," said Veronica calmly, writing away at the *Brief History*. "Montmaray's ambassadors have always been of *noble* birth."

"Veronica!" I couldn't help protesting. "Remember, 'Kind hearts are more than coronets, and simple faith than Norman blood.'"

"Are you suggesting that Simon Chester has a *kind heart?*" Veronica asked, still not looking up. "Although I'll allow the simple faith—a simple faith in his own ambition."

"What's a coronet?" demanded Henry. "Soph? What do you mean about Norman blood? Is it to do with battles?"

I *might* have been able to provoke Veronica into an argument about Simon then, if I'd really tried, but by the time I'd finished my explanation to Henry, Veronica had gone off to the library to check the spelling of some long-dead prince's name and it was too late.

It must be that she's still upset over George . . .

But now the supply ship's been sighted, guessing from the clamor Henry's making. Will finish this later.

Received from supply ship—two tins of paraffin, a box of dried fruit, a sack of flour, a side of bacon, five skeins of khaki knitting wool, new boots for Henry, what looks like a Christmas hamper from the Stanley-Rosses, another mysterious brown-paper parcel that Veronica hid (although not before I'd seen it), and a letter from Toby:

> *Dear All,*
>   *Aunt C is fussing over her broken foot (an absentminded horse stood on it at Lord B's last hunt) and is insisting I spend*

Christmas with her. I will try to get out of it, but she's madly clingy at the moment. Still in shock, I expect, over . . . no, you'll never guess. King Edward has abdicated! Given up the British throne to marry an American divorcée! Isn't it too scandalous? Julia says that the unfortunate woman, Wallis Simpson, has actually been divorced twice. Or divorced once and still trying to divorce the second husband; I can't recall the details. I'll enclose a newspaper article for you to read. Anyway, Aunt C is appalled by the whole thing.

Lady B is devastated, too—claims she gave the Simpson woman "a frank talking-to" at a party in London a few weeks ago and now wishes she'd been even more forceful. I can just see Lady B stomping over, all towering hair and clanking emeralds, to honk at the poor woman. No wonder Mrs. Simpson's decamped to the Continent—I would, too, if that's what it took to get away from Lady B. All I want to know is—why on earth would any mother (even an American one) name her baby girl Wallis?

Anyway, that is the main news here, apart from the Crystal Palace burning to the ground—I don't suppose you've heard about that, either—and the last mutterings of the Talking Mongoose. I meant to send you newspaper clippings about the Mongoose because I knew it would amuse you, but I didn't get round to it. You see, a Talking Mongoose lives on the Isle of Man—a farmer reported seeing it, said its name was Gef and that it sang nursery rhymes and could talk in several languages. A man called Lambert managed to obtain some blurry photographs and a few hairs as evidence, and wrote a book about it. Then someone suggested Lambert might not be a fit person to be a director of a particular company, given his belief in Talking Mongooses and such. So Lambert sued for libel. And won—more than seven thousand pounds—which just goes to show that Believing In The Incredible pays. And I can just see the steam coming out of your ears, Veronica.

What else? Oh—one of my dorm-mates has joined the British Union of Fascists. He tried to get me to go along to a rally the other week, but all he could come up with by way of argument was that the Fascist leader, Sir Oswald Mosley, is "one of us" and "a good sound chap." (Oswald Mosley, another odd name for a baby—try saying it five times fast.) Pemberton, the dorm-mate, seemed rather confused as to the purpose of the rally—to show support for King Edward, I think we finally established, as the (former) King is rather keen on Hitler. The strange thing is that Ant went to a Communist rally last week—he showed me his "Long Live Edward, Down with the Government!" banner, and admitted they got lost on the way to Downing Street and had to ask a policeman for directions. Aren't the Communists supposed to do the opposite of the Fascists? Or is it just that they're both anti-Government in general? You see, this is why I abhor politics—because it doesn't make any sense.

Anyway, I told Pemberton in no uncertain terms that he was being a tremendous bore and that black shirts are very

unflattering for someone of his coloring, so he stormed off to
rugger training in a huff. I suspect he joined the B.U.F. be-
cause he doesn't get quite enough practice bashing up people
on the playing field and thinks Fascist rallies would give him
more scope in this area.

Nothing else, except I failed another Latin test. What a
pity they don't offer Kernetin as a subject; I might have a
chance of passing a test in that.

Love from,
Toby

P.S. Please, please, use your Christmas pudding wishes to
make sure I can come home for Christmas!

This is absolutely typical of Toby. He must have received my
letter about George by now, but does he write one word of condolence? No, he does not. Must not ever acknowledge that
death exists. Must ensure that every serious topic—whether injury to an aunt, royal abdication, or political violence—is
smothered in hilarity. Froth and fairy floss, that's what Toby's
letters are.

I sound cross at Toby, and I suppose I am, a little. No, mostly
I'm cross at Veronica, who is keeping at least two secrets from
me—firstly, the content and origin of all those packages she's
been receiving lately, and secondly, something to do with
George. Because I think that's where she got that mysterious
cloth she was clutching—it couldn't have been in our room all

that time. George must have given it to her just before he died. But why would George have kept anything of Isabella's?

No, this is stupid. I am not going to speculate. If Veronica wishes to tell me anything, I will listen sympathetically, but otherwise I will mind my own business. It's not as though I don't have one or two secrets of my own. And I'm certain it would be kinder to keep at least *one* of them from Veronica.

So back to Toby. He reminds me of our old clown doll, a foot high, round on the bottom, and weighted with lead. Henry and Carlos used to try their best to knock it down, but it always bounced straight up again, grinning wildly. That's Toby. That's why everyone loves him so. Well, nearly everyone. One of our old tutors, who quickly tired of being on the receiving end of Toby's jokes, was mad about Freud and insisted that Toby was the most repressed, most neurotic, most in need of psychoanalysis of all of us. We laughed it off (Toby, of course, laughed the hardest). But even though the tutor didn't know nearly as much about the subject as he thought, he did have a point, because Toby *had* to have been the most affected by our parents' deaths. He's the eldest, so he'd known them the longest—he was most able to understand what their loss truly meant. And worst of all, he was the one who watched it happen.

Not that he ever said a word about it to us—Veronica and I only found out because we overheard Nanny Mackinnon telling Rebecca. This was weeks later, when Nanny and Toby had returned from Spain and the funeral was over (not that there was anything to bury, but there was a service held in the chapel).

You see, Isabella had been invited to a royal wedding in Seville. However, Uncle John was being a bit difficult just then, so it was decided my parents would go instead. Part of their reasoning was that they could take Toby, who used to suffer badly from earaches, to consult a doctor. He had his tonsils removed the day before the wedding and was sitting on a balcony, eating a strawberry ice and waving to the golden carriages passing beneath, when the first bomb went off. No one knew it was a bomb at first; everyone thought it was fireworks. There were a lot of people lining the avenue below, as well as hanging off all the balconies and even the rooftops, and they all started clapping and cheering at the noise. Nanny said she remembered shaking her head as the horses shied and whinnied.

These Spaniards! she thought. *Not a care about what all that commotion might do to the poor ponies, as if it weren't bad enough what they do to those bulls!*

It wasn't until the second bomb exploded that anyone realized what was happening. The bomb landed on the carriage that my parents were traveling in and blasted away the roof, exploding the rest of the carriage into red-and-gold flames. That was when the police started firing into the crowd. In the ensuing stampede, no one was able to get anywhere near the carriage to rescue the occupants, or even to see if anyone had survived the explosion. All the while, the fire was spreading, via the terrified horses, to the adjacent carriages, to people fleeing the avenue, even to the ground floor of the hotel Toby and Nanny were in, although that particular blaze was extinguished straightaway.

In total, three wedding guests, two horses, and a dozen spectators died. No one knows what happened to the bomber, who was later discovered to have sent letters to the newspapers stating he was striking a blow on behalf of Moroccan freedom fighters. (Even though not one of the victims was a member of the Spanish government or the Spanish aristocracy, or indeed, had anything to do with Moroccan repression.)

Perhaps this is one of the reasons Toby dislikes politics—that some of the people who care most about politics seem to have the least compassion for ordinary human beings.

Still, one good thing about politics is that it's managed to spark some signs of life in Veronica. She came into the kitchen just now to read Toby's letter, and proceeded to interrogate me about Mrs. Simpson (lucky for me that Julia had passed on all that scandalous gossip). Not surprisingly, Veronica is taking a very unromantic view of the idea of a king abdicating for love.

"But this woman isn't even divorced yet," she said, perusing the newspaper clipping Toby had enclosed. "She's had two husbands, both still living. Apart from everything else, he's supposed to be the head of the Church of England—he's hardly setting a good example."

"But if he's so terribly in love . . . ," I began.

Veronica was still reading the newspaper article. "She's not of noble birth, not British, she's not even from Europe. No money, apparently, except her current husband's. And how old is she, anyway? She hardly looks likely to produce an heir . . .

Hmm, perhaps it's best he abdicated, then, if he's such a hopeless judge of what's appropriate and what's not."

"So you'd expect Toby to give up the throne if he fell in love with someone you thought was inappropriate?" I asked.

"Give up the throne to whom?" Veronica said. "Who else is there? Unless Henry manages to convince everyone she really is a boy . . ."

As I said, no romantic sensibility whatsoever. Still, at least she's taking some interest in her surroundings again.

Luncheon is over and Veronica, Henry, and I have just finished mixing up the Christmas pudding. Usually it's Rebecca or Alice who makes it, but neither of them has showed any enthusiasm for the task so far (poor Alice has taken George's death very hard), and if we leave it much later, it'll be Easter. We followed the recipe out of *Mrs. Beeton's Book of Household Management* as best we could, but had to improvise a bit. For one thing, not even Veronica knew how much a "gill" of milk was. Also, I don't think Mrs. Beeton ever used goat's milk in her puddings. We didn't have any currants or shredded almonds, either, but we made up for it by putting in raisins and a whole jar of Mary's candied lemon peel. Then Henry knocked the bottle of brandy into the basin, so the pudding mixture ended up with a great deal more than the required "one wineglassful." Henry gave Carlos the bowl to lick afterwards and Carlos turned rather glassy-eyed, then slumped on the hearthrug. I think the alcohol evaporates after the pudding's been boiled for a while, though. I suppose if it doesn't, we'll all be so drunk that we won't mind if it tastes a bit peculiar.

The main point of Christmas pudding isn't really how it tastes, but the Stir-up, when we get to make our Christmas wishes. Henry went first this year after we agreed to measure Carlos's age in dog years, rather than human ones. She took up the wooden spoon with a flourish, screwed her eyes shut, and stirred the mixture the required three times.

"Phew," she said, opening her eyes. "It's like stirring wet sand."

Veronica added a splash or two more of goat's milk. Then Henry stirred for Carlos, holding his giant paw in one hand and the spoon in the other. She accidentally let Carlos's wish slip out, so we each had to say ours then—that's the rule, if one wants them to come true. Henry wished for a proper big tree for her to climb and build a tree house in, like the Swiss Family Robinson. Carlos wished to meet a lady Portuguese water dog so we could have lots of Portuguese water puppies. Veronica wished Toby could come home for Christmas. I said I wished for peace throughout the world, especially in Spain (I actually wished Simon could come home for Christmas). Rebecca said, "Don't you go bothering me with your foolish games, I've work to do"—not that she *was* doing any work. And Uncle John gave an unintelligible grunt.

Veronica and Henry have now finished tying the mixture into a cloth and are hanging it up in the pantry. Oh, here comes Alice across the courtyard. If she'd been ten minutes earlier, she could have had a wish, too. Good heavens, she's wearing her best frock and an actual hat, and it isn't even Sunday. Wonder what's going on . . .

Well. It is rather awful, but I suppose we should have expected it. It's just that I can't see how on earth we are going to manage— no, I'd better tell it in order.

All right. Alice came in, all dressed up, refused a cup of tea, and didn't even want to sit down at the table. All she wanted was a word, please, with "Your Highness." Veronica, she meant. I assumed it was something to do with the supply ship not delivering something she'd ordered, or Basque fishermen sailing too close and getting their nets tangled with ours and Veronica needing to give them an official warning.

"Of course," said Veronica. Henry was standing there, all bright eyes and twitching ears, so Veronica added, "Why don't you come into the library, Alice?"

So the two of them moved off, but they'd barely reached the door when Veronica turned and said, "Come on, then, Sophie."

"Oh," I said, "I don't think . . . wouldn't you rather . . . if it's official business . . ."

Then I thought, *Well, it's just sitting there next to Veronica while she sorts it out, whatever it is, and giving her some moral support.* I must admit, I was also terribly curious. So I trailed after them to the library.

Veronica took the chair at the desk, leaving the chaise longue to Alice and me, although Alice again refused to sit down. She twisted her reddened, work-gnarled hands and refused to meet our eyes, and altogether looked so uncomfortable that I felt very sorry for her.

"It's quite all right, whatever it is," said Veronica kindly. "I'm sure that we can figure out a solution to whatever's bothering you."

"Oh, Your Highness!" said Alice. "I'm sorry to be asking you, I know I ought to be talking to His Majesty, but, er . . ."

As we'd left His Majesty in the middle of a loud conversation with his chamber pot, we both nodded understandingly.

"And young Toby—I mean, His Highness—away at school . . ."

It took a good five minutes of Veronica's coaxing before Alice spat it out. She wanted to ask Veronica's permission for the three of them, she and Jimmy and Mary, to leave Montmaray. Because now that George was gone, God rest his soul, there was no need for her to stay to look after him. She and Mary were the only adults left in the village—and poor Mary, with the rheumatics bad in her knees—and two women just weren't enough to manage the nets and the lobster pots and the gig. It had been enough of a struggle when George was there. And she worried about Jimmy. He thought of Henry as his friend and that wasn't right, anyone could see . . .

"She *is* an awful brat, isn't she?" said Veronica. "It's very good of Jimmy to put up with her."

Alice looked horrified. No, no, she hurriedly explained, she wasn't saying a word against the little princess, only that it was wrong that Jimmy should be on first-name terms with a member of the royal family and getting ideas above his station, and she, Alice, had to think of his future. Which was why she had written to her brother-in-law in Fowey. He'd written back to say he had his own fishing boat now and could take Jimmy on.

"And besides, with Your Highnesses being young ladies now, you'll be leaving yourselves soon and being wed and—"

"I can assure you," said Veronica, sitting up straighter, "that *I* will not be leaving Montmaray."

"Er, no, I mean, yes, of course," said Alice, blinking very fast, so I felt obliged to speak up.

"Alice, you *know* we'd never stand in your way, not if you've decided to leave. And of course we wish you all the best."

"Yes, of course," said Veronica quickly. "And we'll do all we can to ensure you have everything you need to settle comfortably in your new home."

There followed an embarrassing quantity of tears and curtseys from Alice, which made me wince because really, it is we who should be thanking Alice (and Mary and Jimmy), not the other way round. She has always said she stayed behind, after the other villagers left to find work, on account of George, but I know it was just as much for our sake. She and Mary have always helped out with the cleaning in the castle, kept us supplied with milk and cheese and vegetables, shared each catch of lobster and fish, and been on hand to help with household disasters whenever Rebecca was too preoccupied with Uncle John to do anything useful. And Jimmy—what would Henry have ever done if she hadn't had him as a constant companion? I daren't even think of how she will react to the news—first George and now Jimmy taken from her.

Oh, the more I write, the worse I feel. My heart feels so weighed down with worry that it seems to be currently residing somewhere near my knees. Veronica can insist that she—we—will stay on, but how *can* we, really? Let's take a look at our household, shall we, soon to be quite, quite alone on a small island in the middle of the Bay of Biscay, two hundred miles of storm-tossed sea between us and civilization, a household that consists of:

1. One middle-aged man of indifferent health and intermittent sanity;

2. One middle-aged housekeeper, who prefers not to housekeep too much as it interferes with her worship of the man previously mentioned;

3. Two young ladies not yet turned eighteen, neither of whom can cook very well, although between them they have adequate skills in the areas of bookkeeping, plumbing, dusting, historical research, laundering, and storytelling;

4. One ten-year-old tomboy, able to fish, swear, and trap rabbits, but unable to write, make her own bed, or remember to brush her teeth;

5. One dog, several mad cats, numerous chickens, half a dozen pigeons, and far too many rats.

Oh, I wasted my Christmas pudding wish! I should have wished for . . . what, exactly? What could possibly help? I suppose wishing for Simon's presence is as good as anything. At least it would distract me from our current woes.

Boxing Day 1936

This is the first spare minute I've had since Alice and the others left, but now that I've dutifully sat down, pen in hand, to record events in my journal, I realize I don't feel at *all* inclined to relive any of the past ten days or so. Let's see, what has been the worst so far? Henry's rage over the departure of her dearest and only friend? Rebecca's furious outburst when asked if she could possibly spend a little more time on the housework now? Or is it that smelly nanny goat of Mary's, bleating fiercely at the kitchen door if I'm five minutes late for her milking?

No—the worst, the very worst, was Alice and the others leaving. I was determined to be dignified and not cry, especially when I realized Alice must have been planning this since George died. Her brother-in-law didn't even wait for a reply to his letter—he simply appeared on Tuesday morning in his fishing boat and started loading the bags. There were pitifully few of them, with all their clothes, china, linen, and cutlery fitting into an old suitcase of Toby's, a flour sack, and Alice's little wooden chest. The furniture was left behind. Afterwards, I sat at Alice's kitchen table, blinking up at the bunches of rosemary still hanging from the rafters, an enormous lump in my throat, wondering how we'd ever manage without the three of them.

However, despite everything, we are not starving or living in complete squalor. Veronica's talent for organization has come to the fore and we each have schedules pinned up in the kitchen. Rebecca has taken up cooking duties and much of the cleaning, and we're learning to treat her incessant grumbling as mere background noise, the way we do the Blue Lady's moaning (that is, the noise made by drafts in the Blue Room, which overly fanciful types might *imagine* to be a ghost). Veronica and I take it in turns to accompany Henry down to the village every few days to check the lobster pots, collect some crabs, or do a bit of fishing. Henry is in charge of poultry, firewood-gathering, and (at her insistence) rat-catching. I have just finished reading *Goat Husbandry for Pleasure and Profit* (written in 1873, but I can't imagine goats have changed much in the last sixty years), am about to start *The Noble Art of Cheese making*, and have taken over the job of transferring the best bits of the village vegetable garden to our courtyard. No one is willing to tackle the beehives, which were always George's duty. We'll just have to learn to do without honey.

Veronica has also written to Mr. Grenville and Aunt Charlotte explaining the situation and requesting they send at least one servant as soon as possible. She sent the letters with Alice, so we won't have a reply till the new year. I expect both our solicitor and our guardian will say that the best course of action would be for the five of us (six if you include Rebecca, but I'd rather not in the mood she's in) to pack up and move to England, at least until Toby is old enough to live here permanently. However, I can just imagine Veronica's response to *that*.

What else? Oh, Christmas. Well, Aunt Charlotte must have insisted Toby spend it with her. So much for Veronica's Christmas pudding wish—or mine, come to that. I'm pretty sure Simon spent Christmas at Aunt Charlotte's, too. As for us, we tried to put on a cheerful front for Henry's sake, but she was too miserable to appreciate it. To be honest, even I felt my festive spirits evaporate when I went to look for the box of decorations and found they'd been stored directly under a leaky part of the nursery ceiling. Toby's cardboard angels, my tissue-paper snowflakes, a dozen years' worth of paper chains—all reduced to a sodden gray pulp. Even the gold-painted pinecones seemed to have sprouted mold. And it was raining too hard to contemplate gathering any flowers or greenery outside, not that there's much about at this time of year anyway.

In the end, I followed the example of an arty governess we had a few years ago and set up a tall twisted bit of driftwood in the kitchen, with shells strung from the branches on pieces of leftover knitting wool. Henry contributed an angel she carved from a cuttlefish shell. And Veronica and Rebecca managed to cook Christmas dinner together without any major catastrophes. We had roast chicken, glazed ham, and all the vegetables

Henry could salvage from the waterlogged garden. The pudding was . . . well, it had a very interesting texture. Henry dropped her slice on the floor and it bounced. I think we boiled it too long. But Julia and the rest of the Stanley-Rosses had very kindly sent us a hamper stuffed full of mince pies and nuts and preserved fruit, so we had that instead. Afterwards, Rebecca made eggnog and I read A Christmas Carol aloud by the stove while Veronica fixed the leaky tap over the sink and Henry mended a rip in her best fishing net. Uncle John stayed in his room throughout, of course, but the door was ajar, so it was almost as though he were there, too. So it wasn't such a terrible Christmas after all.

Today, though . . . Traditionally, Boxing Day is when we go down to the village and hand out presents and join in the carol singing. This year, we have each set ourselves up in a separate bit of the castle to mope. At least I assume the others are moping. I certainly am. I even had a bit of a cry earlier, which achieved nothing except red eyes and a swollen nose. I'm also ashamed to admit to spending a whole hour hoping that Alice, Mary, and Jimmy were having a really miserable time in Cornwall, and that they now rue the day they ever decided to leave their proper home.

And now Henry has come running in with the news that pirates have anchored off South Head and are preparing to attack.

"Don't be absurd, Henry," I told her.

"Oh, all right!" Henry huffed. "Perhaps not *pirates*, but you have to come and look honestly, I've never seen a flag like that. And they're just sitting there, not fishing or anything."

I'd better go up and see what she's on about.

Henry was right. A strange ship is sitting there, half a mile off South Head. It's not a fishing trawler, nor a freight steamer, nor one of those American cabin cruisers. Veronica is currently wrestling Henry for control of the telescope so she can figure out where it's from, but I could swear its flag has that bent-cross thing that's on the German flag.

Now Veronica has commandeered the telescope. "Yes, I see what you mean. A blue swastika on a white background," she says at last. (That's what it's called, a swastika. There's one on a vase that Great-uncle William brought back from a tiger-hunting expedition in India.) "How odd," Veronica says slowly, returning the telescope to Henry. "The German flag is a black swastika on white and red. Unless it's the Rhineland—do they have a new flag now?"

Well, no wonder none of us recognized it. We know French and Spanish and Portuguese boats, of course, we've seen lots of them. And sometimes we see Moroccans or Italians or Danes—but rarely Germans. I wonder if the ship's something to do with the Spanish war. Aren't the Germans supposed to be helping Franco's side? Except this ship isn't very big. Perhaps they're just lost—we had a terrific fog this morning.

"Ooh, they're getting in a little boat!" Henry has suddenly shouted. "With supplies! And they're—don't, Veronica, you'll make me drop it! There's two of them—oh, you should see their motor, imagine if we had one like that! They're heading for the village. I wonder if they've got a proper chart, they'll go right into the rocks if they're not careful."

"We'd better go down," Veronica says to me. "See what they want."

This is the first time we've had any visitors since Alice, Mary, and Jimmy left. Not that they would necessarily have been much help (nor would George, come to think of it), but I suddenly feel terribly defenseless.

Well. It is evening now and we are unharmed—at least for the moment. By the time we got down to the village, the strangers had already tied up their motorboat at the wharf—we could see it bobbing about on the huge waves.

"Should we tell them it's safer to tie up around in the cove?" wondered Veronica out loud, with a glance at the leaden sky.

"They're trespassing," hissed Henry. We'd wanted her to stay back at the castle but had no way of making her obey us, short of chaining her to the floor. "That's as bad as being pirates, almost. They *deserve* to sink."

"But if their boat sinks, they're stuck here," I pointed out.

For, to our surprise, the ship with the swastika flag had already moved off. We stayed crouched for a while behind the boulders above the village, trying to decide whether to confront the men or not. It was all very well for Queen Matilda, but she had a whole battalion of soldiers following her. Meanwhile, the men went on transferring their things from the boat to Alice's cottage. It made me feel very indignant to see them treating her home as a campsite (even though Alice had abandoned it, as well as us).

I also felt more than a bit frightened. One of the men, the blond one, was very troll-like. I hugged Carlos closer, but it wasn't much comfort—he's big and occasionally loud, but not much of an attack dog. I found myself wishing desperately that we had a man around for protection (unsurprisingly it was Simon, rather than Toby, who sprang to mind). However, we had no men, or none of any practical use, so Henry and I just looked at Veronica, waiting for her to tell us what to do. At last she sighed and said, "Well, they'll probably come up to the castle eventually. At least this way, we'll find out what they want straightaway."

Henry agreed to sneak around the back and keep a lookout, in case anything happened. She promised to rush back to the castle and raise the alarm if it looked like we were in any danger (not that I could imagine Rebecca caring much if we were, or doing anything very helpful). Then Veronica and I called Carlos over (he'd grown bored and wandered off to harass puffins) and the three of us marched down the track, making as much noise as we could. The troll saw us first and set down a leather case that looked as though it housed a typewriter.

"*Guten Tag*," he said, with a wary glance at Carlos.

Veronica gave him her best frown. "Good afternoon," she said. "Er . . . *Deutsch?*"

"*Ja,*" said the troll, adding something else in rapid German. Veronica shook her head. "Do you speak English?"

The troll turned around and called out to his companion, who hurried over. This one was an elf—big, sad eyes, an enormous forehead, and pointed ears. He bowed and said something in French, less than a quarter of which I caught. Veronica and I are both competent at written French (Veronica is better than competent), but our speaking and listening skills are terrible due to not being allowed to practice them inside the castle. The Fitz-Osbornes were never very keen on the French, not after Napoleon ruined our perfectly good curtain wall, but Uncle John has taken this dislike of all things Gallic to new depths since the Great War. He smashed up our old radio, the big one, two years ago when he caught us listening to Radio Normandie. Mind you, that's nothing compared to how much he loathes the Germans.

Meanwhile, Veronica was explaining—or attempting to explain—our limited French proficiency, in French. She must have succeeded—the elf's liquid eyes became even sadder. "*Español?*" Veronica asked hopefully. The elf shook his head. "English?" she said.

"My English is . . . not so good," he said, but it was a lot better than our German.

"So, what are you doing here?" Veronica asked, trying to regain the sense of righteous irritation she'd lost in all that language-negotiating. "Do you know you are trespassing?"

I won't attempt to reproduce the entire conversation, as it was lengthy and multilingual, supplemented with notes that the elf, Otto Rahn, exchanged with Veronica on pages from his notebook. However, he seemed most apologetic when Veronica introduced us and made a point of using our royal titles when he addressed us after this, which mollified Veronica somewhat. He even knew a little of the origins of the FitzOsbornes, having just visited an estate in northern France that had been owned by the family at the time of the Norman conquest of England. Herr Rahn, it turned out, was a scholar from Berlin with an interest in medieval history. That was why he was here.

"But Montmaray Castle isn't medieval," Veronica said. "It isn't even a castle. *Ce n'est pas un château moyenâgeux.*"

"No, of course, Your Highness," said Herr Rahn. Then he explained that he was tracing the path of some heretics who'd fled France in the thirteenth century, trying to escape the persecution of the Church.

"You think they came *here?*" said Veronica. We were all using exaggerated facial expressions and gestures to compensate for the poverty of our vocabulary, and at this she narrowed her eyes and shook her head. "There's no record of any inhabitants before 1542."

"Perhaps . . . perhaps their ship is . . ." He pointed to the bay.

"Wrecked," I contributed.

"Then there won't be anything to see," said Veronica.

He smiled. "We thought perhaps to speak to the . . ." He gestured around the abandoned village and shrugged. "But perhaps, Your Highness, we may visit your library?"

Veronica frowned and shook her head again. "I'm afraid not. We do not allow visitors." She was no doubt imagining how violently Uncle John would react if he encountered the men, although I had my own reasons for wanting them to stay at a distance. The troll, for one—he'd finished unloading the boat and was now lurking in the background, eyeing Veronica in a way that made me uneasy. Herr Rahn looked as though he wanted to put forward more of an argument about the library, but just then a gust of wind nearly toppled him.

"You should put your boat around in the cove," I said, with an apologetic glance at Veronica. I was starting to like *him*, if not the troll. "A storm is coming, a . . . um, *tempête*." I pointed to the clouds, then the boat, then gestured around the rocks to the sheltered cove where we usually keep our boats in winter.

"Oh, yes," he said. "Thank you. Hans!" He issued instructions to the troll (it was clear who was in charge) and the troll lumbered off towards their motorboat.

"We will not disturb you," said Herr Rahn, turning back to us. "Our ship is gone to take supplies from Brest, but will return . . . er, for one week."

"Well," said Veronica, with another frown. "I suppose you must stay, then. But you must remain here, in the village. You must not come to the castle. The paths are slippery and the cliffs very dangerous. *Vous ne devez pas venir au château.* It is forbidden, *verboten*." She nudged Carlos with her knee and he gave a deep, threatening woof, the effect spoiled somewhat by his simultaneous tail-wagging.

"I understand," said Herr Rahn, patting Carlos on the head.

Carlos grinned up at him. At that moment, lightning forked over the sea and the sky started to spit at us.

"We'd better go," I said.

"*Au revoir,*" Veronica said, and Herr Rahn clicked his heels together and bowed very nicely to both of us.

Henry was waiting for us behind the boulders, her face shining. "I knew it!" she cried. "I knew they were pirates! I sneaked into Alice's cottage and—"

"Oh, Henry, you didn't!" I said.

"You *told* me to spy on them," said Henry.

"I said to *watch*," said Veronica. "From a distance. What if they'd seen you?"

"They didn't notice a thing," said Henry. "Anyway, listen, one of their bags was open, a big canvas one—"

"Please don't tell us you stole from them," I groaned.

"Of course I didn't," Henry said indignantly. "Well, not anything they'll miss."

"Henry!" said Veronica. "You're going back there this instant and—"

"No, wait—there was a gun inside it! A pistol, a black, oily one."

Veronica and I stared at her in horror.

"Oh, I didn't take *that*," said Henry. "I swear, Veronica, I didn't even touch it. No, there was this paper—blank paper for writing letters, you know, with a secret symbol at the top. I just took one page, so you could figure out where they came from."

I leaned into Veronica's shoulder as she unfolded the thick piece of cream paper that Henry had handed her. The letterhead design consisted of an upright sword with a two-stranded loop around the blade, surrounded by the letters DEUTSCHES AHNENERBE. Below this was a single line of text—"*Reichsgeschäftsführer W. Sievers.*"

"Well? What does it say?" asked Henry, tugging at Veronica's sleeve. "They had all sorts of equipment, radio-looking things. I bet they're German spies!"

Veronica stared at the paper a moment longer. Then she pushed it into the pocket of her trousers. "You are not to go anywhere near the village while those men are here," she said.

Henry, predictably, began to protest.

"No!" said Veronica sharply. "This is not a game. Do I have your word that you will stay away from them?"

Henry pushed out her bottom lip. "But what does it say? Who are they?"

"Henry!" I said. "They're armed. It doesn't matter who they are—if they catch you poking around, they could shoot you!"

"Do I have your word?" said Veronica again.

"Yes," sighed Henry.

"Good," said Veronica. Then the rain started to come down in earnest and we ran for it.

It's taken me nearly an hour to write this much, thanks to Henry's interruptions. She keeps popping up beside my elbow with fresh ideas for defending the castle from the men.

"And there's the old cannon in the henhouse," she has just informed me. "We could clean all the rust and droppings off, and hoist it up into the gatehouse with the pulley system."

"And then what?" I asked. "Drop the whole thing on their heads as they pass under the murder hole? Do you even know how it works?"

"There's a cannonball in the Great Hall," said Henry. "Under the piano—Jimmy used it to squash that big rat. All we'd need is gunpowder. What is gunpowder, anyway? Can you make it out of things from the pantry?"

"Go and brush your teeth," I said.

"Isn't Veronica back from the library yet?" Henry asked.

"Bed, Henry," I said. "Now."

"Well, Carlos can stay here to guard you," she said, trailing towards the stairs. "Stay, Carlos." Even though Carlos, curled up in front of Vulcan and steaming slightly, had showed no sign of moving. I can't say I blame him. It always takes a while for the seasons to penetrate the castle walls, but winter seems to have finally managed it. Veronica, over in the library, must be freezing. I'd better take her another hot brick for her feet.

No, I'll be honest—I just want a chance to talk to her properly, now Henry's out of the way.

When I knocked, Veronica was sitting on the chaise longue, surrounded by piles of newsprint and stray sheets of writing paper. The uncharacteristic confusion should have given me an indication of her state of mind, but I was too anxious to find out about the men to pay much attention.

"So, did you figure it out?" I said. " 'Ahnenerbe'?"

"What?" said Veronica. "Oh. That."

"*That?*" I said. "Isn't that what you've been looking up?" I glanced at the mold-spotted English-German dictionary by her elbow.

"Oh. Well, yes, it means 'ancestor' or 'heritage' or something," said Veronica. "I knew that. But I was sure I'd seen that word somewhere before. So I went through all these newspaper clippings." She gestured at all the paper.

"Where did all these come from?" I asked, staring. It's not as though we can afford newspaper subscriptions.

"Oh, Daniel sent them," said Veronica, leaning over the arm of the chaise longue and starting to gather them up.

"Daniel?" I said. "Who's . . . you mean Daniel, our old tutor?"

"He's not that old," said Veronica, looking a bit pink when her head finally came up. "He's only twenty-six."

"Daniel Bloom? He's the one who's been writing to you? Sending you all those mysterious packages?"

Veronica affected unconcern. "Well, who else could it have been?" she said. "The Basque captain?"

"I can't believe Daniel's been writing to you all this time!" *And that you didn't tell me*, I failed to add. I sat down abruptly next to her. "Oh, *Veronica.*"

"What does it matter whether he's been writing to me or not?" She gave me the sort of look she gives Henry when Henry io being particularly obtuse. It had more of an effect on me than it ever does on Henry.

"Well," I said uncertainly. "And . . . and you've been writing back?" I shifted a bit and there was a rustling sound underneath me. I retrieved the bit of writing paper I'd accidentally sat on, began reading the first line ("Dear Veronica . . ."), then dropped it at once, embarrassed.

"It's not a *love* letter," said Veronica. "You can read it if you want, but I doubt you'd be interested. Politics and history, that's what they're all about."

I took a deep breath. I was trying to be Sensible—trying, in fact, to be Veronica. I decided not to think about Daniel for a moment. "All right. But what does this have to do with the Germans?"

Veronica leaned forward. "Daniel sent me a monograph published by the Ahnenerbe. It was about genealogy, about how the Nazis are looking for historical evidence of a superior Germanic culture." She gave a sudden smile. "Daniel has a theory that all historical study is motivated by political ambitions. He teases me about my *Brief History* sometimes. This was more proof for him, you see—the Ahnenerbe is funded by the Nazi government."

"So?" I said. "Don't most governments employ historians?"

Veronica had stopped smiling. "The Nazi government is not most governments. Hitler is the worst kind of dictator. The Nazis burn books, censor the press, murder their enemies—"

"You don't know that," I said.

"The Nazis burnt down the Reichstag."

"They didn't," I said. "That was the Communists. I remember, that was why all those Communists were expelled from the German parliament . . ."

Veronica was shaking her head. Was she listening to me? Or was I too unimportant for her to pay me any attention at all? I felt my face heat up.

"Is this what *Daniel* says?" I exclaimed. "*He* sent you that dreadful book about Hitler, didn't he?" Groping for something that would wound, I hurled an accusation that even I, as hurt and angry as I was, didn't really believe: "*He's* why you've suddenly taken against the Fascists! He always did go on and on about them. And you're just blindly following him!"

Veronica stared at me, her eyes slitted, her mouth tight. I felt a sudden thrill of fear. We never fought. Not like *this*. But something in me wanted it. It was like sitting shivering at the window, watching a storm close in, longing for the first terrifying flash of lightning to be over.

Then Veronica's shoulders sagged.

"You're upset because I didn't tell you about the letters," she said flatly.

"No," I lied.

"Because I don't think you could be jealous, not of Daniel," she said, glancing away. She sighed. "I am sorry I didn't tell you, Sophie. But I knew Henry would tease, and I really didn't think it was that important."

"That's . . . all right," I said. I took a deep breath. "And I'm sorry that I said that you were . . . following him. I know you wouldn't. Only he's not . . . Veronica, he isn't a Communist, is he?"

Veronica folded her arms. "What does that matter?"

I could think of several reasons why it could matter, starting with the murder of the Russian royal family, but I kept my mouth closed. I'd just had another thought—what if Veronica . . . Could she possibly be in *love* with him?

"I'm not *marrying* him," she said, reading my thoughts. "We're merely exchanging letters. Truly, I doubt he's even noticed I'm female. Now, do you want to hear about Herr Rahn?"

"Yes," I said quickly, even though I was certain Daniel was well aware Veronica was female. It was difficult to miss, and had been even when she'd been fourteen and he was our tutor.

She stood up and went over to the desk. "In the monograph, they made reference to a historian called Otto Rahn. He wrote a book a few years ago called, called . . ." Veronica shuffled through her papers. "Here it is—*Kreuzzug gegen den Gral. Crusade Against the Grail.*"

If Veronica had wanted to divert me from the subject of Daniel, she'd succeeded admirably. "The Grail?" I said. "You mean, the *Holy* Grail? As in King Arthur and Tennyson and . . . That Grail?"

"Possibly not what we imagine to be the Grail, but yes, Herr Rahn is searching for the Holy Grail."

I goggled at her. "And he thinks it's *here?*" I said. "At

Montmaray? Wouldn't someone have found it by now, or at least mentioned it to someone?"

"I suspect that's why he wants to see the library," said Veronica.

"Unless he thinks those people, the heretics from France, had it with them when their ship sank. Imagine, the Holy Grail at the bottom of South Head!"

"There is no Grail," said Veronica. "Really, Sophie, think about it. Christ was a carpenter. He would have drunk wine, even at Passover, from a clay cup or a wooden one—how could a cup like that possibly have survived two thousand years?"

"How do you know what God can or can't do? Anyway, perhaps it's something else—not a cup."

I shouldn't have said the word "God"—Veronica was getting that peevish look she gets whenever religion is mentioned.

"Perhaps it is," she snapped. "Perhaps Herr Rahn would agree with you. Nevertheless, Herr Rahn's quest is part of the Ahnenerbe research, which is funded by the Nazis. And that enormous blond man with Herr Rahn is no more a medieval scholar than Henry is. I believe he's a member of the SS." She took in my blank look. "Hitler's personal army. And Himmler, the head of the SS, is said to take a close personal interest in the activities of the Ahnenerbe."

"Oh," I said in a small voice. I was thinking of that dreadful book of Daniel's, the tortured enemies of Hitler staring miserably out of its photographs.

"Yes," said Veronica grimly. "Oh."

"But . . . but have you ever come across anything about the Grail in here?" I asked, turning to look at the bookshelves.

"I haven't read everything in here," said Veronica. "And I haven't been looking for anything about the Grail."

"Yes, but . . . ," I said.

"No," said Veronica. "I've never seen any reference to it."

I gave a half laugh. "Well, except for Edward de Quincy's poem."

"What?" said Veronica, frowning.

"Oh, you know, that line in 'The Voyage of King Bartholomew':

> *And hoisting brave Benedict o'er his head*
> *Gazed down upon glimmering gold and red,*
> *The Holy Grail ris'n from the depths to aid,*
> *And with fresh strength—the sea monster was slayed."*

Veronica's frown deepened. "I'd forgotten that bit. But no historical scholar could possibly take anything Edward de Quincy FitzOsborne said seriously. Hardly anyone even reads him nowadays. How would Rahn know about him? I can't imagine he spends much time reading obscure English poetry."

"Yes, I suppose you're right . . . ," I started to say when I had a horrible thought. I remembered Toby's letter, his note to me about the poetry game and the German Ambassador being so impressed with Simon. But surely Simon wouldn't have said . . . and the German Ambassador couldn't have *believed* him . . . could he?

"Anyway, for some reason, Herr Rahn and his Nazi employers think they can find the Grail here," said Veronica.

I looked down and saw that my hands had somehow twisted themselves into a knot. "What will they do when they don't find it?" I whispered. "If they think we're hiding it from them?"

Veronica only shook her head.

"Then shouldn't we . . . I don't know, let them at least look through the library?" I said.

Veronica stared at me. "Have you gone *mad*? Think about—"

"Just so they can see there's nothing here!" I added hurriedly. "We could make sure Uncle John's out of the way when they arrive, tell Rebecca so she keeps him locked in his room."

"Absolutely not," said Veronica shortly. Then she sat down at her desk with her back to me and began to sort through the papers on it with quick, sharp movements. I sat there, waiting, but she didn't say anything further. After a while, I got up and went to the door. I could see Veronica reflected in the dark windowpane, one of Daniel's letters clenched in her hand. She didn't look like a girl in love, I have to say. She just looked very tired.

28th December 1936

I awoke this morning with a plan, of sorts. First, though, I went to the library and found Tennyson's *Idylls of the King*. It had been a while since I'd read it. "The Holy Grail" was in the middle, brimming with fantastic visions and mad knights and castles being torn asunder. The Grail, Sir Percivale claimed, had been carried by Joseph of Arimathea from the Holy Land to Glastonbury. I suppose Joseph's journey could have taken him via the Bay of Biscay and Montmaray, and his ship could have sunk or its cargo been washed overboard. Except Percivale said the Grail had actually reached Glastonbury safely "and there awhile it bode," until it disappeared years later due to the general wickedness of the population. So Tennyson wasn't much help.

Then I flipped through Edward de Quincy FitzOsborne's *Collected Works*, but it was just as I'd remembered—one brief reference to the Grail that came out of nowhere and disappeared immediately. And one can be certain that if there'd been a shred of evidence that the Grail had come anywhere near Montmaray,

Edward de Quincy would have written a hundred pages about it in bad iambic pentameter.

The awful thing was that I could well imagine Simon trying to impress the German Ambassador and making Montmaray seem more important than it actually is. Montmaray is important to *us*, of course, but not to outsiders—we have no citizens of historical note (Edward de Quincy doesn't really count), and there is no unique wildlife, no highest mountain or biggest waterfall or longest river. All we have is a lot of rocks and shipwrecks, and while some of the shipwrecks probably do contain treasure, anything down there on the seabed is quite irretrievable. But Simon is a true patriot, no matter what Veronica says, and I must admit he seems ambitious. So why wouldn't Simon be tempted to embroider a little, to choose to be entertaining rather than strictly accurate in what was, after all, a social gathering, not a conference for history professors. Perhaps the German Ambassador, aware of the Ahnenerbe research, had asked specifically about the Grail; perhaps Simon, wanting to please, had given a response that was not *wholly* based on the known facts . . .

I can just imagine what Veronica will say and do if she discovers this. Not that it's Simon's fault if the Germans have put two and two together and come up with fifteen, but she is just itching for an excuse to annihilate Simon. All it would require is one of her acerbic letters to Mr. Grenville, asking why he permits his clerk to run around in Society impersonating a diplomat, and Simon would lose his job. I can't allow this to happen.

I am going down to explain things to Herr Rahn. Or at least find out what he's up to.

I have put this down on paper in case I don't come back.

Signed, *Sophia Margaret Elizabeth Jane Clementine FitzOsborne.*

I was praying like mad all the way down that it would be all right, and that seemed to work—perhaps Rebecca's onto something after all, with all that kneeling and muttering in front of altars.

Not that it began very well. I needed Carlos to go with me for protection (the troll had seemed wary of him), and Carlos was in the kitchen with everyone else.

"Just going for a walk," I said to them, dragging a very reluctant Carlos towards the door (he'd been drooling over the fish Rebecca was cutting up for stew).

"Why?" said Henry, quite sensibly. The rain was still streaming down the windows, and the wind, when I opened the door, was icy.

"I just need some . . . some fresh air," I said as a blast of it threw me sideways into the doorframe.

Rebecca snorted. Veronica looked up from the scribbles on Henry's slate and narrowed her eyes.

"You know, I think I'll come with you," Henry announced, scraping back her chair.

"I think *not*," said Veronica at once, "when you were confined to bed for more than a week not so long ago and still have five sums to finish."

And during the ensuing argument, I managed to slip out unnoticed.

Carlos was quite happy to be outside once we got past the drawbridge and he remembered all the rabbits and puffins out there for the chasing. We headed for the village first, even though I suspected the men would be out exploring. I was right—we eventually came across them on the Green. The troll was wheeling a long stick with a disk on the end and calling out measurements to Herr Rahn, who was writing them down in his notebook.

"Good morning, Your Highness!" cried Herr Rahn when he caught sight of me. Too late, I realized I'd forgotten the English-German dictionary.

"Morning," I said, because there really wasn't much good about it. The rain was whipping back and forth, stinging my face, and my hands were frozen. "I was just . . . er, taking the dog for a walk."

The troll scowled at Carlos, then wheeled away towards the far end of the Green, his black oilskin flapping behind him. "How are you getting on?" I continued. "With your . . . ah, research?"

"Oh," said Herr Rahn, who had a nice smile. "Not so bad, thank you. But I was wanting to ask—what is that?" He pointed to the cross at South Head, shrouded today in a mist of sea spray and rain.

"That's the war memorial," I said. "Um, *monument aux morts*. The Great War, you know. A hundred and fifty-seven

Montmaray men died in a single day." Massacred by Herr Rahn's countrymen, I didn't add. After all, it wasn't *his* fault—he was too young to have been in the war.

"Very sad," he said. "That must have . . . er . . . This is why the village is . . . ?" He gestured downhill at the desolate cottages.

"Partly." I nodded. "And also the influenza epidemic in 1918. *La grippe*."

"Ah, yes," said Herr Rahn softly. "In Germany, too."

It was so terribly unfair, that epidemic. The soldiers who'd managed to survive the Great War, the wives who'd waited for them, the children who'd barely known their fathers—so many of them struck down by disease just as peace was declared. Veronica once told me that across the world, twice as many people died of the influenza as were killed in the Great War. And Montmaray, isolated as it sometimes seems, was nevertheless part of that world. The Great War demonstrated that to deadly effect, and so did the epidemic.

I sighed heavily. "So, with most of the young men dead, a lot of the villagers went back to Cornwall. To find work."

He nodded slowly. Then the troll called out something and Herr Rahn wrote some numbers in his notebook. He saw my curious glance and gave another shy smile.

"Geometry," he explained. "A pity there is no sun, I hoped to measure the sun at dawn, but . . ." He shrugged. "May I ask, how did the village folk use this . . . this . . . ?" He swept one arm around.

"The Green?" I asked. "Oh, well, they used to have hurling matches once. It's a bit like football—"

His entire face lit up. "Yes, I know it! The silver ball is being thrown up, like the sun rising. And to touch the ball is good luck."

"That's right," I said, a little surprised. "We have the ball up in the castle now."

"And other celebrations?" he asked. "Midsummer?"

"Yes, the bonfire is set up there," I said, pointing to the middle of the Green. He gave a sigh of satisfaction. "But what does this have to do with your research?" I asked. "I thought you were studying French heretics?"

"Ah!" he said, eyes sparkling, and I was reminded of Veronica preparing to launch into a complicated historical explanation. "The Cathars—the French heretics—knew Sacred Geometry. It is from the Druids. They worshipped the sun, and that is why the Church, the Roman Church, was against them. I have been in France and also Spain, Italy, Switzerland, Iceland—"

"Iceland!" I exclaimed in wonder.

"Yes, but mostly France, where there is . . . oh, it is difficult to explain in English! I wrote a book . . ."

"*Crusade Against the Grail,*" I said before I could stop myself.

He stared at me. "Have you read this? It is not in English."

"Er, no," I said. "I've heard of it. So you *are* searching for the Grail? It isn't here, you know." I peered up into his eyes, anxious to make him understand this. "There's no record of it ever being seen here, nor spoken of, nor even—"

"Ah, the Grail," he said, smiling. "What is the Grail? What do you think?"

I frowned. "Well, in Tennyson, Sir Percivale said it was the cup that Christ drank from."

"Yes," he said. "There is also, in medieval German, *Parzival*—have you heard of it? And the opera by Wagner, too. But they are not right; the Grail is before Christ. There was the legend of the Grail and then the Church tried to make it their own."

"Then what is it?"

"The Grail of the Cathars, the Pure Ones?" he said. "Perhaps a perfect crystal to hold the sun. But I think it truly is *Sophia*. Wisdom."

"Wisdom?"

"Do you not know what your name means?" he asked. "Wisdom. *Sophia*. What so many have searched for, so many years."

"Well, I should have been named something else, then," I said. "I haven't any wisdom."

"Are you sure?" he said, smiling. "Well, if not—then wisdom is *there*," and he nodded towards the castle. "In books. The wisdom of others before, who see and think and write."

"Oh," I breathed, picturing an infinite line of writers bent over papyrus and vellum and parchment, scribbling down the knowledge of the ages. But at that moment, the clouds above us cracked open and rain began to pelt down. The troll turned and squelched towards us, looking mutinous, and Herr Rahn regretfully folded up his notebook.

"We must go . . . but you will join us? For tea?" he said.

"Oh, no, no, I should be getting back," I said, suddenly recalling the black gun Henry had seen. I tried unsuccessfully to hold back a shudder.

"You are cold," said Herr Rahn, observing this with a look of concern. "Are you sure you would not like hot tea or—"

"No, no, I'm fine, thank you!" I cried. "Come on, Carlos!" And I ran all the way back to the castle, not even stopping to worry about the sea surging below my feet as I flew across the gaps in the drawbridge.

Veronica had the big kettle boiling when I burst into the kitchen, and she sent me straight up to the bathroom with it.

"You *are* an idiot," she sighed, coming in ten minutes later with another jug of hot water. "I thought Henry was the one I had to worry about. What on earth were you thinking, going out in this weather?"

I sneezed and wondered that myself. Veronica sat down on the wooden lid of the loo and gave me an expectant, exasperated look. I opened my mouth to recount my conversation with Herr Rahn, then closed it again. After all, she'd just called me an idiot. Besides, I wanted to prove I could keep secrets just as well as she could.

"Could you please pass me the towel," I said instead.

She tossed the towel at me and then folded her arms.

Peering through damp clumps of my hair, I realized that she was prepared to sit there for as long as it took. This *was* Veronica, after all.

"We talked about the war," I said.

"Really?" said Veronica, blinking. "Which one?"

"Which . . . the Great War!" I said. "What else? Herr Rahn was wondering about the memorial cross."

"Ah," she said. "And did you tell him what happened?"

"I told him a hundred and fifty-seven Montmaray men died in a single day."

"A hundred and fifty-eight," said Veronica.

"A hundred and fifty-seven," I said. "Don't you recall that Toby and I counted all the names on the stone one summer?"

"Don't you recall that Aunt Charlotte refused to pay the engraver's bill because Edwin Davy's name was left off?"

"Does it *matter*?" I burst out, tossing the towel back at her.

"I expect it mattered a great deal to Edwin Davy's widow," said Veronica, hanging the towel neatly on its hook. "But as you point out, it's doubtful a couple of Nazis would care much about a single dead enemy soldier. What matters to them is having access to the library. You *did* stress that they mustn't come anywhere near here, didn't you?"

I pressed my lips together, grabbed my comb, and began to yank it through my hair, realizing only then that I'd failed to find out whether Simon had played any role in the Germans' arrival. What if he *had*? And oh, I hadn't asked Herr Rahn not to mention Simon to Veronica . . .

Veronica crossed her arms. "Because I would have thought that any talk of the war would lead quite naturally to your explaining that Germans could never be welcome here."

I worked away at a stubborn knot, thoughts whirling furiously. *Had* I emphasized they mustn't come near the castle? Well, I'd *implied* it. Herr Rahn seemed an intelligent and sensitive man. How *else* would he think we'd feel about Germany, given the long shadow cast by the memorial cross?

"At least, I *assume* that was your purpose in wandering through the freezing rain to converse with a couple of Nazis," continued Veronica relentlessly. "To *warn them away*."

I threw my comb down. "Herr Rahn is not a Nazi!" I shouted. "And it's none of your damned business what the purpose of my conversation was!"

Veronica raised nothing more than her eyebrows, and those only a fraction of an inch. "Really, Sophie. When we're trying to encourage Henry to use more ladylike language." She stood, straightened the bath mat with one foot, then strolled towards the door. "And if you insist on having rendezvous with Herr Rahn," she said coolly over her shoulder, "at least try to conceal your departures from Henry. I spent the remainder of her lesson extracting another promise from her to stay away from those men."

The thought that Veronica was entirely correct—about Henry, about trying to avoid the Germans—did nothing to improve my temper. Why is she always calm and collected and correct? Why do I always do and say such stupid things? In attempting to avoid trouble for Simon and Montmaray, all I've managed to do is make things worse.

Oh, how could Herr Rahn *possibly* call me wise?

I am writing this sitting up in bed, in the hope that scribbling down all my unhappy thoughts will make them less worrying. I hate that Veronica and I are quarreling. I hate it even more that we're at odds at the exact time we most need to support each other—for I have a very bad feeling about our German visitors. I can't help liking Herr Rahn, but the other man—Hans—gives me a creeping, prickly sensation, as though . . . well, I suppose I can say it here privately, in this journal, knowing it won't be subjected to a blast of Veronica's withering logic. All right. He reminds me of my Isabella dream. Not the dream itself, just the feeling I get when I have it. There, I've said it. I know I'm being melodramatic and fanciful, but there it is.

Dinner tonight was a watery imitation of Alice's fish stew. Afterwards, we huddled around Vulcan with the door to Uncle John's room open so Rebecca could keep an eye on him, and I read Tennyson aloud because it was the closest book at hand. I let Henry choose the poem to try to distract her from her increasingly wild plans for defending the castle. Naturally she decided on the poem that seemed most likely, in her view, to contain exciting battles: "The Passing of Arthur." There certainly were plenty of bloodthirsty descriptions (she made me read the bit about "the crash of battle-axes on shattered helms" twice), but it made me uneasy for quite another reason. I'd never before noticed how strongly it related to our own King—I kept glancing at Uncle John's doorway, hoping he wasn't paying attention as I read about poor dying King Arthur saying,

> ". . . for on my heart hath fallen
> Confusion, till I know not what I am,
> Nor whence I am, nor whether I be King.
> Behold, I seem but King among the dead."

And then, even worse, was Bedivere's lament,

> "The King is sick, and knows not what he does."

Even Rebecca looked up from her knitting at that and shook her head. Altogether, it was a very uncomfortable evening. And it will probably be an uncomfortable night, if only because now I've spooked myself into having a nightmare.

Perhaps I should take a leaf out of Rebecca's book and say a prayer. The Lord's Prayer, or that old Cornish one:

> From ghoulies and ghosties and long-leggedy beasties,
> And things that go bump in the night,
> The good Lord deliver us.

29th December 1936

I need to write down what has just happened. I need to set down the truth. If I write lies or if I write nothing at all, this journal is worthless. I *can* do this. I *must* do this, in case . . . well, in case anything happens. Anything *else* happens.

All right. This is what happened tonight, every single terrible thing that I can remember.

I was dreaming, the Isabella dream, just as I'd feared. I hadn't had it for weeks, not since George died. This time it was worse than ever, because when I leaned over the edge of the boat, my sleeve got tangled up in the unraveling shroud and it dragged me over, pulled me under. The water was black, wet cloth curled round my face, I couldn't breathe . . .

I thrashed so hard that I woke myself up. But I must have fallen asleep again, because suddenly I was King Bartholomew, running across the drawbridge, the sea monster lunging at me out of the Chasm, its mouth yawning like a cave, each sharp tooth a glittering sword . . . and then I was in the Great Hall with Toby and Veronica, all of us engaged in a frantic search for Benedict, which was missing from the chimneypiece. "This is all Rebecca's fault!" snapped Veronica, and Toby knocked over the suit of armor, which slumped to the floor and groaned.

I woke properly then, to find the room glowing in moonlight. The sea monster was glinting at me from the tapestry. Bartholomew, his sword dangling from one tiny fist, looked sad and helpless.

Then I heard it again, the noise that had woken me. I struggled out of my tangle of blankets and stumbled across the room.

"Veronica," I whispered. "Veronica, wake up!" I shook her shoulder. She muttered and turned over. "There's someone downstairs!" I said, louder than I'd intended.

She sat up abruptly and pushed her hair off her face.

"I heard a noise," I said, although I wasn't so certain now. Perhaps I'd still been dreaming. Then it came again, the clink of metal against stone. We stared at each other.

"Check Henry's all right," said Veronica. While I was still fumbling for my dressing gown, she pulled her jersey over her nightgown and darted out the door.

I couldn't find my shoes, and I didn't think to snatch up my candle until after I'd stepped into the moonless gallery. It was as though I'd fallen back into my dream, into the depths of the inky water. I groped my way along the wall, listening to my thudding heart and the harsh sound of my breathing.

"Rebecca?" I whispered, pushing her door open when I finally reached it, but her bed was empty, her candlestick missing from its place on the bedside chest. Nothing unusual about that, though—she often sits up all night beside Uncle John's bed.

I padded over to the connecting door to Henry's room and peered inside. Henry, I saw with a rush of relief, was flung across the width of her bed, one foot exposed to the cold, her tufted head half buried beneath the pillow. I crept forward and pulled the blankets straight. She stirred, grumbling a little, then was still again. Carlos, curled on the end of her bed, raised his head enquiringly, eyes gleaming silver.

"It's all right," I whispered. His head sank back down onto his front paws, eyes already closing.

Back in the gallery, I halted, biting my lip. Should I go back to my room to fetch a candle? Should I search the other rooms in case anyone was hiding there? But why was I thinking *anyone*? Because, of course, the intruders could only have been the German men. Except why would they be wandering around the castle in the middle of the night? *Because Veronica warned them not to come here*, said a voice in my head, *and they were so very, very curious . . .*

I pictured the gun, gleaming black inside the open canvas bag, and I clenched my teeth to stop them chattering. That was when I heard voices spiraling up the tower stairs. *Veronica!* I thought. *If they've hurt her—*

I whirled around, banging my elbow but too scared to cry out, and blundered towards the stairs. My body tight with cold and fear, I half fell down the final few steps. I glimpsed the flicker of a candle, the white slash of Rebecca's face, and—oh God—a dark huddled mass on the floor . . . Then Veronica stepped in front of me, arms outstretched.

"Don't look," she said, but I'd already seen. My hand jerked to my mouth.

There was a person on the floor. No, a body—it was no longer a person. There were legs, an arm, a head turned away from me. The rest was hidden under the hearthrug, but even in the dim light, I could see the puddle seeping across the kitchen floor, darker than water, glistening and viscous.

"Who . . . ?" I choked out, feeling the blackness rising from the floor, misting my vision.

Veronica grabbed my arm, her nails digging through my sleeve. "Stop that!" she said. She turned around. "Rebecca! The blanket!"

Numbly, I realized the unmoving legs were clad in gray trousers and shiny black boots. One of the Germans, then. I was too cold and dizzy to know whether I should feel relief at this.

"Sophie, listen," said Veronica, tightening her grasp on my arm and shaking harder. I'd have bruises later, I thought irrelevantly, looking down at her hand. "You have to go outside, head off the other one. Get him away from here somehow, while I figure out . . ."

Veronica's voice trembled and died, and it was this that made me take a deep breath, pull my arm free, and reach for the candle on the table. Veronica needed me. The candle wavered in my hand but didn't go out, and I took courage from this. Rebecca emerged from Uncle John's room, clutching a blanket.

"He's in the courtyard," Rebecca said hoarsely. "The other man. We heard him."

"Lock the door," Veronica said. We all glanced at the kitchen door and its rusty, never-used bolt. Rebecca moved towards it. "Please, Sophie," Veronica added, nodding at the other door, the one that led into the Great Hall.

I took another deep breath and then did as she told me. Walking into the Great Hall, which was lit only by streams of moonlight and the flickering candle, was worse than even my dream. Dark shapes crouched like monsters preparing to pounce. The clocks whirred threateningly. There was a rustling noise from near the piano that ceased the instant I stopped to listen. I held the candle higher and forced myself to concentrate on my footsteps. Nearly there . . . just another yard or so, and then . . .

The chapel door was ajar. Had Rebecca left it that way? Or was it . . .

"Stop that!" I told myself aloud. Then, clenching my jaw so hard that it cracked, I crept forward.

The chapel, as far as I could see in the shaky light, was empty. I stepped inside and raised my candle. Well, there was no reason for him to be in here, nothing to see—the walls were bare, the altar unadorned, the stained-glass window featureless in the dark. I turned and made my way towards the main chapel doors, the double ones that led out into the courtyard. Unbolting them, I pulled one open a crack. I peered out. The full moon slid behind a cloud.

Then an icy breath snuffed out my candle.

I whimpered and then clapped my hand over my mouth, too late. It was only the wind, of course, but I was spooked beyond all rational thought—even more so a second later when I heard the scritch-scratch of mice (I simply couldn't face the possibility they were rats) in the corner.

Matches, I need matches, I told myself. There were probably some on the altar (I thought of Rebecca on her knees before it), but as I turned, I caught a flash of light from the library tower far brighter than any candle. I pushed the chapel doors open a little further and looked out. He was in there, all right. *Veronica needs you to do this,* I reminded myself. I edged outside and began to tiptoe across the courtyard towards the tower. Then I remembered the gun and realized that sneaking up on him was a very stupid idea. It was impossible to stomp in bare feet, though, and when I reached the open door of the library, I saw that the man bent over Veronica's desk was completely unaware of my presence. My heart pounding, I coughed loudly and shoved the door against the wall.

Herr Rahn jolted upright, pointing his torch directly at me. My arm shot up to shield my face.

"Your Highness," he said, lowering the torch at once. "I . . . I apologize."

I clutched the doorframe, my eyes blank with that flash of white light. "You shouldn't be here," I said.

"I am sorry," he said. "But . . . but the books, I had to see . . ."

Blinking at him, my vision slowly clearing, I realized he was blushing. "You'd better not have disturbed anything," I said, his embarrassment giving me the nerve to speak so severely. Also, I'd realized he didn't have the gun with him—or if he did, it was so well concealed that he probably wasn't intending to use it in the near future. "My cousin will be very cross," I added, frowning in what I hoped was an authoritative manner and crossing my arms hard across my chest to conceal their trembling.

"No, no, I promise I was only looking at the bookshelves," he said. I turned and stared at the door, praying he'd take the hint. "It is a very fine library," he said hopefully. "Perhaps Her Highness would be so kind as to . . ."

"Not now!" I burst out in frustration. Would he *never* leave? "It's one o'clock in the morning!"

"Er, no," he agreed. "But—"

"You really should go," I said.

"I do apologize," he said, and he looked so sad and gentle-eyed that I felt quite sorry for him. Then I remembered what was lying in the kitchen and felt even worse. Herr Rahn bowed his head and moved towards me, his glance falling on the desk and its framed photographs as he passed. "That is a very handsome young man," he said with a shy smile.

"My brother," I said, without needing to look to know whom he meant.

I shut the library door behind us and walked Herr Rahn out through the courtyard to the drawbridge.

"Good night," he said as we stood under the remains of the portcullis. I saw him give it a bright, inquisitive glance and then repress an urge to ask about the design.

"Good night," I said. I waited till his dot of torchlight had bobbed all the way across the drawbridge and onto the rocks beyond the Chasm. Then I turned back towards the castle.

It was only at that moment that I began to wonder what had actually *happened*. The two men must have separated to search for the library. I had assumed, without any conscious thought on the matter, that Rebecca had come upon the German—Hans, I now knew—in the kitchen and hit him over the head with the frying pan. She wouldn't think twice about it if she believed anyone might be a threat to Uncle John, especially if she'd been startled awake. But that didn't explain the pool of blood. Could so much blood come out of someone's head? Wouldn't there just be a bruise? Unless she'd used a knife . . . My insides suddenly seized up, and I bent over and was sick in the courtyard mud.

Oh, God help us, I remember thinking. For are any of us nonbelievers at moments of despair?

I stumbled back into the kitchen to find the hearthrug lying crooked and damp over freshly scrubbed flagstones. Veronica was at the sink, wrist-deep in murky water, but she whirled round at the sound of me.

"Well?" she asked.

"He was in the library," I said. At any other time, this invasion of her private domain would have been met with outrage, but she only nodded. "He's on his way back to the village," I said. "I *hope*."

"Right," she said grimly. "Good." She let the water drain

away and started wringing out the cloth she'd used to clean the floor.

"Veronica!" I said when she gave no sign of being about to say anything else. "What *happened*? Who . . . and where's the . . . What did you do with it?"

"Quiet!" said Rebecca, edging backwards out of the pantry. "You'll wake him."

I felt a bubble of laughter rise and pop in my throat. "You can't wake him!" I cried. "He's *dead*!"

Veronica dropped the cloth and hurried over, wiping her hands on the hem of her nightgown. "Shh!" she hissed, glancing up at the ceiling. She pushed me down onto one of the chairs and crouched beside me. "Listen," she said, "He . . . Father woke up, he must have heard the Germans talking in the courtyard. He went into the Great Hall and took down Benedict, and then, when the blond one saw the unlatched door and came into the kitchen—"

"Oh God, no," I moaned, covering my face with my hands.

"We must hide that body," said Rebecca.

"Are you mad?" I said, lifting my head. I looked at Veronica, but for once she wasn't arguing with Rebecca. "Are you *both* mad?" I said. "We have to tell Herr Rahn! This is his friend, we can't just—"

"They're SS," said Veronica fiercely. "I saw the insignia on his tunic. Do you understand? Part of the German army, Hitler's special forces. What do you imagine they'll do when they find one of their men has been mutilated with a sword?"

"They were *trespassing*," I said, a fresh wave of nausea rising at the picture Veronica's words evoked. "In the middle of the night! A man has the right to defend his—"

"They'll say His Majesty is insane!" cried Rebecca, looking more than a little insane herself with her gray hair hanging in hanks around her white face and—oh God, was that *blood* on her nightgown? "They'll take him away, lock him up, oh no . . ." Her voice rose in a wail.

"Quiet!" said Veronica. "You'll wake Henry!"

"You can't possibly agree to this," I said to her.

Veronica shot a glance at Rebecca and lowered her voice. "Sophie, you didn't see it. The body was all . . . it's horrible. It wasn't just self-defense. We can't let the Germans see what he did to the body, they'll . . . You know what they're doing in Germany to their enemies. What could they do to *us*?"

There was a sudden noise from the stairwell and then Carlos skidded into the room, followed closely by Henry. Veronica jumped to her feet.

"What's going on?" said Henry, rubbing her eyes. Carlos went over to the hearthrug and sniffed. I lunged at him and dragged him away by the scruff of his neck.

"Nothing," said Veronica. "Just . . . Rebecca thought she heard something and it scared her a bit, that's all. Now go back to bed."

"Why's the floor all wet?" said Henry, frowning at her feet. "And what's—"

"Henry!" shouted Veronica. "Go upstairs at once!"

"Wait," I said. It never does any good to order Henry around; I've learnt *that* lesson. "Perhaps she can help."

Veronica's jaw dropped, but before she could say anything, I'd knelt down beside Henry. "Listen," I said. "We think the Germans may have come up here, snooping around. You know how Uncle John gets with strangers, we have to keep them away. Now, if only someone could go up to the gatehouse and keep a watch . . ."

"I can!" said Henry at once.

"And if you see anything—they'll probably have a torch or something—run back as quick as you can and tell Rebecca."

"Should I take Carlos?" she said eagerly.

He tilted his huge head up at us. "Yes, he can sit at the bottom of the ladder," I decided. "Here, you can have my candle." I handed over the candle, bent in the middle from where I'd been clutching it, and Henry scooped up the matches from the table.

"And if I see anything," she said, "I can give a secret signal, like a bat screech or—"

"Yes, yes," said Veronica, pulling off her jersey and tugging it over Henry's head. "Now go, quickly."

"But what are *you* going to do?" she said.

"Search the grounds, patrol, that sort of thing," I said, feeling as though I'd landed in the middle of one of her dreadful adventure books.

She nodded and then the two of them were gone.

"Where's Uncle John?" I finally thought to ask.

"In there," said Veronica, nodding at his room. "He seems to have come over all strange, Rebecca could hardly get him into bed. He's just lying there now."

"Shock," I said knowledgeably, having firsthand experience of it now. "And where's the . . . ?"

"In the pantry," said Veronica. We all winced.

"And what, exactly, are you saying we should do with it?" I said. It was easier to think of the body as *it*, rather than *him*. And by then, I'd begun to accept the awful truth—that hiding it was the only possible course of action.

Veronica turned away from me. "Well, I thought we could dig a hole in the courtyard or hide it in the woodshed or something," she said. "But if they search the castle—and they *will*—they'll find it. We'll just have to throw it off the cliff. It's perfectly plausible that he was wandering around on the rocks in the dark and he slipped. And the body won't last long in the sea, they never do."

Her voice wavered then and I was glad of that, at least. If she'd sounded cold and rational, I'm certain I would have hated her at that moment.

"But . . . but what about Henry, up in the gatehouse?" I said. "If she goes out onto the curtain wall, she'll see us for sure."

"I didn't mean into the Chasm," said Veronica. "It might wash up into the firewood cave if we do that. I meant around the other side. The ledge that runs below the Napoleon hole."

I shook my head in disbelief. "That's impossible!" I said. There was—theoretically—a way down to that ledge from the castle, starting near the drawbridge, but not even Henry would have attempted that steep, narrow, slippery path at night, let alone with a heavy bundle.

"No," said Veronica. "We can go through the tunnels."

I stared at her, aghast.

"One of them leads to that ledge, I've seen the plans," she said. "Well, a sketch, at least, from John the Third's reign. And another tunnel heads off it. As far as I could see, it comes out in the middle of sheer escarpment, which is even better for our purposes."

I must have turned as white as my nightgown. Veronica touched my arm.

"I can't do it by myself," she said softly. "And it's probably better if Rebecca stays with *him*—who knows what he might do next."

"The . . . the tunnels under the chapel?" I stuttered. "With the rats and the damp, and you don't even know where they go . . . Oh, Veronica!"

I thought I'd been so brave going out through the courtyard to see off Herr Rahn. And yet that was nothing, nothing at all, compared to what she was asking now.

But even as I thought this, I knew there was no one else to help her.

"Shoes," I said desperately, trying to fill my head with practical things so the terror wouldn't overwhelm me.

Veronica frowned. She said she wasn't sure if we shouldn't stay in our nightclothes, in case Herr Rahn came back—it would look less suspicious; we could pretend we'd been awoken again by a noise and were just having a look around. But, as I pointed out, we were going to be carrying a blood-soaked, body-shaped bundle—how could we not look suspicious? We might as well be warm and well shod.

So I ran upstairs to grab our clothes, and when I came back, Rebecca and Veronica had dragged the body as far as the Great Hall. It was long and bulky, wrapped entirely in the blanket and tied around with a bit of old rope Henry had been using for skipping. I pulled on my skirt and tied my shoelaces, trying frantically not to think about the dark, spreading patch around the middle of the bundle. Then Veronica and I each lifted an end and we staggered off.

It was much, much heavier than George had been. Rebecca followed us as far as the chapel, muttering anxiously and sending wide-eyed glances over her shoulder. She had taken the man's torch, and it traced a wobbly path for us behind the altar, picking out the steps leading down to the crypt. I'd never had reason to go anywhere near it—there hadn't been anything left of my parents to bury, and my FitzOsborne grandparents had died before I'd been born—but Veronica said she'd been down there once to do rubbings of the tomb inscriptions, so she led the way, backwards. I took the torch from Rebecca, tucked it under my arm, and kept my eyes on my feet as I followed, shuddering with each step.

I reached the bottom of the stairs and we set the body down. Glancing around fearfully, I saw the place wasn't quite as horrifying as I'd imagined. The ceiling was low, but the floor was dry and smooth. Two rows of fluted pillars ran the length of the space, and between the pillars and the walls lay the stone tombs, forty or fifty of them. The nearest were carved with effigies—a crowned figure with his hands crossed over his chest, another clutching a scroll, a woman with a featureless face—but most were unadorned, inscribed with no more than a name and a date.

Veronica took the torch from me and played it over the scroll-holding figure. I edged closer and realized who it was. Why, it was Edward de Quincy FitzOsborne! I let out a breath in a near laugh. Good old Edward! They were family, I realized, Fitz-Osbornes just like me—I had nothing to be afraid of, not really.

"I wonder," Veronica mused aloud, setting the torch on the floor, "if we could . . ."

Then, to my horror, she curled both hands around the stone lid of the tomb and tugged.

"What are you doing?" I screeched. Family or not, I had no desire to see what was inside that tomb.

"It'd save us a long trip," she puffed. "Come on, give me a hand."

"You can't . . . you're not putting it in there!" I said. "That's our great-great-great-great-uncle!"

"He's nothing but dust by now. And he wouldn't mind, if he knew why we were doing it."

It was only my desire to avoid the tunnels that made me go over to help, but even with both of us pulling, the lid refused to budge. It wasn't just the weight of the lid—it seemed to have been sealed somehow.

"I suppose that's one of the first places they'd look, anyway," said Veronica with a sigh. "It was worth trying, though. Well. The tunnels are supposed to be down the other end."

We picked up the bundle again, which seemed to have grown even heavier, and stumbled on. After about twenty yards, the floor became rougher and began to slope upwards. The rows of pillars ended, and several yards later, so did the crypt itself. But there was no sign of any tunnel entrance, not even one buried under rubble. I'd hoped for an archway, a lamp set into the wall, perhaps even a helpful signpost, but there was only black granite, curving overhead like a frozen wave. Veronica frowned and moved the torchlight over the rock face.

"It's supposed to be a square hole, large enough for a man to crouch inside," she said. She started to retrace her steps, shining the light into the niches I'd only just noticed, which were carved at irregular intervals into the wall. Some of them gleamed dully, the light bouncing off neat little piles of bones. I shivered as Veronica and the light grew more distant, although it wasn't particularly cold—indeed, the air was warm and stale. "It has to be on this side," floated back Veronica's voice. "Except . . . oh, this is nothing but solid rock, I swear . . ."

I followed her, more because I wanted the light back than because I thought I'd be any help in the search. The floor smoothed out again and I read the tomb inscriptions as we paced past them. King John the Third. John the Conqueror. Benedict. King Stephen. Yet another John . . .

Wait a minute.

"Veronica," I said. "Was there a King Benedict?"

"No, of course not," she said, climbing on top of a tomb to shine the torch into the niche above it.

I took a deep breath. "Then why is there a tomb here with his name on it?"

Veronica whirled around and pointed the torch at the tomb I was indicating. "Of course," she breathed. *"Benedict will protect the House of FitzOsborne, now and for eternity!"*

We tugged at the lid and it slid back to reveal not bones or dust or ashes, but a square of black.

"You," Veronica said, beaming, "are a genius."

But the warm glow of pleasure at her praise rapidly cooled. The torchlight barely made a dent in the deep darkness below the rim of the tomb. I could hear a *drip, drip,* and worse, a rustling noise. Rats—no, *bats*—no, something even more repulsive . . .

"I'll go first," said Veronica. "Then push that thing down to me and you follow once I've pulled it out of the way."

"But what if the tunnel's blocked? And then someone closes off the lid and we get stuck down there and—"

"Listen!" said Veronica, but my teeth were chattering so hard I could barely hear anything—not anything good, at least. "Put your hand down. Feel the fresh air? Smell the sea? This leads to the cliff. And think how close the chapel is to the curtain wall. Fifty yards, even less. You can walk across the courtyard in half a minute—we won't be down there long. Look, it's . . ." She had dropped to the bottom of the hole—there seemed to be some metal rungs hammered into the walls—and was crouched down, shining her torch ahead. "It's perfectly . . . well, it's a bit low, but . . ."

If I thought any more about it, I'd never do it. I clenched my teeth, hauled the bundle of body up over the foot-high edge of the tomb, and shoved it over. Then, flinching at the thud as it hit the ground, I lowered myself down beside it.

The tunnel was, as Veronica admitted, cramped. It was also damp, icy, and malodorous. The torchlight played crazily over the rough-hewn granite as we stumbled along at a crouch, scraping our elbows and knees raw. Something soft brushed against my face at one stage and I jerked my head away, smashing it into the roof of the tunnel. I felt wetness trickle down my forehead then, but I didn't stop to wipe it away—I think I was afraid that if I halted, even for a second, I'd give in to the hysteria building up in my chest, fall down in a screaming heap, and never get out of there.

Finally, after what seemed like hours, the tunnel widened and split. One fork led off at an angle; the other continued, more or less in a straight line.

"This one," said Veronica, pointing to the right. I didn't argue, even though I was terrified we'd end up wandering in a never-ending circle down here. But she was correct, as always—a few yards on, she came to an abrupt stop and I staggered, almost falling lengthwise over the bundle. I thrust my head forward and realized where we were.

The tunnel mouth opened halfway up the west face of the cliff on which the castle was built. I peered downwards, careful not to lean out too far. A ledge, about a yard wide, lay below us. Veronica tested it with her foot, then crawled out onto it and felt for the edge.

"It'll hold us," she said, and we dragged the bundle out and laid it on the rock. I'd been so anxious about our trip through the tunnel that I'd managed to put aside the thought that we'd been dragging along with us a person—a dead one, a murdered one. Now I was forced to think about it all over again. I hadn't liked Hans at all, but he probably had a mother, a sister, maybe even a wife or fiancée, and they would never get to visit his grave or even know how he died. It wasn't *his* fault that he'd ended up like this. My eyes filled with tears.

Meanwhile, Veronica was undoing the rope and unwinding the blanket.

"What are you doing?" I said, blinking hard.

"We're pretending he fell off a cliff, and he wouldn't have done it tied up in a blanket," she said. "Now give me that torch."

"You're not throwing that away!" I yelped, snatching it back.

"What if his body washes up without it?"

"You said it wouldn't! You said the sharks would eat it! Anyway, he could have dropped the torch somewhere! How are we going to get back without any light?" My voice sounded so high that I didn't recognize it. Veronica looked ready to slap me, and it probably would have been a good idea.

"He wore it strapped into that holder, it wouldn't have fallen out!" she snapped. "And we can't take it back to the castle— what if they find it? How do we explain why we have it?"

"And what about the gun?" I cried. "Herr Rahn didn't have it when I saw him."

Veronica frowned down at the body. "Well, *he* doesn't seem to have it. Do you think Father took it off him? Or Rebecca did?"

I shook my head. All at once, I was too exhausted to think about any of it anymore. I just wanted it to be over. I barely even flinched when Veronica hefted the top end of Hans's poor un- wrapped body and I saw the mess of blood and . . . other stuff coming out of his middle.

"On the count of three," said Veronica, and then we heaved him off the ledge. Halfway down, he slammed into a jagged bit of rock, and for a heart-stopping moment I thought he'd been impaled there—but he crashed on down the cliff face and landed in the ocean, the splash swallowed up by the crash of the waves. We stood there a moment without speaking. I remembered my dream of Isabella, and thought of George and all the other dead Montmaravians shifting about beneath the waves, reaching up their cold white arms towards Hans and pulling him down to the seabed.

"He was trespassing," Veronica reminded both of us after a while. "We told him not to."

"But he didn't deserve to *die*," I sniffed.

"We didn't kill him," she said. "We couldn't have done anything to save him. The only thing we did was bury him at sea, rather than let his family bury him."

There wasn't much else to say after that. We threw the rope and the torch over the ledge, but Veronica wanted to take the blanket back and wash it or burn it or something—there was too great a chance it would float. Even leaving it in the tunnel seemed too risky.

I don't remember much of the crawl back up the tunnel. It must have been pitch-black, but I honestly don't remember it. I do remember climbing back into Benedict's tomb, up the metal rungs, and banging my knee against the lid as we slid it back in place.

When we finally reached the chapel, Veronica took a candle from the altar and we made our way back to the kitchen, where Rebecca stood staring at us from the doorway of Uncle John's room. I could well imagine what a sight we presented. Our elbows were raw; both of us had skinned knees; and when I gingerly touched the sore part of my head, my fingers came away stained crimson. But there were more important things to worry about just then than a bit of blood.

"Where's Henry?" I asked.

"She came in a while ago, said the man had been wandering around on the other side of the Chasm," whispered Rebecca hoarsely. "Then he seemed to go off towards the village. She went back up to the gatehouse."

"We'd better get her," Veronica said, but I pointed out it

would be better if we cleaned ourselves up first. There was the blanket to dispose of, too.

In the end, we left Rebecca cutting the blanket into strips with the scissors while Veronica and I went up to the bathroom and tried to set ourselves right. I felt like Lady Macbeth, scrubbing and scrubbing at bloodstains that could never come out. It was only the knowledge that Henry was waiting for us to reassure her that stopped me from curling up on the floor in a whimpering pile. At this, I thought, Oh, *this is what it must be like to be a grown-up.* Which was not a particularly comforting thought—I would have given anything to return to innocent childhood at that moment. But one glance at Veronica's grim countenance as she pulled a comb through her hair made me realize that the less of the burden I shouldered, the more she would have to bear—and she didn't look as though she could carry much more.

After that, we fetched Henry and assured her that the castle was safe, sneaked out to hide the bloodstained strips of blanket under a pile of straw in the henhouse until we could think of a better way of disposing of them, checked that Uncle John was still asleep, put Henry back in bed a second time after admitting that yes, I'd met Herr Rahn, but that I'd seen him off and everything was now fine—and then tried to fall asleep ourselves. I didn't try very hard. I was afraid I'd see Isabella drifting towards me, staring at me with her dead, knowing eyes, tangling me up in her shroud, trying to tug me down to the depths of the sea where the dead German lay.

So I sat up instead and wrote all this, and now the horizon is a thin band of silver. Soon I will get up and hide my journal in its secret cranny, and then I will have to face whatever horrors the new day brings.

New Year's Eve 1936

I haven't been able to write anything for two days—I've been too afraid to sneak this book out of its hiding place—but now the German soldiers have left. As with my last entry, I'm sticking to Kernetin in case this book falls into the wrong hands. It makes writing rather slow going—however, I'm determined to set down as detailed a record as I possibly can.

Well, the day before yesterday—that was awful. Herr Rahn returned to the castle early in the morning and loitered apologetically under the gatehouse until Henry came out to feed the hens. She quickly summoned Veronica and me. Herr Brandt, his colleague, appeared to be missing, he explained to us. It was possible Herr Brandt had gone for a walk near the castle. Had we seen him?

Veronica did all the talking, to my relief. No, she said, she had not seen anyone walking around here. When and where had Herr Rahn last seen him?

At this, Herr Rahn caught my eye and blushed.

"Yes, I'm aware of *your* midnight excursion," Veronica said severely.

Herr Rahn bowed his head and admitted he had left his colleague by the gatehouse the previous night. After meeting me, Herr Rahn had returned to the village, expecting Herr Brandt to follow—but Herr Brandt had not turned up.

Veronica said that she wished Herr Rahn's colleague had taken heed of her warning about approaching the castle—the mist could descend unexpectedly and the cliffs were slippery, steep, and terribly dangerous, even for those of us familiar with them. But perhaps Herr Brandt had taken their boat out?

"No, no," said Herr Rahn, his forehead now corrugated with worry.

"We could have a search party," Henry offered brightly. "We could take Carlos. He's good at sniffing things out."

I felt the blood drain from my face. Veronica managed to conceal her anxiety about this suggestion far better than I did (although, I realized later, the only evidence was hidden in the henhouse, with enough competing smells to confound even Carlos). Fortunately, Herr Rahn misinterpreted my expression and hastened to reassure me.

"No, no, I am certain Herr Brandt is all right, but the cliffs—"

"I think we should look around the rest of the island first, before worrying about the cliffs," said Veronica firmly. "I expect he's sprained his ankle or something and settled down to wait for help. We'll meet you at the village in an hour to help you look."

Herr Rahn was so effusive in his gratitude that I felt quite miserable. It made it worse, somehow, that the dead man now had a complete name. I could just picture a Frau Brandt in a dirndl and cross-stitched apron, fretting about her faraway son.

"If he *did* go wandering round the cliffs," said Henry thoughtfully, leading the way back to the kitchen after Herr Rahn had departed, "he'd be dead now. He was so heavy and flat-footed—did you see him walking? And if he fell in the water—well, he doesn't look like the sort who knows anything about currents or swimming, not the way he brought their boat into the wharf that day. He'd be drowned in a minute."

"Don't," I said shortly. I'd had only a few hours' sleep and was in no mood to listen to Henry's morbid ramblings. But the news was equally bad inside—it seemed Uncle John hadn't woken at dawn, as he normally did, and was "laying funny."

"He's breathing, isn't he?" snapped Veronica when Rebecca came to report this.

"He needs the doctor!" shouted Rebecca. "He's not right!"

"How can she tell?" wondered Henry aloud from the doorway. And when I joined her, I had to admit he looked pretty much the same as always, lying on his side, refusing to make eye contact or say a word. The only departure from his usual behavior was that he hadn't yet seized a nearby object and hurled it in our direction.

"Sit back down and eat your breakfast, both of you," ordered Veronica, although I noticed she managed to swallow even less than me. Rebecca went up to the gatehouse to raise the doctor's flag and the rest of us walked down to the village to take part in Herr Rahn's pointless search. We investigated the coves, took him up to the viewing point near the memorial cross, and trained his binoculars on all the possible places Herr Brandt might have gone exploring. Herr Rahn explained he had already radioed his colleagues on his ship for help, but they would not be able to reach the island for a day or two.

"They don't have a doctor on board, do they?" asked Henry innocently. "Because our uncle's been taken ill. We've just put up the doctor's signal flag for him."

"Your . . . uncle?" said Herr Rahn, looking confused.

"I'm sure he'll be all right after some bed rest," said Veronica hastily. She must have been imagining how Uncle John would react if a German doctor marched into his room. I certainly was. Just then, I had a horrible thought. Where was Benedict? Had Rebecca had the sense to clean the blood off it and put it back over the chimneypiece?

"I did not know your uncle is living in the castle," Herr Rahn was saying.

"He's quite old," said Henry. "And a bit mad."

"Henry!" I said loudly. "Go and show Herr Rahn around the Great Pool. There might be footsteps in the mud if Herr Brandt slipped in. Veronica and I will search the bushes at the edge of the Green."

"But—" said Henry.

"Please do as you're told," I said, fixing her with a glare, and she was astonished enough by this to obey at once. The moment they were out of earshot, I grabbed Veronica's arm and asked if she knew what had happened to Benedict. Her eyes widened.

"I told Rebecca to keep it out of sight," she said. "She took it into his room and I hoped she'd . . . but I didn't check. And I forgot all about it this morning. One of us had better go back and make certain."

"And get rid of that blanket," I said.

We looked at each other despairingly.

"I'll go," I said. Veronica was better at talking to Herr Rahn than I was. I was terrified that at any moment I would blurt out the awful truth.

I hurried back to the castle and was thankful I had. It turned out Rebecca had wiped Benedict clean on a rag, then shoved sword and rag under Uncle John's bed. It was fortunate Uncle John wasn't his usual self—I was able to slip into his room and retrieve both items without too much difficulty. Rebecca was no help. She hadn't even done the breakfast dishes. Fuming at her uselessness, I poked the rag inside Vulcan; gave the sword a hasty polish; retrieved the scabbard, which had been flung under the piano; and hung both sword and scabbard over the chimney-piece in the Great Hall, cursing Rebecca all the while for making us keep the horrid thing sharpened all these years.

Then I ran back outside to the henhouse to retrieve the strips of blanket we'd hidden in the straw. I thought of throwing them into the Chasm, but as Veronica had pointed out, it was all too possible they'd wash up in the firewood cave. Instead— gagging at the stench of stale blood and bird droppings—I buried them in the kitchen garden beside the carrots. I had just enough time to wash my hands and brush some of the mud off my clothes before the others came down over the hill and across the drawbridge.

"We're just going to walk along the curtain wall, see if we can spot anything," said Veronica.

Poor Herr Rahn was quietly frantic by that stage. "I am very much afraid that . . . I said to him not to go near the cliffs, but . . . surely he must be found by now if . . ."

Veronica and Henry led him up the ladder while I stayed below with Carlos. Their heads emerged a minute later above the parados and Herr Rahn sent me down a feeble smile. I had had enough at that; I hurried inside and shut myself in the upstairs bathroom for a good hard cry. Then, somehow, I managed to fall asleep on the bath mat. Veronica discovered me there half an hour later.

"Well, he's gone back to the village," she said. "I gave him a quick look at the kitchen, but managed to talk him out of searching the whole house. I told him it was impossible anyone could get upstairs without us noticing and that the place wasn't big enough to get lost in, but that we'd have a look anyway. His colleagues will be here tomorrow or the day after." She sighed. "The important thing is to keep Henry away from them."

I blinked at her, feeling heavy-eyed and stupid. "What about Uncle John?" I asked.

She sat down on the edge of the bath beside me. "We'll just have to keep them away from him. I've no idea how. I'm certain they'll want to question him, he's the one supposed to be in charge here."

"We'll just say he's ill," I said. "He *is* ill, isn't he? If he stays quiet the way he's been today, it should be all right."

"What's the chance of that happening?" said Veronica bitterly. "You know he'll throw a fit when he sees men in uniform, let alone hears them speaking German."

"Well, Rebecca will just have to keep him quiet," I said. "It's not as though she's doing anything else useful at the moment."

Then there wasn't much else to do but wait for the ship with the blue swastika to reappear, which it did today at noon. A motorboat much like Herr Rahn's was soon launched off the side, but Henry, telescope glued to her eye, reported that this time there were four men aboard. "Maybe five," she added as the boat neared the shore.

"Ought we to go down and meet them?" I asked Veronica in a low voice, drawing her away from Henry. "It might seem more welcoming."

"But we aren't welcoming them," she pointed out. "We don't want them anywhere near here. They shouldn't have been here in the first place."

"Still, if we're friendly, they might be more sympathetic when we say we don't want Uncle John questioned."

Henry's shout interrupted our discussion. "They've docked! Ooh, that motor's fast. Don't you wish we had a motor like that?"

"Are they wearing uniforms?" Veronica asked.

"Brown, with big black boots. No, one of them's wearing all

black. Now Herr Rahn's talking with them. He's sticking his arm straight out and the others are sticking theirs out, too, like in that newspaper picture of Hitler." Veronica and I exchanged anxious looks. "Now they're unloading things . . . they're going into Alice's house, no, one of them's gone behind a rock and he's undoing his trousers . . ."

"Yes, thank you, Henry, that's enough," said Veronica, taking the telescope from her. "No, Sophie, we'll wait for them to approach us." She sighed. "Pity we can't raise the drawbridge any more, or lower the portcullis."

"Pity I haven't got the cannon working yet," said Henry. "But I've got my catapult all ready."

I then explained to Henry that this was a moment for diplomacy rather than battle.

"Why?" she asked. "Veronica just said they were trespassing."

"Why were you eavesdropping on my private conversation with Sophie?" said Veronica.

"It wasn't private, you were standing right next to me! What was I supposed to do, pretend my ears had fallen off?"

"Anyway," I interrupted, "the point is that there are six of them and—"

"Six of us," said Henry.

"Six men, six *armed* men," I said.

"As opposed to three girls, a feeble old man, his useless housekeeper, and a dog," said Veronica.

"Don't call me a *girl*," snapped Henry. "And I bet Carlos is a better fighter than any of them."

"We are not fighting anyone," I said firmly. "We are going to help their search as much as we can and ask that they leave Uncle John alone. You know he isn't well and that sometimes he can be a bit—"

"Mad," said Henry, nodding.

"And so we'll ask them—nicely—to stay away from the castle."

"*Tell* them," said Veronica.

"Tell them *nicely*," I said.

An hour later, I looked out from my post on the roof to see the men come marching—well, not exactly *marching*, but certainly not strolling—towards the drawbridge. We ran downstairs and hurriedly arranged ourselves in the kitchen. Veronica seated herself at the head of the table facing the unlatched door, her hands folded in front of her, her head straight and still, looking as though a heavy golden crown were balanced on top of it. Carlos stood at attention at her right, trembling with alertness. Henry and I placed ourselves on her left, my hand on Henry's shoulder part reassurance and part restraint. Rebecca had already locked herself in the bedroom with Uncle John. We waited silently, the very air tense.

At last came the knock on the door.

"Come in," said Veronica sharply.

All at once, the room darkened as half a dozen men crowded through the doorway. Herr Rahn managed to push his way through to the front.

"Your Highnesses, may I present SS-Obergruppenführer

Gebhardt," said Herr Rahn. A tall man with white hair and eyes the color of ice gave a perfunctory bow. "SS-Obergruppenführer Gebhardt—Her Royal Highness, Princess Veronica of Montmaray. Her Royal Highness, Princess Sophia. And Her Royal Highness, Princess Henrietta."

We each nodded, even Henry, who had scowled at the sound of her full name.

"Your Highnesses," said the tall man, in a voice as cold as his eyes. His English was impeccable. He was clearly very important—his posture alone managed to indicate he outranked every other German in the room. "As you know, one of our men is missing. We have not found any sign of him on the island. We request permission to search this . . . this castle." He glanced around the kitchen, at the broken windowpane and shabby dishcloth, and I knew I wasn't imagining the disdain in his expression.

Then Veronica stood up, her invisible crown seemingly welded in place, and all of a sudden, the German officer looked much shorter. "As *you* know," she said, "we have helped Herr Rahn search all the possible places on this island a man could become lost. You are welcome to search the henhouse, the woodshed, the gatehouse, even the cucumber frames if you wish, but we have already searched the house and I think it highly unlikely that—"

"We will start outside," interrupted the officer. He barked out orders at the men, four of whom rushed out the door and scattered. "Then, if we have no success, we will search in here."

"If you've already decided to invade our home, I hardly know why you bothered asking for permission," said Veronica, sending Herr Rahn a scornful look. He looked down at the flagstones, his face coloring.

Gebhardt thrust out his jaw. "The nephew of our esteemed Führer's personal physician has gone missing. On your territory, may I remind you. We would expect *every* cooperation from you."

"And may I remind *you*," snapped Veronica, "that Herr Rahn and Herr Brandt trespassed upon sovereign territory when they docked without notice at our wharf. We generously allowed them to stay. We also warned them against approaching the castle and explained the dangers of the cliffs, and yet I discovered that Herr Rahn, for one, chose to disregard my warnings and break into our library at midnight—"

"Sovereign territory!" scoffed Gebhardt, aiming a contemptuous kick at the nearest chair. Carlos started up a deep, almost inaudible rumbling in his chest. I edged closer to him, still hanging on to Henry's shoulder.

"And now Herr Brandt, apparently sharing his colleague's disregard for common sense, has disappeared in the middle of the night and you hold *us* responsible?" Veronica continued.

"You," said Gebhardt, pointing one bony finger at her, "ought to—"

"WOOF!" shouted Carlos, startling Gebhardt into a backwards stagger. He tripped on the chair he'd disarranged, lurched sideways, and would have dashed his head against the sink if Herr Rahn hadn't grabbed his arm.

"Control your dog!" Gebhardt yelled, his face suddenly crimson. "Or I will shoot it!"

"Don't you dare!" Henry wrenched herself away from me and threw herself across Carlos. Veronica stepped quickly in front of both of them while I tried to drag them backwards.

"Now, there is no need . . . ," Herr Rahn began, glancing anxiously at Gebhardt. At that moment, two of the men appeared in the doorway.

"*Ja?*" snarled Gebhardt.

The men shook their heads. Gebhardt pointed to the tower stairwell behind me and rapped out something in German. The men brushed past us and ran up the stairs. I was pleased to hear one of them bang his head against the lump of rock at the first bend, placed there for the exact purpose of thwarting invaders.

"And do you suppose Herr Brandt is hiding in our laundry hamper?" said Veronica in her most caustic voice. "Has fallen asleep in the bath? Became engrossed in the alphabet mural on the nursery walls and forgot to return to camp?"

"Veronica!" I whispered urgently. "Don't antagonize him!"

"You should listen to the girl's advice," spat Gebhardt.

"And you, Gebhardt," said Veronica, "should be advised that landing soldiers on sovereign territory without permission and threatening innocent women and children breaks international law. Your Führer may think he got away with it in the Rhineland, but I assure you that there are no German sympathizers in Montmaray and we will use every diplomatic means to ensure that you face the consequences of your contemptible actions!"

The other two men marched in from the courtyard and were directed towards the Great Hall as I clung on grimly to Henry and Carlos, who were both shaking with fury. Meanwhile, Veronica and Gebhardt glared daggers at each other. Eventually the men upstairs clattered back down, one rubbing his forehead, the other shaking his head apologetically at his commanding officer.

"Where else is there to search?" snapped Gebhardt.

"You could try the cliffs," suggested Veronica coolly. "Or the sea below."

I saw the indecision in Gebhardt's face. He had almost accepted that Herr Brandt had fallen to a watery death; he was nearly ready to turn and march out. The only thing stopping him was his pride, which refused to concede that Veronica could be right. I held my breath as several long seconds went by. Finally he snorted, shook his head, and took a step towards the doorway.

And then it happened.

There was a heavy thump and the door to Uncle John's room rattled.

"Who is in there?" cried Gebhardt. He strode over to the door and hammered on it. "Open at once! *Schnell!*"

There were a few more thumps and then the door was wrenched open from the inside. Uncle John suddenly appeared in all his unkempt glory, Rebecca hanging off one arm. She tried to tug him back towards the bed, but he had caught sight of the

German men (all six of them now gathered back in the kitchen) and he let out an almighty roar.

"Huns!" he bellowed. Then he threw his chamber pot at Gebhardt.

Gebhardt shrieked and flailed; Rebecca screamed; Carlos leapt at Gebhardt; the German soldiers ran around the kitchen, tripping over chairs and one another; and Herr Rahn attempted to placate Uncle John, receiving an elbow in the stomach for his pains. Suddenly Uncle John stopped roaring and crumpled onto the flagstones.

"You've killed him!" howled Rebecca.

"Out of the way!" ordered Veronica. "All of you!" The Germans fell back and she dropped to her knees by his side, groping for a pulse, then turning her cheek to his gaping mouth.

"He's breathing," she said. "You"—she pointed to the two nearest Germans—"you carry him back to bed. And you"—she glanced at Gebhardt, who was still spluttering—"radio for medical assistance at once. Tell them the King of Montmaray has had a stroke." She got to her feet and followed Rebecca as Uncle John was carried into the bedroom.

"Well?" I cried. "Aren't you going to get help?"

"We will radio immediately," said Herr Rahn, answering for his officer. Gebhardt was otherwise occupied, stripping out of his drenched, foul-smelling tunic with one hand and clutching at his torn trouser leg with the other. The two Germans shuffled out of the bedroom. Then, with a final snarled vow of retribution from Gebhardt, all six of them departed.

They did seek medical assistance, it turned out, but it was on behalf of Gebhardt rather than Uncle John. Carlos had torn a chunk out of Gebhardt's leg and they were worried about rabies (unnecessarily, as we've never had rabies here on Montmaray; not that I felt any desire to reassure them). Herr Rahn sneaked back half an hour later to tell us this. He and one of the soldiers had stayed behind for a final search of the island, while Gebhardt and the others had returned to their ship.

"And your uncle?" asked Herr Rahn.

"He's the same," I said. "Breathing, but not moving." We were beneath the gatehouse again—Rebecca had threatened Herr Rahn with a red-hot poker when he'd appeared at the kitchen door and I'd had to chase after him.

"I am sorry," he said, looking miserable. "But you will be leaving now?"

"Leaving?"

"Leaving Montmaray," he said. "You have family in England, yes? The young princess told me. It will be safe there."

"Safe from what?" I said, my heart starting to beat harder.

He glanced over his shoulder, then leaned closer. "Sophia, Gebhardt is a man who . . . He cares nothing for the Grail, nothing for wisdom! Gebhardt . . . *il veut la vengeance.*"

"Vengeance?" I said.

"I am a *scholar,*" he said urgently. "Not a soldier. I join the Nazis because I must, but I . . . I do not agree with . . ."

There was a shout from the other side of the Chasm.

"I must go," he whispered. "I am sorry. For everything. *Au* revoir." Then he gave one of his heel-clicking bows and was gone, hurrying over the drawbridge.

And now, as I sit here writing, the old French clock strikes once, which means it must be past midnight. It seems the new year has staggered in without anyone noticing. Oh, when I recall the New Year's Eves when Isabella was here—the champagne, the fireworks, the music . . .

But what is that awful wailing noise? Is it Rebecca? Do I even *want* to know? No, but I had better go down and find out.

1st January 1937

King John the Seventh of Montmaray is dead; may he rest in peace.

It is evening now, and I've yet to feel any emotion at all. Maybe it's lingering shock after all the other events that preceded it. Or perhaps it's simply that he was such a small part of our lives. He shouted a bit and threw things on occasion, but we'd learnt to ignore that. Mostly he was merely a brooding presence on the other side of a closed door. Isn't that sad, that the most positive thing I can say is that I was largely indifferent to him?

I'm more worried about the effect this will have on Veronica, who has never really been indifferent to him. Of course, she was the target of most of his furies, increasingly so as she grew more and more like Isabella—in looks, at least. I think that sometimes he actually believed Veronica *was* the wife who'd left him. Veronica hasn't said a word about him today, though, or cried (Veronica never cries), or behaved in anything other than her usual manner. This may be because she's been kept so busy, mostly with letter-writing—to Aunt Charlotte, to Toby, to Mr. Grenville, to the bank, to various diplomats and foreign ministers, to the Anglican bishop who conducted my parents' funeral service, and to a dressmaker in London who specializes in mourning clothes. By some miracle, a northbound steamer stopped this afternoon upon seeing our doctor's flag, which we'd forgotten to take down, and they agreed to take the letters for us.

As for me, I've also been occupied—cleaning up the disarray left by the German searchers, mostly. Meanwhile, Rebecca is keeping vigil by Uncle John's side in the chapel. Freshly bathed, his hair cut, his beard trimmed, dressed in clean robes, he looks a good deal better than I can remember him looking in years. He really does appear as though he's sleeping. It seems almost unfair that he should be so at peace when he's caused so much trouble. But I daren't allow myself to start thinking about whatever revenge Gebhardt is plotting—even if he doesn't suspect Uncle John had a role in Herr Brandt's disappearance, he certainly wants retribution for the chamber pot–throwing. Not to mention Carlos's ripping his leg open and Veronica's defiance and . . . No. Not thinking about that. Not thinking about any of it; it's just a waste of energy when there's nothing I can do about it.

The only bright spot is that Toby and Simon will be coming home now for the funeral, perhaps as early as Tuesday if they can find a ship straightaway. To think that I was once concerned about how I would behave the next time I saw Simon! That I worried about my incessant blushing and my inability to put sentences together in his presence and my unmanageable hair! How trivial it all seems now, how silly and childish . . .

It's nearly midnight. But I have to get this down on paper, and there is no chance whatsoever I will sleep now, not tonight.

I was writing in bed earlier this evening when Veronica sat down abruptly by my side.

"I have to tell you something," she said.

I looked at her face and felt my heart clench. "Oh God," I said. "What now?"

"Not . . . now," said Veronica. "No. A long time ago."

I took a deep breath. "Go on."

But she stayed silent, her hands clenched in her lap, her knuckles chalk-white. She shook her head and stared at the rug.

"It's all right," I said feebly. "I mean . . . well, if it was a long time ago, it doesn't . . ." I was about to say it didn't matter, but judging by the set of her mouth and her shuttered eyes, it mattered a great deal, and all at once I knew the only thing that could make her look like this. "Is it . . . to do with Isabella?" I whispered.

Veronica glanced at me, startled. "How did you know?"

Again I saw the shroud unraveling in the icy water, the face falling to one side, the dark eyes with all the life washed out of them. I bit my lip. "Is she dead?"

Veronica stared at me and then nodded.

"Oh, *Veronica*," I said, tears welling up. I wanted to put my arms around her, but her face, pale and bleak, held me back. I groped for the words that would unlock hers. "But . . . how do you know? What's happened?" *A long time ago*, she'd said, and I remembered Isabella's unlined face in the water.

Veronica closed her eyes for a moment. Her bottom lip was bloody where she'd been gnawing at it, but her eyes were dry. How does one comfort a person who never cries? I pushed my blanket aside and moved closer, but didn't dare to touch her. "You can tell *me*," I said.

"I thought I could, but I can't," she said. "I don't know how."

"Pretend," I said. "Pretend it's a story for Henry. A made-up story."

"A Gory Story," said Veronica, with a harsh sound that could have been a laugh.

"Yes," I said, inching closer until finally my side was tucked against hers. She was freezing. I tugged at my blanket until its folds covered her legs. "Go on. Once upon a time . . ."

Veronica nodded. "All right. Once upon a time, there was a queen . . ." Then she stopped.

"Who was very beautiful," I urged.

"Of course," said Veronica, with a twist of her mouth. "According to *Tatler*, anyway. She wasn't born a queen, though. She was only one because she married a king."

"Was he handsome?" I said, slipping my hand into the crook of her elbow and squeezing it. I was heartened when she didn't push me away. I moved my head closer to her shoulder.

"No. Nor was he particularly rich. Still, he was a king."

Veronica paused. "She thought he looked very distinguished in his uniform when she first saw him. She was only eighteen then, and very easily impressed. She didn't understand what war does to soldiers. Especially soldiers who manage to get most of their men killed."

"It wasn't his fault," I said. "Not really."

"It was," she said. "He knew it was. It changed him. He took it out on everyone around him. Especially her. Especially when she didn't do her duty, when all she could produce was a *daughter*."

"But everyone celebrated when you were born! There was a feast in the village, George said. With fireworks and dancing and everything."

"That was for Toby," said Veronica. "Six weeks later."

I opened my mouth, then closed it.

"Only boys counted, you see," said Veronica. "The kingdom followed Salic Law—"

"Followed *what*?" I said, unable to stop myself. But I'd said the right thing after all—Veronica started to sound more like her usual self.

"It's a law governing succession, thought to have originated with the Salian Franks about fifteen hundred years ago," she said. "Although it only stated women couldn't inherit land. Later it came to mean that a kingdom couldn't be inherited by a woman or her descendants. Or so the French argued in the fourteenth century when Edward the Third of England tried to claim the French throne through his mother, who was the daughter of Philip—"

"Right," I said. I had a vague recollection of Toby and Veronica arguing in a desultory manner one rainy afternoon about whether Toby would still inherit the throne if Veronica had a son before Uncle John died—assuming Isabella hadn't returned in the meantime and given birth to a boy. I shook my head. "Your story," I said firmly. "Go on about the queen."

Veronica sighed. "Well, the queen didn't have a boy. She didn't even like the child she *did* have, especially when the child turned out to be far too interested in books and not at all pretty." Veronica ignored my protests. "Fortunately," she went on, a bit louder, "the king's younger brother had a sweet wife who not only produced a boy, but two girls besides. However, little did they know that there was a curse on the kingdom—"

"There was not!" I said, sitting up straighter.

"Yes, there was," said Veronica. "A bad-luck curse. Due to the king's smashing up all the looking glasses in the castle, on account of going mad after sending his men to their deaths during the war. And sadly, the king's brother and his wife were the ones who paid the price."

"They died," I said softly.

"Yes," said Veronica, and we sat there in silence for a moment, pressed against each other.

"But the queen," I said at last.

Veronica said nothing.

"Pretend it's a story," I reminded her.

She looked down at her fingers, pleating the blanket, as though they belonged to someone else. "Well. The queen became tired of the mad king, and her unsatisfactory daughter, and having to look after her nephew and nieces, and being stuck on an island far away from parties and . . . and things. So she decided she needed to go away for a holiday."

"A holiday?" I asked. "Just a holiday?"

"I don't know," said Veronica. "Maybe a holiday. Maybe she wanted to leave forever. Nobody knows, except perhaps . . . except the king. And he was mad, remember. And violent. Afterwards, no one dared ask him. Anyway, she happened to see a ship passing by just as she was thinking of leaving. So she packed a small suitcase and she left the castle. She went down to the village and ordered a man on the wharf to row her out to the ship."

"George?" I whispered.

"That . . . that may have been his name," said Veronica, her voice faltering for a moment. She took an uneven breath and went on. "It was evening. Winter. There was a storm brewing. And the man—George—well, he happened to have been the manservant of the king's father, a long time ago, before the war. He knew the king wouldn't want the queen to leave. The queen belonged to the king, you see, and he knew the king would be very angry with his manservant if he just . . . just allowed her to go. So he tried to argue with her. She wouldn't listen. She climbed into the rowboat and picked up an oar. Well, of course he had to climb in after her—anyone could see she didn't know one end of an oar from the other. He took up the oars and pulled away from the wharf, still arguing all the way out onto the deep

water. He could just see the black hulk of the ship on the hori
zon. And then he stopped rowing. He refused to go any further."

Veronica looked down at her hands. I held my breath,
waiting.

"She was very angry by this time," said Veronica. "She lost
her temper, and she hit him and hit him. He raised his arms to
protect himself, to restrain her, but he still had hold of the oars,
and in the confusion she stumbled and fell against the side of
the boat. Her head slammed into the edge. She went very still
then. Perhaps she was dead. He wasn't sure."

I felt an icy shudder wash over me. I was in that boat, surrounded by all that cold black water.

"The big ship sailed past the island and off into the darkness, and she continued to lie there, silent, unmoving. So he
took a long white shawl out of her suitcase, and he wrapped it
around her. And then he buried her under the waves. That was
what they did in that kingdom, with people who died. Unless
they were part of the royal family—then they were laid to rest in
the crypt beneath the castle. But this woman wasn't part of the
royal family anymore, he told himself, she'd tried to escape, she
wasn't worthy . . ."

"Don't," I said, tears starting to roll down my cheeks. But I
knew this was the only way she could tell it. The words were
spilling out of her now, mercilessly.

"And then he rowed back to the island. It wasn't until he
reached the wharf that he realized he should have thrown
her suitcase overboard, too. But who could say—perhaps the

gathering storm would have washed it ashore and then there would be questions, and the man didn't want his king to have to answer any questions. After all, everyone talked about how the king had become mad and violent and perhaps—perhaps they would think the king had killed her. So the man hid the suitcase in his cottage. He lived by himself, so it was safe there. He was going to tell everyone that he'd seen a launch from the ship collect the queen, that she'd had it all planned out. But only one person ever asked, and that was the king's housekeeper. Maybe the king had sent her to investigate. The housekeeper didn't care much, anyway—she'd never liked the queen and was glad she was gone—so the man hardly had to bother to get his story straight. It was a bit sad for the queen's daughter, but she was better off without her disloyal mother. And the man was always careful to take special notice of the daughter, and he indulged her whenever she wanted to talk about history—did I mention she was very interested in books and things?"

"Stop," I said, my breath hitching on a sob. "Stop it."

"I'm sorry," said Veronica, and finally her voice broke. She put her arm around me and pulled me closer. Taking a ragged breath, she whispered, "I'm sorry, Sophie. It's just a story."

"That cloth you had," I said at last, wiping my face with my palms. "It was from her suitcase."

"Yes," said Veronica.

"And George told you all this," I said. "Just before he died."

"Not all of it," she said. "He told me where the suitcase was hidden. He told me most of it. Some I guessed. It makes sense."

I glanced at her face, which was pale but composed now. "I'm glad I know the truth."

I wanted to tell her of my dream, but I couldn't think how it would be of any comfort to her, so I kept silent. And after a while, she stood up, tucked the blanket around me, said she was going to check on Henry, and left the room. Then I wrote all this down.

5th January 1937

I have never been so glad to see Toby in all my life. Veronica, Henry, Carlos, and I practically dragged him out of the boat when it docked this morning, barely stopping to acknowledge the other two passengers.

"Ugh," said Toby, trying to disentangle himself from Henry, who'd thrown herself around his neck. "Don't squash me, I'll be sick again." And he did look a bit green, although nowhere near as bad as the short, round stranger next to him, who had one hand over his mouth and the other clutching at his stomach.

"Sick as dogs, both of them, all the way from the Channel," said Simon, coming up behind with the bags.

"You needn't sound so smug," said Toby. "Just because *you* spent the trip strutting round on deck, scoffing bacon sandwiches."

"Well, it might have helped if you hadn't drunk all that brandy the night before."

"*Gentlemen,*" groaned the stout man. "Please."

"Oh, I do apologize," said Toby. "Everyone, this is the Reverend Webster Herbert."

"Are you the Bishop?" asked Henry, looking at his black suit with interest.

"No, afraid we don't rate a bishop anymore," said Toby cheerfully. "But never mind! Mr. Herbert, may I introduce my cousin, Princess Veronica, and my sisters, Princess Sophia and Princess Henrietta-who-prefers-to-be-known-as-plain-old-Henry. Oh, and this is Prince Carlos." Carlos gave the Reverend Mr. Herbert a friendly whack in the stomach with his tail. Then there was a lot of jostling over the luggage and we all started up the path, everyone talking at once.

I positioned myself behind Simon and I heard him say to Veronica, "My condolences on the loss of your father." And Veronica nodded and said "Thank you" in a very civil manner. It may just have been the calming presence of Toby, but nevertheless I took their lack of open hostility as a good omen, particularly as the clouds had parted for a brief moment and there was a hazy glimmer of rainbow over the sea. Miraculously, the peace held all the way up to the castle, all through the complicated allocation of bedrooms, all through luncheon, coming unstuck only when the grown-ups (for the first time, I had no hesitation in classifying myself as one) sat around the table afterwards discussing the funeral arrangements.

It was a pity Aunt Charlotte couldn't have been there to tell us all what to do, but her foot was still in plaster and the doctor had forbidden her to move further than her drawing room. Unfortunately, Toby seemed to have misplaced the lengthy list of instructions she'd given him, and it turned out that Mr. Herbert hadn't had much experience in burying kings.

"It's quite straightforward," said Veronica. "The funeral service is mostly out of the Book of Common Prayer, and Toby, as the new King—"

I blinked. I'd always known Toby was heir to the throne, but to think that now he actually *was* King—or would be, after the coronation ceremony . . .

"—leads the responses throughout. Then we carry the body down into the crypt and Toby removes the Royal Seal—"

"That round thing with the FitzOsborne crest engraved on it?" asked Toby.

"Yes, according to tradition, the King wears it round his neck on a gold chain," said Veronica. "It's for stamping into sealing wax on official letters, so you'll need to—"

"No!" said Rebecca from the doorway of the Great Hall. We all turned around.

"What's the matter, Rebecca?" said Veronica. It was the most Rebecca had said since Uncle John had died. We waited a bit, but nothing else was forthcoming. Veronica sighed. "As I was saying, Toby puts the Royal Seal around his own neck, and then . . . well, he should remove the crown as well, but I think that's in Aunt Charlotte's safe. At least I hope it is, it certainly isn't here. It wasn't part of the original ceremony, anyway. After that, Toby grasps Benedict in his right hand and—"

"No!" cried Rebecca, still in the doorway, now shaking her head wildly. "No!"

"Do you think," Veronica snapped at Simon, "that you could *possibly* attempt to discover what it is that your mother finds so objectionable?" Simon, who'd already risen from his chair, scowled at Veronica. Mr. Herbert, sitting across the table from me, looked overwhelmed and still slightly seasick. I felt a bit queasy myself, remembering the last time the King had grasped Benedict.

"Why don't we discuss this later?" Toby suggested brightly. "Mr. Herbert probably wants to unpack and have a rest, anyway."

"Good Idea," said Simon, herding his mother towards Uncle John's room. Veronica stood up, glared at Simon, and then led Mr. Herbert upstairs. Toby slumped back in his chair.

"I *thought* they were being too polite to last," he sighed. Then he looked over at me and reached out a hand. "Oh, Soph! Poor *you*. Has it been just dreadful?"

"Yes," I said, considering. "Yes, it really has. And you don't even know a quarter of it."

He grimaced. "I gathered that, what with Henry babbling about Nazi pirates trying to shoot Carlos, and Rebecca reduced to monosyllables."

"We'd better go up and get Veronica, and then you can find out—"

"No, you tell me," he said. "Honestly, Soph. I'd rather hear it from you."

"Let's go up to the gatehouse, then," I said after a moment. "So we don't get overheard."

We took a blanket and two hot bricks with us, and huddled together on the floor. Then I told him everything—about the Nazis arriving on their futile and possibly Simon-inspired quest for the Grail; about Hans lying bloody and mutilated on the kitchen flagstones; about the terrifying trip down the tunnels with the corpse; about Uncle John throwing the chamber pot at Gebhardt—all of it. I'd forgotten what a good listener Toby could be—he gasped in all the appropriate places, urged me on when I stumbled, asked all the right questions. I hesitated when I came to Isabella. But I knew Veronica would want him to know, so I went on, describing my dream and my vision at George's funeral, and then Veronica's terrible revelation.

"My God," he breathed at the end. "And George actually . . . my *God*." He stared at me. "Oh, Sophie. You sound so *calm*. You've been so brave and . . . oh, Sophie!" He flung his arms around me.

"No, I haven't," I mumbled into his shoulder. "I was absolutely terrified all along and—"

He let me go so he could peer into my face. "That's what I mean. You were so scared and you did it anyway. That's even braver than Veronica—because she's always had nerves of steel." He frowned. "How *is* she, anyway? I haven't had a second alone with her yet."

I shook my head. "The usual, just quieter. And when I think about how awful I felt when . . . well, when Mother and Father died." He nodded quickly. "And the same thing's just happened to her, losing both her parents at once."

"Except it's not as though she actually *liked* Uncle John. And Isabella's been gone for years."

"Toby!" I said crossly. "Even so! And finding out about George . . ."

"Yes, I know," said Toby. "She really does need to have a good howl or *something*. Well, maybe she and Simon can have one of their enormous rows and she can throw a plate at him, let it out that way."

Henry burst in at that moment, desperate to show off her new knot-tying skills to Toby, and she dragged him down to the courtyard. I gathered up the blanket and no-longer-hot bricks and went back to the kitchen, where I found Simon peering inside the kettle.

"How's Rebecca?" I asked.

He shook his head. "I gave her a sleeping powder. I'm just making tea—would you like some?" It turned out Toby had brought with him not just tea, but white sugar, tinned shortbread, and my favorite fig-and-ginger jam, all of which he'd appropriated from Aunt Charlotte's pantry.

"Oh," I said. "All right, then. Thanks." I sat down and realized I hadn't once blushed since Simon had arrived. Perhaps I really *had* become Sensible after all. Then our fingertips brushed as he passed me the sugar, and I shivered. Or perhaps not.

"So," he said, looking at me over his cup. "How *are* you?"

"Um," I said. I couldn't remember his ever asking me this

before. "I'm . . ." I couldn't think of any polite yet truthful way to end that sentence, so I cleared my throat and began again. "You know, I really can't believe that Toby is . . . well, that he's *King*."

Simon's face lit up in a rare, uninhibited grin. "I know! King Toby! Imagine!" Then he sobered at once. "But this *does* change things, of course. I know *you* were planning to leave Montmaray anyway. But the others—well, you understand that things are different now. With the villagers gone and my mother not . . . er, able to look after you, not at the moment . . ."

As though Rebecca had *ever* looked after us! Simon must have seen me suppress a snort, because he went on hurriedly.

"They *can't* stay here, Sophia, it simply isn't practical." He leaned towards me and gazed earnestly into my face. I felt my heart begin to beat a bit faster. "The Princess Royal's expecting all of you to return with Toby and me—I've arranged for a ship to pick us all up in a few days." He half smiled at me and sat back. "I'm so glad I can rely on *you* to help me persuade them to do the sensible thing."

My heart went back to its usual speed. Simon didn't care how I was at all—he just needed to tick off another one of his duties on the list Mr. Grenville had given him: "Item 7(a): Ensure all three (3) FitzOsborne girls board ship for England." I put down my cup heavily, sloshing tea into the saucer.

"Veronica won't leave Montmaray," I said. "You know that. And I'm *not* leaving her here by herself." I pushed back the terrifying memory of Gebhardt's threat, of Herr Rahn's warning, and

I raised my chin, Queen Matilda–style. "Anyway, Toby only has six months of school left, and then he can live here all the time."

Simon shook his head. "Oxford. That's what the Princess Royal wants."

This was news to me. "Do they *really* let boys who fail all their school tests go up to Oxford?"

"My ears are burning," said Toby, coming in from the courtyard with Henry. He draped his arm across Simon's shoulders and plucked a sugar cube from the bowl on the table. "What scandalous things are you saying about me now?"

Simon slapped Toby's fingers away. "We're discussing your future," he said. "Specifically, your academic future."

Toby groaned. "Oh, Aunt Charlotte's been going on about Oxford again, hasn't she? I've told her a thousand times how thick I am."

"Nonsense," said Simon severely. "You're lazy, not stupid. And think of all the useful people you'll meet there."

"All right, then, here's the plan—I'll get Veronica to disguise herself as me and she can go to all my lectures instead."

"And that's another thing," said Simon. "The girls can't possibly stay—"

"Ahem," I said loudly, with a meaningful look in Henry's direction. Any objections Veronica might have to leaving Montmaray would be mild and reasonable compared to Henry's, especially if Henry realized it might involve her going to school. Fortunately, she'd been too busy trying to impress Toby with an acrobatic display to have heard anything.

"And that's nothing!" she cried, upside down by the sink, when she saw us all looking at her. "I can do five cartwheels in a row!"

"But not in *here*, Horrid Hen," said Toby. "Courtyard, please."

"But you'll come and watch?"

"Certainly, as soon as I've finished ordering around these loyal subjects of mine."

"Ooh, I forgot you're King now. Yes, Your Majesty!" She tumbled to the floor, gave a demented sort of curtsey, and ran off, giggling.

"I wish *I* could forget," muttered Toby. "And is it my imagination or has Henry somehow grown *younger* over the past three months?"

"She always goes through an overexcited phase when you get back," I said. "And it's been a difficult time, and no one's been paying much attention to her lately."

"I expect she misses Jimmy, too," he said, rubbing his face. "It was so odd, seeing the village deserted. Wasn't it, Simon?"

"Odd, but inevitable," he said. "And to return to the subject, Sophia and I were just discussing what will happen while you're finishing your education. You know it isn't practical for the girls to stay here—"

"Toby!" came a cry from the courtyard.

"Oh, let's not talk about it right now," said Toby, going over to the door. "Ooh, Henry, do that again! Brilliant! You'll have to teach me."

Simon gave me an "Isn't he hopeless!" look, but instead of smiling sympathetically, I frowned and took the tea things over to the sink.

We didn't get around to any further discussion until this evening, after dinner had been cleared away and Henry sent upstairs with the Meccano construction set that Toby had brought her.

"I do hope your mother is feeling better," said Mr. Herbert to Simon, with a nervous glance at the door. Rebecca was still asleep in there—no one had felt any inclination to wake her up for dinner.

"I expect it's just that Rebecca's very upset about Uncle John, and talking about the funeral makes it seem more real to her," said Toby.

"I don't know," said Simon slowly. "I wonder if it's more than that . . ."

"Well, she was here when Grandfather died," I pointed out. "So she probably remembers how the ceremony went."

"Then it's a pity she isn't able to share this information with us in coherent sentences," said Veronica. "However, we'll just have to make do with four hundred years' worth of documentation from the library. Now, Toby, did the Foreign Office let you know whom they're sending to represent the British government?"

"Ah . . . Simon?" said Toby.

"A diplomat by the name of Davies-Chesterton," said Simon. "But unfortunately, the British royal family is a bit preoccupied with other matters at the moment, what with the abdication—"

"Yes, yes," said Veronica. "And the Spanish royal family is in exile."

"And the French ambassador didn't reply," said Simon.

"Well, that would be because my late father cut all diplomatic ties with France in 1918," said Veronica, a note of impatience creeping into her voice. "What about the Portuguese?"

"They sent a very nice letter of condolence," said Simon.

"And the Germans?" said Toby lightly, but no one laughed except Mr. Herbert, who gave a polite, confused titter. Simon frowned, and I wondered how much Toby had told him. Most of it, I assumed. After all, Simon was one of us, really. The Germans were as much his problem as ours.

"I hope you've also informed all the Montmaravians currently living in England," Veronica said to Simon.

"I'm sure they're aware of the tragic news," said Simon rather evasively. I couldn't really blame him. They're probably scattered all over the place by now, and even if he had everyone's address, not all of them can read. It might be asking a bit much, anyway, expecting them to travel all this way to pay their respects to a man who'd been responsible for the deaths of so many of their relatives.

Veronica, of course, took a different perspective on Simon's failure to contact them. Simon's jaw tightened as she went on to express this opinion rather forcefully. He shoved an errant lock of hair back and took a noisy breath. I stared at him as he sprang loudly to his own defense. Simon hadn't changed at all since I'd last seen him—but I realized that *I* had.

It was as though I'd put on a pair of spectacles—or taken off rose-tinted ones, perhaps. He was as handsome as ever, and yet somehow diminished-looking. I could see, finally, that Veronica was right about him in some ways, but that Toby was, too. Simon was clever *and* ambitious, genuinely concerned about Montmaray and even more interested in himself. He was neither as courageous as Veronica nor as charming as Toby, but was nevertheless compelling in his own way. And I *still* (I'm ashamed to write) wanted him to kiss me! Being a grown-up is very complicated and confusing . . .

Not surprisingly, I took in very little of the rest of the conversation.

"Good, that's sorted then," I suddenly heard Toby say. "Who's up for a game of Squid?"

I excused myself from this, ostensibly so I could come upstairs to organize mourning clothes, but really so I could pace around the bedroom having a big think. After a while, I stopped muttering and pacing, and sat down on the bed to write all this down by flickering candlelight (even more flickering than usual, due to a bothersome draft).

There's not much I can do about our mourning clothes, anyway. Henry refuses to wear her dress and has appropriated Toby's old black tailcoat and pin-striped trousers. Veronica's dress is too tight around the bust, but she plans to leave the top buttons undone and wrap a shawl around herself for decency. Mine is scratchy and desperately in need of a sash, except the only one I can find is a fuzzy tartan one from an old dressing gown . . .

Oh, really! How can I possibly be worried about how I look as I prepare for my uncle's funeral! I will think about *that* instead. Yes, what a relief it will be—that solemn ceremony, the stately rituals set down on parchment centuries ago, a dignified regal farewell. Oh, if only certain other deceased people had had such ceremonies to lay them to rest, I might be having fewer nightmares now.

7th January 1937

I read over that last paragraph and I shake my head in disbelief. How could I *possibly* have imagined that anything would go according to plan when it comes to FitzOsbornes and Montmaray? I ought to have *known* that Rebecca would . . . No, I'll tell this properly. Life here might be utter chaos, but my journal will rise above the confusion.

So, yesterday. We woke to find ourselves encased in fog, the dense, gray, suffocating sort that feels as if the castle has been hoisted into the middle of a bank of clouds. It wasn't until midafternoon that some wisps of clarity began to appear. Henry went up on the roof with the telescope, but there was no sign of any ships, let alone ones bearing diplomats.

The rest of us took turns keeping vigil in the chapel, at Mr. Herbert's request. He was worried Rebecca would wear her knees to nubs in front of the altar and insisted she take a break. Surprisingly, she gave in—either she was impressed by his clerical garb or she remembered that Simon was here and that he needed her to cook him meals. Veronica took PAYN–POLK of the *Ency-clopaedia Britannica* in with her for her stint (she's been working her way through its twenty-eight volumes ever since I can remember). I took Carlos. I thought he might come in handy if Herr Brandt made a gruesome spectral appearance. Nothing unexpected happened, though, except for a mouse scuttling across Carlos's tail in the near dark. I'm not sure whether Carlos or the mouse was more horrified.

Actually, I didn't mind taking my turn in there, once I'd found a spot that allowed me to avoid looking at Uncle John, who was laid out in front of the altar. For one thing, I didn't have to worry about accidentally bumping into Simon when I was in the chapel (the castle is feeling rather crowded at the moment). For another, the cold flagstones and the austere surroundings made me feel a little like a medieval penitent—rather appropriate, given my confusing thoughts of the day before. I knelt down and asked God to take away my desire to kiss Simon, or to transfer it to someone more suitable. I think it worked to *some* extent. I did feel a twinge of irrational jealousy at dinner when Toby draped himself across Simon's shoulders in his usual familiar manner—but at least I recognized this for the lunacy it was.

Then, today, we awoke at dawn to the most tremendous crash. My initial thought was that Henry had finally figured out how to make gunpowder, but no, it was merely a thunderstorm, the heavens deciding to clash right above the castle. It lasted for a good three hours—torrents of rain, zigzags of lightning, thunderclaps that seemed to shake the very foundations of the castle. Veronica and I ran around in our nightgowns, putting empty chamber pots under all the ceiling leaks, then got started on boiling up enough water for everyone to have a proper wash, which took quite a while.

We all looked most peculiar when we finally came down in our mourning clothes—except Rebecca, who has worn her black dress for the past five days and consequently looked very familiar, if a bit disheveled. She also seemed a little more like her regular self—she clipped Henry over the ear when Henry spilled the milk, glared at Toby when he took a piece of toast meant for Simon, and hissed at Veronica for no reason at all that I could see. She still wasn't speaking in actual words, but she looked intimidating enough that Mr. Herbert cornered Toby, Veronica, and me after breakfast.

"I just wondered if . . . Are you *quite* sure Mrs. Chester is all right about the funeral arrangements? Only she seems a little . . . and I would rather not upset anyone at this tragic time . . ."

Toby said that Simon would have let us know if Rebecca had said anything.

"Oh," said Mr. Herbert. "Well! I'm sure that's all right." Then he chuckled. "After all," he added, "it's not as though Mrs. Chester is likely to have any violent objections right in the middle of the funeral!"

Toby, Veronica, and I glanced at one another. I knew they were thinking the same thing I was—that that was *exactly* the sort of thing Rebecca was likely to do. But just then the black cat scampered up to present Veronica with a twitching, head-less rat. And what with all the screaming (it turns out Mr. Her-bert has an even greater aversion to rats than I do) and mopping up of blood, we forgot about Rebecca for the time being.

The storm, still churning away over the bay, had put paid to any hopes that the British diplomat (or anyone else) might arrive, so after a quick squint through the telescope at the turbulent, empty seascape, we decided to begin. Toby and Simon had carried half a dozen of the uncomfortable chairs from the Great Hall into the chapel and arranged them in a row in front of the altar, but Rebecca disapproved (non-verbally, but heartily), so they took them back out again and found some old cushions and we knelt on those. The damp of the flagstones seeped through immediately, chilling my kneecaps.

Not a single ray of sunlight pierced the stained-glass win-dows. There were candles flickering on the altar and in the niches in the walls, although not nearly enough of them—they merely served to intensify the gloom. Worse, I had an uninter-rupted view of Uncle John, who lay with his hands wrapped around Benedict's hilt. For one dreadful moment, I thought I saw a smear of blood on the blade. I squeezed my eyes shut and said my anti-ghoulies prayer, though, and when I opened my eyes again, the bloodstain had disappeared.

Once everyone was arranged to Rebecca's satisfaction, Mr. Herbert cleared his throat and began. We got all the way through "In the midst of life, we are in death" and "The Lord gave and the Lord hath taken away," all the way up to Toby standing before the altar and saying, "Let us commend our King, John Edward Stephen Tobias Henry Bartholomew, to the mercy of God," when Rebecca lurched to her feet.

"Stop!" she cried.

Veronica groaned. Simon shuffled sideways on his knees and tried to tug his mother down beside him, but she was having none of it.

"Stop!"

Mr. Herbert looked over at Toby helplessly.

"What's wrong, Rebecca?" Toby whispered—as though there were other mourners in the chapel who mustn't be disturbed.

"You have no right to stand there!"

Toby looked down at his feet, bemused. Henry started shaking with silent giggles. I poked her hard in the ribs and she subsided into hiccups.

"You are not the heir of His Majesty!" Rebecca shouted. "You are not the true King!"

Her face was red; her chest heaved with emotion; her hands were clenched—she seemed utterly mad and utterly sincere. I just knelt there, gaping up at her. But Veronica got to her feet and dusted off her knees.

"Go on, then," she sighed. "As you are determined to turn this funeral into some histrionic travesty—"

"How dare you!" Rebecca cried. "You don't care about this funeral! You never loved His Majesty! *I* loved him!" And to everyone else's embarrassment, she broke into noisy weeping. Simon stood up and tried to push his handkerchief at her, but she shook her head. Instead, she grasped his shoulder and turned him to face the altar.

"Here," she sobbed, "*here* is the true King! Yes—my son! Simon, the firstborn child of King John the Seventh!"

If she had hoped for exclamations of shock or outrage, she must have been disappointed. Apart from Henry's hiccups and the hissing of the candles, there was complete silence.

Simon was the first to speak. "Mother," he said quietly. "What . . . ?"

She clutched him closer. "I promised His Majesty . . . I *swore* I wouldn't tell a soul while he lived. But he always meant for you to be king; you were always his favorite."

"How interesting," said Veronica, through what sounded like clenched teeth. "But perhaps you could save your fantastic tale for a more appropriate time—after dinner, say, when we often read each other fairy stories by the fireside. For the moment, the Reverend Mr. Herbert has a funeral ceremony to conclude. Simon, perhaps you could escort your mother to her room so that she can have some sorely needed rest. No doubt she is hysterical after a difficult few days. Mr. Herbert, please continue."

"Oh," he said, glancing around. "Well, should I perhaps . . . ?"

"*I* think," Toby said. We all turned to look at him. "I think that . . . that we should hear what Rebecca has to say."

Finally there was uproar. Veronica started shouting at Toby.

Rebecca continued to wail. Mr. Herbert made squeaking noises and batted his arms around, and Carlos started barking loud enough to wake Uncle John.

"Enough!" I cried. "Please!" I gestured at Uncle John. "Can't we just . . . I mean . . ." I ran out of words then, but it seemed to be sufficient. Everyone quietened.

"Perhaps," Mr. Herbert ventured, suddenly remembering he was supposed to be in charge, "Mrs. Chester could . . . er . . . speak? And then Her Highness could . . ." Veronica, white-faced with fury, glared at him but gave a sharp nod.

Rebecca, still clutching Simon's arm, grew teary again as she glanced at Uncle John. "It's true. Simon is His Majesty's son. Look look at his face."

We all stared at the dead man and then at Simon. It was true; there was a suggestion of Uncle John in Simon's face. But I had no idea what Phillip Chester, Rebecca's husband, had looked like. Perhaps he'd also had that brow, that nose. And in any case, the most striking feature of Simon's face was his deep, dark eyes—Rebecca's eyes. Although now I came to consider it, they were also Veronica's eyes . . .

"Are you claiming," said Mr. Herbert, "that . . . that your son is the legitimate issue of yourself and . . . ?"

"We were as good as married," sniffed Rebecca, scrubbing at her face now with Simon's handkerchief. "We made private vows in front of this very altar."

"Don't be absurd," said Veronica at once, very coldly. "The late King may or may not have had . . . dalliances with village women before the war, but there would never have been any question of his marrying one of them. He was always destined to wed someone of noble birth, and so he did. And even if there *had* been a child—"

"Simon," interrupted Toby. "Did you know about this?"

Simon shook his head. He was as pale and tense as Veronica, but unlike her, his eyes held a faint glimmering of excitement. He didn't believe it . . . and yet, if it turned out to be true, he would be very, very pleased about it, there was no doubt about that.

"I promised His Majesty," whispered Rebecca. "Not to tell, not while . . ."

"How convenient," sneered Veronica. "Now that there's no one left to contradict your ridiculous story, you think you can spread a lot of lies to further your son's ambitions."

"Veronica, really," said Toby. "Simon had no idea."

She turned on him then. "And you! The only reason you're giving this any credence is that you're terrified at the thought of taking on a king's responsibilities! How much easier to hand them over to Simon Chester, who's cleverly made himself so indispensable to you!"

"Stop it," said Toby, in a very low voice. "I know you don't mean it, Veronica. It's just that you're upset and I can understand why, it must be awful, especially with your poor mother . . ."

"Don't you dare mention her!" snapped Veronica, and before anyone could move, she had stormed out of the chapel. Toby, looking distressed, took a few steps after her, then stopped.

Henry tugged on my sleeve. "I don't understand," she whispered to me. "How could Uncle John get married to Aunt Isabella if he was already married to Rebecca? And why is Veronica—"

"Not now, Henry," I said.

"Soph?" said Toby, falling to his knees beside me. "Please, could you go after Veronica? She'll talk to *you*."

Rebecca had moved closer to the altar and was staring down at Uncle John's face with a ghastly, triumphant expression. It was this more than anything else that made me tug Henry to her feet and lead her and Mr. Herbert into the kitchen, where I sat them down and made them tea. I left Henry teaching Mr. Herbert the complicated rules of Squid and went in search of Veronica, eventually finding her, as I should have known, in the library. She was halfway up a ladder on the second floor, her face buried in a heavy leather-bound volume.

"Veronica?" I said tentatively. "Are you all right?"

"What? Oh, hello." There was a dust-colored smudge across her black skirt, and a cobweb dangled from her ebony hair clip. "Ha! Just as I thought . . ." And she backed down the ladder, a couple of thick books tucked under one arm. She sat on the lowest step, placed the books on her lap, and beckoned me over. "Look at this. Village child claims to be the grandson of King Stephen, appears to be the very image of King Stephen's son. The court rules that illegitimate offspring have no claims to heredity and Bartholomew the Second retains the throne. The story's confirmed in Edward de Quincy's journal." Veronica gave the thickest book a friendly pat.

"But wait a minute," I said. "Does that mean . . . do you think Rebecca's telling the truth? That Simon really is . . . who she says he is?"

Veronica shrugged. "If Rebecca had any proof, she'd be waving it in our faces, and she's not. Doesn't matter. What matters is that Simon Chester can't possibly inherit the throne. Toby is the eldest living legitimate male relative of the late King—the throne is his."

It shouldn't have surprised me that the question of who should be king was foremost in Veronica's mind. However, Rebecca's outburst had other implications.

"You know, if Simon really is Uncle John's son," I said, "that makes him your . . . well, half brother. And it means Rebecca is my aunt. Sort of."

"Don't be so *revolting*, Sophie," said Veronica with a faint shudder. "Anyway, what happened? Is the funeral over?"

I shook my head and explained it had been postponed. The coronation, traditionally held seven days after a king's funeral, seemed destined to be even more postponed. I couldn't see Rebecca backing down on this, no matter how many relevant documents Veronica pulled off the library shelves. And if Simon was convinced that Rebecca was telling the truth, not to mention Toby . . .

As usual, Veronica seemed able to read my mind. "I suspect Toby might regard Simon's taking over the throne as a lucky escape for him," she said quietly. "However, *we're* going to convince him otherwise." She brightened. "Oh, and I must write to

Aunt Charlotte at once. I'm sure she'll be *very* supportive of our position when she hears of this."

She gathered up all her books and we went back to the kitchen. Rebecca appeared to have locked herself inside Uncle John's room and was thumping around in there, possibly in some sort of tribute to him. Henry was beating Mr. Herbert at Squid, and Toby and Simon had disappeared. Veronica sat down next to Vulcan and started scribbling down notes while I went looking for the boys. They weren't in Henry's room, which they'd been sharing due to the leak in Toby's room. Nor were they in the nursery, the Blue Room, the Gold Room, the attics, up on the roof, in the chapel (poor Uncle John looked quite forlorn lying there, alone and unburied), in the gatehouse, or anywhere in the courtyard. It was only after I'd given up and was washing my hands in the bathroom that I heard a low laugh and realized they'd hidden themselves away in the Solar. I shoved open the door at the far end of the bathroom.

"I've been looking all over for you—" I started crossly, then broke off. Toby and Simon were scrambling up from where they'd been half sitting, half lying against the wall. Both looked flushed; Toby looked guilty.

"How's Veronica?" said Toby at once.

"What do you care?" I frowned.

"Sorry, we were busy talking and lost track of the time," said Simon, smoothing back his hair. "There was rather a lot to discuss, and we preferred not to say it in front of Henry."

I stared at him. "Sorting out which one of you is going to be king?" I said in a voice that sounded remarkably like Veronica's. Simon blinked at me.

"Now, Soph—" began Toby.

"Don't 'Now, Soph' me!" I cried. "Veronica's right—you *don't* want to be king, do you?"

There was a pause.

"Perhaps Simon would do a better job of it," said Toby.

"Perhaps *Veronica* would do a better job of it," I said. "In fact, I'm certain she would. But it's not going to happen, is it? She's already looking up things in the library and there's no way . . . Besides, when Aunt Charlotte hears about this—"

"I've a great deal more influence over Aunt Charlotte than either of *you* have," said Toby. The set of his mouth reminded me of Henry at her most stubborn. It made me absolutely furious.

"Don't you dare threaten me!" I shouted.

"You have *no* idea—" Toby began.

"Stop it! Both of you," said Simon. We stopped it. "Look," he said. "Things are a bit strange at the moment, but there's no need to shout at each other like this."

"I'm sorry, Soph," said Toby quickly. "I've just been very . . . upset."

He hadn't looked at all upset when I'd pushed the door open. He'd been smiling and leaning against Simon, practically sitting in his lap. If I was being honest with myself, it was *that* that had bothered me the most. If Toby had been a girl, I would have been burning up with jealousy (well, obviously, if

Toby had been a girl, he wouldn't have gone off alone with Simon and ended up sprawled over the floor with him, but still). Even as it was, I envied Toby for how close he was to Simon, for having the sort of friendship with Simon that I could never have. And this made me ashamed of myself, especially as I was supposed to be finished with my ridiculous infatuation with Simon. So although I was still angry on Veronica's behalf, I grudgingly accepted Toby's apology and offered an (insincere) apology of my own. Then we all went downstairs.

A couple of hours later, the funeral started again and this time continued to the end without interruption. After the blessing, we stood and carried Uncle John down to the crypt, stopping before one of the few unoccupied tombs (I tried not to think about the last time I'd been down there). As a compromise, Simon and Toby removed the Royal Seal together and handed it to Mr. Herbert for safekeeping. The Oath of Accession, the traditional method of introducing the soon-to-be-crowned King, was omitted altogether. Finally the stone lid was scraped back into place over Uncle John and we trooped back upstairs into the chapel to snuff out the candles.

The funeral dinner was a dismal affair. Rebecca was stomping around upstairs, occasionally bursting into unintelligible rants. The rest of us poked at the rabbit stew on our plates and said very little. As soon as possible, I escaped to the library so I could find a book to bury myself in. I wasn't in the mood for Jane Austen or even the Brontës. I wanted something with no romance at all, something sharp and cynical, so I ended up with *The Importance of Being Earnest.* It was as I was settling myself in bed with it, wondering what the time was and wishing that *I* had a watch like Simon's, that I had a horrible thought. I must have made some sort of strangled noise—Veronica glanced up from the letter she was writing.

"What?" she asked.

"You don't think that Toby and Simon are . . . ," I said, then bit my lip. I looked at Henry, sprawled across Veronica's bed with her half-built Meccano train engine. Veronica raised her eyebrows impatiently. Henry kept working away with her tiny screwdriver, the tip of her tongue poking out the corner of her mouth. "Well, that they're a bit like Oscar Wilde and that boy?" I whispered.

"Oscar Wilde?" said Veronica blankly.

"The writer!" I said, waving my book at her. "The one who went to prison!"

"Did he?" said Veronica. "Why? Was it for sedition or forgery or something?"

"No, no, it was for . . ." I hesitated again. If I said "the love that dares not speak its name," I might have to explain further. This would cause problems, not only because Henry was in the room, but also because I wasn't entirely sure what it meant. Well, I knew in general terms, but . . .

"It was for indecent behavior," I ended up whispering at Veronica.

"Oh," she said without much interest, turning back to her

letter. "Well, I wouldn't be surprised at anything *Simon Chester* gets up to."

Henry lifted her head at that. "Veronica, is *Simon* going to be King now, instead of Toby?"

"Over my dead body," said Veronica, her pen scratching across the paper.

"Is that what your letter to Aunt Charlotte says?" Henry exclaimed. "Ooh! Can I write one, too?"

"Why not?" said Veronica, handing her a piece of paper and a pencil. "And what do you want?" I glanced around and saw with a start that Rebecca was in the doorway, looking furious. I suspected she'd heard everything, even the Oscar Wilde bit, although she was glaring at Veronica, not me. She snarled in our general direction, then disappeared.

"You can do a letter as well," Henry said to me, not having noticed this. "Or you can help me with mine. I'm going to do mostly pictures. I'm doing one of Toby wearing a crown."

I shook my head, my mind still full of Simon. I was almost certain now that *Toby* had given Simon that gold watch; it fitted with the accounts Veronica had been going over. It was Simon's birthday at the start of the school year; I was sure of it . . .

I groaned and buried my head in my pillow.

"I know how you feel," said Veronica sympathetically. "It's an awful situation, isn't it?"

I agreed in a muffled voice that it was completely awful.

"But there's nothing else to be done about it at the moment,

so why don't you update your journal? It's important that we
have a record of these events."

I sighed. Then I went out and got my book from its hiding
place in the gallery and I wrote all this down.

8th January 1937

Mr. Herbert's yellow hair is sticking up all over his head from his clutching at it, making him resemble nothing so much as a stout hen with very ruffled feathers. "My dear child," he clucked at me when I poured his tea this morning. "I would feel far easier if you and your sister and cousin would join me. Your passage *is* booked aboard the ship, you know, and I believe the Princess Royal is expecting you . . ."

Mr. Herbert has also made several attempts to talk Toby into returning to school, but Toby says he wants to make sure we are all right. Simon assured Mr. Herbert that he'd accompany Toby back to London himself in a fortnight or so, once Rebecca was feeling more "herself" (not an appealing prospect—I think I preferred her silent). Simon implied that our entire household would be leaving with him. He only dared say that because Veronica was in the library at the time, though.

Poor Mr. Herbert—he can't comprehend our resistance. He himself can't wait to leave this cold, dripping, rat-infested castle, populated as it is with madwomen and ghosts and people who have no idea who their fathers are. He is refusing point-blank to take sides in the king debate, saying only that he will consult with Aunt Charlotte as soon as he returns and promising to pass on all our letters. There is a thick wad of them. Even Simon wrote one, although I'm pretty sure Veronica contrived to burn it before the package went into Mr. Herbert's bag.

Luckily for him, Mr. Herbert won't have to endure Montmaray much longer. The ship carrying Mr. Davies-Chesterton from the British Foreign Office arrived this morning. Toby and Simon are down in the crypt with the young man now, showing him the tomb. It shouldn't take long for him to pay his respects—he didn't even have a wreath; it fell overboard when he was getting out of the launch. He is a very *junior* diplomat. He looks about fourteen. He looked even younger when Veronica was ticking him off about his having missed the funeral. He made the crewman who brought him across from the ship come with him up to the castle, as though he were afraid he might otherwise be left stranded here.

I wonder how he'd react if he were in the kitchen now, because Rebecca has just burst in and is raving on and on about Death. I really do wonder if she's gone a bit mad. Apparently she was off telling the bees about Uncle John's demise—*if* there are any of the poor little creatures left, that is; I wouldn't be surprised if they'd all drowned, in this weather. It *is* an old Cornish custom, telling the bees, but there's nothing in the tradition that says one can't wear a raincoat or a hat if it's pouring. She looks like an elderly Ophelia risen from a watery grave—sodden hair straggling over her face, black dress plastered to her body—as she staggers towards the stairs. I suppose it's rather appropriate, given Uncle John's Hamlet-ish behavior over the years. Now I'm trying to imagine the two of them as beautiful, tragic young lovers, torn asunder by cruel fate. It isn't really working. It does explain Rebecca's hatred of Isabella, though, and the way she's treated Veronica all these years. Did Isabella know about Simon, I wonder? Was it that knowledge that helped her decide to leave?

Thank heavens I've switched to writing in Kernetin—Mr. Herbert just peered over my shoulder. I'm sure he'd be scandalized by a young lady writing about It, particularly if he managed to read last night's entry about Simon and Toby. Oh, and now Rebecca's stumbled back downstairs with some black cloth to drape over the kitchen garden: otherwise the plants will wither, the crop will fail, we'll perish of starvation, and so on. Where did she get all that black stuff from, anyway?

Oh, she really is *too* much—that's my mourning dress! Admittedly it was a bit big around the waist, but I was going to take it in. It was the first new frock I've had in ages! Oh, the others are leaving now . . .

Goodbye, Reverend Mr. Herbert. Goodbye, Mr. Davies-Chesterton. Heavens, Simon must be the only person in the world who can manage to look dashing in that old macintosh.

No, I'm not going with them. I am going to console myself

over the loss of my frock with some of that fig-and-ginger jam
and a leftover breakfast scone . . .

The most dreadful, terrible, *awful* thing has happened!

I *should* have gone down to the wharf with them, I really
ought to have gone, but Toby said he and Simon could manage
the bags themselves and it was raining so hard and I couldn't
bear the thought of trailing after the two of them, watching Toby
with his arm around Simon's shoulders, or worse, Simon tou-
sling Toby's hair and laughing at Toby's jokes . . . but now I can't
help thinking that if only I'd gone, it wouldn't have happened.
Or if I'd been firmer with Henry and insisted she stay; or if I'd ordered Carlos to go along with them . . .

Oh God, poor, poor Toby! And I felt so *angry* yesterday
when I found him in the Solar with Simon, so full of sick, jealous fury that for a moment I actually wanted to hurt him. It's as
though I'm being punished now for thinking such horrible
thoughts, because it's far worse to see Toby in pain than to have
suffered such an injury myself. The snapped bone was actually
sticking out through his skin . . . Ugh, I think I'm going to be
sick just remembering it . . .

Back now, having hung over the basin for a bit. Wasn't actually sick, as it turned out.

All right.

What happened was that Simon, Toby, and Henry took Mr.
Herbert, Mr. Davies-Chesterton, and the crewman down to the
wharf. The two passengers were bundled into the launch with

Mr. Herbert's luggage, the crewman tugged the rope free of the pylon and jumped in himself, and the launch was wrenched away by the waves, disappearing almost at once in the spray and the mist.

Simon isn't sure what happened next. He said Henry had been doing handstands and cartwheels along the wharf, and that she must have slipped. Toby lunged to catch her, both of them dangerously close to the edge. It might have been all right even then, except for the wave that suddenly crashed over them— not even an ordinary wave, but one of those ten-foot terrors. Simon, turning around at that moment, said they vanished completely in the white water. When it cleared, Toby was clinging to the side of the wharf, his legs battering against a pylon, and Henry was lying on the wharf, clutching at Toby's arms, screaming for help. Simon ran over, almost skidding into the sea himself, and yanked Toby to safety, shouting at Henry to run back to the castle and try to signal the ship. But there was no point; it had already gone, vanished into the fog.

By the time Veronica and I got there, Simon had pushed Toby's dislocated arm back into his shoulder (mercifully, the freezing water had numbed it) and carried Toby to Alice's cottage. There hadn't been much he could do for the leg, though. Even Veronica looked daunted when she tore away Toby's trousers. The break was halfway down his shin, the bone having carved itself through the flesh like a serrated knife. It was the most horrible thing I've ever seen—worse than Hans Brandt, even, because I knew that *he* wasn't suffering, not anymore, whereas Toby clearly was. In the end, we gave Toby a mug of brandy (Veronica had had the foresight to grab a bottle of it, as well as bandages, before we ran down), and then I went outside with Henry while Veronica and Simon pushed the bone back into place and strapped it all up with a splint.

Henry was in hysterics. She blamed herself entirely, and I can't say I did much to disabuse her of that notion. If she hadn't been showing off, hadn't been her usual foolish, reckless self, Toby wouldn't have put himself in any danger. It's a terrible way to learn a lesson, though. We could hear Toby's screams from outside, even over the wind and the rain. I think Veronica did most of the surgery. Simon said afterwards, rather shakily, that his main contribution had been lying on top of Toby to stop him moving.

The trip back up to the castle was a nightmare, too. We tried to fashion a stretcher, using a blanket and the oars from the rowboat, but it didn't work very well, especially up the steep bits. Toby ended up limping part of the way, propped up by three of us, until he put his good foot in a rabbit hole. We managed to catch him before he hit the ground, but he'd blacked out by then, what with all the brandy and the blood loss and the pain. Simon and Veronica carried him the rest of the way.

Now Toby is lying in Uncle John's room (*former* room, I should say; I'll have to stop thinking of it as his). We evicted Rebecca—there was no way we were going to try getting Toby up that staircase. He has three blankets (held up over his leg with the aid of the folding tea tray) and the warming pan, but he's still shivering. Henry went out to raise the doctor's flag, but it was torn off the flagpole at once—it's probably flapping over France by now. In any case, who would see it? Dusk is falling and there are no ships. There are few at this time of year anyway, but with the war in Spain, shipping around here has almost ceased entirely. Oh, if only the Germans had left their radio equipment! And if only we knew how to use it! What on earth are we going to *do*?

9th January 1937

Toby has a solution. Personally, I think he's still suffering the effects of all that brandy yesterday, but it's not as though we have many other options.

We are going to send his pigeons off with messages.

Henry has been dispatched to collect them. I warned her not to use the one that follows Spartacus around all day because it thinks it's a hen, but she says there are a few that keep to the loft Toby built. I'm worried they'll have forgotten all about their former home in the Stanley-Ross attics. However, Toby says it's only been eighteen months since Rupert gave them to him, and that during the Franco-Prussian War, one pigeon remembered its way home after four years' confinement in a palace loft. Besides, he says, he's tried sending messages to Rupert with them before.

"And?" says Veronica.

"Well, I forgot the family'd be at their London house, not in the country, and so . . . but one of the birds got home safely!

We're just not sure how long it took, because Rupert wasn't there to check till a few weeks later."

"A few *weeks*—" Veronica begins, but she restrains herself from saying anything further. Toby looks dreadful. I've never seen him so pale and pinched-looking. He claims his leg is feeling much better this morning, but if that's true, it's only because it must have been agony before.

I have just finished copying identical messages onto five scraps of cigarette paper, inserted them into their little metal cylinders, and attached each to a spindly red pigeon foot. The message is: "SOS Toby FitzOsb gravely ill at Montmaray. Pls. send help." I wanted to put in a "Thank you" in advance, but there wasn't room. At least the sky is clearer today—Veronica found an old book about homing pigeons in the library and it said they can become confused in fog. I'm more concerned about the enormous distance—more than four hundred miles, the first two hundred over sea.

"In 1862," Veronica reads aloud, "a champion bird traveled from Saint-Sébastien to Liège, a distance of six hundred and fifteen miles, in a single day, with more than a dozen other birds released at the same time arriving the very next morning."

Her valiant attempts at cheering us up may have helped Toby—he has fallen asleep at last—but they're not helping me much. I don't think any of Toby's birds are champions. One of them looks as though it has mange. Even if one arrives intact, even if Rupert is at home and is checking the lofts regularly, even if he is able to telephone Aunt Charlotte at once (does she even have a telephone?), even if she is able to bully the English authorities into sending a ship for us in this weather—it could be a week till help arrives. I'm not sure Toby can manage that— I'm not sure *I* can.

Henry has just tiptoed in to say the birds got off safely—she went up on the roof to release them. I've never seen her so subdued. It would be an immense improvement if it weren't so disconcerting, particularly as Rebecca has also stopped talking to us. She isn't even talking to Simon anymore. She's probably sulking about Toby having taken over "His Majesty's" room and Simon agreeing with us about it.

Rebecca really has gone crazy, I'm sure of it. I heard her in her room upstairs yesterday, having what sounded like a loud conversation with Uncle John. Of course, she could have been talking with his ghost. It would be just like him to ignore the rest of us, especially at a time when we're desperate for any help, supernatural or otherwise.

10th January 1937

What a day.

We were startled from our luncheon (all of us except Rebecca perched on chairs around Toby's bed) by the buzzing of an aeroplane engine. My heart immediately leapt into my throat. I'd been too worried about Toby to dwell on Gebhardt's threats—the whole thing had started to seem like a nightmare I'd had months ago—but all my apprehension returned in an instant. Could the Germans have returned by aeroplane? Had they sent *fighter* planes? Judging by Veronica's expression, she was thinking the same thing. But then Henry, who'd dashed out to the kitchen to peer through the doorway, ran back in.

"It's Julia!" she cried. "Julia and Anthony!"

Close enough. It was Anthony. Even Toby, the only one who'd had any faith in the pigeons, was astonished. It had been just twenty-four hours since we'd sent off our SOS.

"Rupert found your birds in the loft this morning—the poor chap's been home with the flu since Christmas," Anthony explained as I pushed a mug of soup into his hands. "I telephoned Julia from Brest this morning, just about to fly home after delivering medical supplies to the boys in Spain—and gosh, Toby, I should have kept some back for *you*, you look absolutely—"

"Never mind about that," said Toby faintly. "How many birds?"

"Oh . . . two, three? Not sure. But there I was, all refueled and ready to take off—more than ready, actually. Had some Fascists take a few potshots at me near Madrid, and those French mechanics are hopeless."

"Oh, Anthony!" I said. "Did they actually hit you?"

"Well, there was a bit of damage," he said. "Need to get her back to England, really, to find out what's what."

"But it's safe to fly now?" asked Veronica anxiously.

"Oh, yes!" said Anthony, a bit too heartily. "Except . . ."

"Except?" urged Veronica.

"Well, she's only a two-seater, you know. Toby, of course— need to evacuate him, but I can't say I feel comfortable leaving you ladies here alone even a day or two with whatever those bloody . . . er, those awful Nazis are planning."

"What?" we all cried. Because we hadn't said anything to Anthony about Otto Rahn or Gebhardt, not one word.

"Er . . . didn't you get Julia's telegram?" he asked.

"We haven't received any mail since Christmas," said Veronica. "We don't get regular deliveries in winter, the weather's too rough."

"Oh," said Anthony. "Er. Right."

"What did it say?" I asked.

"Well, that's the thing. I don't know, exactly. Only that Julia's father—well, you know he's a cousin of Churchill's . . ."

We all nodded impatiently.

"And his brother's something in intelligence and, er, they picked up something about the Germans and Montmaray."

"The Nazis are planning an attack?" said Veronica sharply.

"Well, I don't know an attack, exactly," he said. "Actually, I'm not sure what . . . but it will be fine, I'm sure, if you're out of here by then. I'll fly Toby back and I'm sure we can squash in young Henry. Then I'll come back for all of you ladies straightaway. Or send someone—one of the chaps I was at school with has just bought himself a de Havilland Dragonfly, beautiful twin-engine, seats five."

Toby was shaking his head violently and shoving at the blankets, trying to push himself upright. "No, Ant, take the girls and come back for me."

"Toby, lie down!" said Veronica.

"Simon's here, he can look after me and—"

"No," said Veronica firmly. "You need a doctor. Besides, you're King." She held up a hand as Toby began to protest. "We don't have time to argue about it; it'll be dark in a few hours."

And to everyone's shock, Simon stood up at once. "She's right. Henry, get dressed in your warmest clothes. Sophie, could you pack them some food for the journey? I'll get a stretcher organized. Toby, what do you need from upstairs?"

Sometime in the last few weeks, "capable" has replaced

"handsome" as the attribute I most admire in a man, so I very nearly fell back in love with Simon at that moment, and I thoroughly regret ever having said anything bad about Anthony's mustache. Between them, they got Toby all the way to the aeroplane waiting on the Green, settled him and his strapped leg in a comfortable position, and fitted Henry in beside Toby. Then Simon helped Anthony do something vital regarding the propeller.

Despite the urgency of the situation, it was so hard to let them leave. I couldn't help feeling that I'd never see them again, or that they would never see Montmaray again—a feeling only intensified when Veronica thrust a hastily wrapped bundle at Anthony and asked him to deliver it to Aunt Charlotte.

"Of course," he said. "Er, what is it?"

But the rest of us had already worked it out. It was a collection of the most important pages of her *Brief History of Montmaray*. Henry started howling then and tried to scramble over Toby's lap to throw herself at Veronica. Toby's eyes also started welling up (although that was possibly physical, rather than emotional, pain—there wasn't much room in the cockpit, and Henry wasn't being as careful as she ought). And I sobbed unashamedly into Carlos's fur.

"Oh dear," said Anthony. "Oh dear."

"Anthony, just go!" shouted Veronica, stuffing Henry back into the cockpit. *"Please."*

But Anthony was already pulling down his goggles and fiddling with the controls, and Simon was kicking away the rocks propped in front of the wheels. The plane started to trundle down the Green and we ran for cover, ducking our heads. As before, it seemed impossible that such an enormous, unwieldy machine could lift into the air, but there it went—a hop, another hop, and then it was gathering itself up and soaring off over the island. Within minutes it was impossibly distant, a silvery blur against a leaden sky, and I prayed harder than I ever had before that it would arrive safely.

12th January 1937

I know this journal is important. Keeping a careful record of these last days at Montmaray is my duty—my *only* duty now. But there's nothing to write. We have been waiting for nearly two whole days and still no one has come—neither Germans nor rescuers.

Simon and Veronica spend the time bickering; Rebecca sits and stares into space and mutters away to an invisible companion. I busy myself with housework, despite knowing that it's a complete waste of time and energy. I've also made several half-hearted attempts to pack some essentials into Veronica's satchel in case we need to leave in a hurry. (But what is truly essential? Food? Photographs? Bandages and iodine? And what about all those things that can't fit inside a satchel—the sea monster tapestry, the portraits in the Great Hall, Benedict?) I also showed Simon the entrance to the tunnels in the crypt, in case we need an emergency escape route . . . but truthfully, none of us wants to consider this too deeply, not even Simon. The rest of the day, and long into the night, I read and read till my head aches, hoping to avoid sleep as long as possible. But it's no good. Isabella's always there, waiting for me to close my eyes. It's as though she doesn't ever want me to forget that she's floating below the surface of the bay, the ends of her shawl trailing behind her, her dead eyes open and watchful. What does she *want?* What is she trying to tell me? I feel so terribly sorry for her, but *I* can't do anything to help her.

And now Simon has just stormed through the kitchen and out the door. I can hear the squelch of his boots as he picks his way through the mud of the courtyard—he seems to be heading towards the gatehouse. He's forgotten to take a macintosh and it's raining again. He'll catch his death of cold if he's not careful. And here comes Veronica, equally grim-looking, although at least she has a word for me.

"Library," she says. Now she's disappeared, too.

Oh, this is *mad.* I'm going to go upstairs to sort through my clothes and decide . . .

What's that noise? It sounds like . . . Now Simon's running in, he's shouting, it's . . .

Aeroplanes. Seven. German.

We are in the firewood cave. The tide is rising. The waves lap at the rocks, inches below us. I write this by the last slanting rays of afternoon light—in English, as you can see, not Kernetin, because I want whoever finds this journal to know what happened to us.

The German aeroplanes came from the south, early this afternoon. They swooped low over the island, the village their immediate target. Veronica, on the top floor of the library tower, saw the first bomb hit. She said it not so much fell as seemed to be drawn down, as though George's cottage had hooked it on a line and reeled it in. She saw the cottage walls bulge and shatter before the explosion reached her ears; by that time, she'd already snatched up the King James Bible and was hurling herself down the stairs and out the door.

We all raced into the chapel, clutching whatever we'd had close at hand—this journal, in my case. Simon scooped up my half-packed satchel; Rebecca had a blanket around her shoulders; I dragged Carlos along. Veronica pushed the Bible towards me and turned to run back into the Great Hall for Benedict, but Simon grabbed her arm.

"No!" he roared. "No time! Get down!"

And he was right: the engines were whining louder and louder. I looked up through the stained-glass window just as the leading aeroplane roared over the courtyard. A white flash lit up the gatehouse, and the drawbridge folded up and plummeted into the Chasm. The noise was like nothing I'd ever experienced. It was more than noise; it was a rush of fury, a shock wave that set all the bones in my skull vibrating. Just as I threw my arms over my face, the glass exploded into a storm of glittering jewels. Then I felt someone tug me around the altar and suddenly we were stumbling down into the crypt, groping our way through the darkness as crashes far above us shook the pillars and the floor. Carlos pressed close to my legs, trembling all over.

"Sophia!" I heard Simon bellow. "Over here!"

Veronica had located Benedict's tomb, and they were tugging at the lid. Already, acrid smoke and the powdery smell of crushed stone were filtering into the crypt. Veronica vaulted down into the tunnel first; then Simon helped his mother over the edge of the tomb. I gave Carlos a leg up and a shove, then stuck my journal in the waistband of my skirt and followed him. Landing awkwardly on one ankle, I set off at a limping crouch, Simon so close behind me that I could feel his heart hammering against my back.

It was quieter down there, with only a dull rumbling and an occasional thud to remind us of the destruction going on above. Not being able to see what was happening only made it worse, though. I was terrified that the next hit would bring hundreds of tons of rock crashing down upon us. We reached the place where the tunnel split in two and turned left, our path twisting and sloping downwards. My feet slid about on the slippery rock. Behind me, Simon cracked his head against the roof and swore. All at once, Carlos stopped, so abruptly that I tumbled over his back and into Rebecca. Looking ahead, I could see the glow of daylight outlining the walls of the tunnel.

"Where are we?" Simon shouted.

I could hear the crash of the ocean, could taste it in the dank air. With a thrill of horror, I realized that we'd trapped ourselves in a tunnel that led straight into the Chasm. The tide was rising—we could drown here or climb back up into the castle to burn to death, if we weren't crushed to pulp first. I must have whimpered; Simon put a hand on my shoulder.

"Move over, I'm going through to the front," he said. "Veronica!"

But there was barely enough room for me to turn around. There was no chance Simon could squeeze past. At any rate, we soon heard Veronica's voice.

"What?" shouted Simon. "What did she say?"

"We're below the drawbridge," I relayed. "Not far from the firewood cave."

"How far above the water?" asked Simon.

"A foot or so," came Veronica's reply. Then, "There's a ledge. I'll try to reach the cave."

"Veronica!" I screamed. "Don't!" Now that we were close to the open air, the whine of the planes had become audible once more. I imagined a pilot spotting her tiny figure and veering round to capture her in his sights.

"Damn it!" said Simon. "I should have gone first."

At our urging, Rebecca crawled forward a bit and flattened herself against the rock. Craning my neck over her shoulder, I was able to see a little more. From the tunnel mouth, a narrow ledge, overhung with tatters of drawbridge, wound itself up towards the castle. Veronica had squeezed herself onto the ledge and was peering ahead.

"Well?" said Simon into my ear. "What do you think?"

All I could think was how grateful I was that Toby, with his broken leg, and Henry, my reckless little sister, didn't have to face this. Veronica glanced over her shoulder, noticed my frantic waving, and edged backwards. We ended up in an awkward huddle at the tunnel mouth, Rebecca and I squashed in the middle.

"We can reach the firewood cave," Veronica said. "That ledge is a foot wide."

I disagreed vehemently. It was more like eight inches, and bits of it were missing altogether. "And they're bombing directly above it!" I cried. "They'll see us!"

"No, they won't, not from above, not with that rock overhang," said Veronica. "And the Chasm's too narrow for them to fly through."

"But the cave will still flood at high tide," I argued. "And—"

"And we need to get to the *other* side of the Chasm," put in Simon impatiently. "The castle's too dangerous, even if we could reach it from here—all that falling rock, those unexploded bombs—and besides, the boats are both tied up near the village."

"Why didn't I think of that?" said Veronica. "Let's just take a stroll across the drawbridge, shall we? Oh, I forgot, it's been *completely destroyed!*"

An involuntary sound, almost a laugh, emerged from my mouth—even in mortal peril, Simon and Veronica were still managing to snipe at each other.

"Don't be stupid!" snapped Simon. "That raft of Henry's is in the cave—we'll cross the Chasm on it, keep close to the rock on the other side, then steer around to the cove where the boats are."

I turned, as much as I was able, to stare at him. It was a plan worthy of Henry herself. It was completely insane. However, we couldn't stay squashed in the tunnel forever, not with the waves surging towards our feet as we spoke. The only real question was whether to wait for the planes to stop or not. The bombardment seemed to have been going on forever, although it had probably been no more than ten minutes. I found it hard to believe it would ever stop, but Simon pointed out that they would run out of bombs or fuel eventually. After a bit more heated argument, Veronica told us she was going on ahead and stepped back out onto the ledge before I could try to stop her.

I shoved Rebecca aside at once and craned my neck after Veronica. I was suddenly aware of the frantic thud of my pulse in my ears, and it was this that made me realize the engine noise had died down. It sounded as though a couple of the planes had peeled off from the rest and flown away while we'd been arguing. There hadn't been any really loud thuds for a while, either. Still, I had more than bombs to worry about as I monitored each careful step of Veronica's. At one terrifying point, her foot slipped off the ledge and she staggered sideways, managing only at the last moment to fling herself back against the cliff face. But at last she scrambled up into the cave, reappearing a moment later to beckon us up.

Rebecca went next, with a sure-footedness that surprised me

until I considered she'd spent more time on this island than any of the rest of us. Simon and I then resolved that I should lead Carlos (who, with his tail tucked between his hind legs, looked decidedly unenthusiastic about the plan), with Simon prodding Carlos along from behind.

I sent up a silent prayer and stepped out onto the ledge. Carlos took a mouthful of my skirt and whined, trying to tug me back. I murmured some rather unconvincing encouragement and started to inch along sideways. I pressed as much of my back as possible against the cliff face, one hand fumbling for the next rock hold, the other stretched out and clenched in Carlos's scruff. I dared not look down into the churning water, or up at the sky, or anywhere else except at my feet. One or two planes still roared overhead, to Carlos's distress—at one point, he halted in midstep and refused to go on. We cowered there together, frozen in place, for what felt like whole minutes, until Simon screamed at us and I managed to lift one foot and move it a few inches in the right direction. A couple of yards on, I was forced to crouch as I passed under the place where the remains of the drawbridge were still attached. Then finally, finally, I was clambering up the last rock. I took hold of Carlos and pulled while Simon gave him a push from below; then all at once the three of us were in a shaking heap on the cave floor.

Somewhere above us came another crash, and we scuttled for the furthest corner of the cave, Veronica's arms reaching out and hauling me to safety. Huddled beside her, I buried my face in Carlos's neck, inhaling his familiar wet-dog scent and trying very hard not to sob. I knew that if I started, I might never manage to stop.

"Listen," said Simon at last. The roar of the planes was a low drone; the last three were flying away.

"But will they come back?" I said, raising my head. Surely Gebhardt had had enough vengeance by now. "They won't want to destroy the whole island, will they?"

No one answered. I looked around. Veronica and Simon were now bent over Henry's raft in the corner, examining it with near-identical expressions of disapproval (the two of them looking more than ever like brother and sister). The raft was slightly longer than it was wide and made entirely of flotsam and jetsam—curved planks that seemed to have come from a boat, a dismantled tea chest, some thick branches that were almost logs—all of it lashed together with old rope and fishing line and even bits of fishing net. There had been an attempt to insert a mast in the middle, but all that remained was a jagged hole.

"Hopeless," murmured Veronica. I suspect it was only habit that made Simon argue with her.

"Look, there's some rope attached," he said. "We could throw it onto a bit of the cliff on the other side of the Chasm and pull ourselves . . ." His voice trailed away. The other side of the Chasm is mostly sheer cliff face, and even if it weren't, it's doubtful the rope would reach that far or that any of us would be able to toss it so accurately. And the water is far too deep and turbulent for even the strongest swimmer. Veronica immediately pointed this out.

And since then, for the past hour or so, Simon and Veronica have been arguing about the best way to improve the raft's seaworthiness as they fiddle round with spare planks, bits of rope, and the firewood ax.

Meanwhile, I've been sitting here, writing frantically, as Rebecca has an impassioned conversation with thin air . . .

We eventually agreed we had to do *something*, with the tide rising and no food and no fresh water, and the castle end of the tunnel probably buried under rubble by now. There was nothing else for it. I helped Veronica and Simon carry the overhauled raft to the edge of the rock and slide it on top of the water. It listed a bit to one side as it bobbed up and down, but it stayed afloat.

"It won't hold all of us, though," warned Simon.

"Carlos can swim beside it," said Veronica, and Carlos, back to his old self now the aeroplanes had gone, thumped his tail. "You take one of us and come back for the others in the boat."

"I'll take Mother—" Simon began.

"No," said Veronica at once. I could tell what she was thinking—that the two of them would take the rowboat and leave us here to die.

Simon must have gathered this, too. He flushed and clenched his jaw. "Fine," he said. "Sophia's the smallest, I'll take her."

At some point in the past, I might have dreamt of Simon choosing me above everyone else; of Simon and me together, alone in a boat as sunset drew close. But I looked at the raft and all I could think was, "They went to sea in a Sieve, they did. In a Sieve they went to sea! And when the Sieve turned round and round, everyone cried, 'You'll all be drowned . . .'"

"Perhaps we should just wait here a bit longer," I remember saying feebly, but no one paid me any notice and the next thing I knew I was crawling towards Simon, who was kneeling in the middle of the raft and holding out a hand to steady me. The raft dipped under our weight, sending icy water sloshing over our calves. Then Carlos leapt into the sea with a great splash, drenching both of us. I turned quickly to Veronica, intending to give her my precious journal for safekeeping, but already the current had wrenched us away.

"Veronica!" I screamed.

"See you soon!" she shouted bravely. She raised her arm in farewell. It cast a long shadow—the sun was sinking. I hurriedly stuffed my journal back in my waistband, pulling my damp jersey over the top of it. Beside me, Simon was lying flat, trying to steer with a long plank, but it was no good—the water was too deep, the swirling currents too strong, the walls of the Chasm now out of reach. Everything was moving much too fast. My stomach heaved in protest.

"We'll just have to wait till we reach a smooth spot," Simon panted, dragging his makeshift paddle up. "Then try and steer towards the other wall . . . Aarrgh!"

A rush of dark water came at us just as another wave slammed into us from the side, and suddenly we were whirling around wildly, clutching at each other and at the edges of the raft with numb fingers. Like the Jumblies, my head was green and my hands were blue, except in my case it was from seasickness and cold. I retched and shivered as wave after wave of salt water slopped over the tilting surface to which we clung. At one point, I felt even death might be preferable to much more of this.

Mustn't give up, have to get to the boat, for Veronica's sake, I told myself, over and over again. Then I remembered Carlos.

"Carlos?" I spluttered. "Where . . . ?"

"Look out!" cried Simon, and jerking around, I saw a black cliff looming towards us with frightening speed. Dizzy, not even sure which side of the Chasm it was, I flung out the paddle to stop us crashing headfirst into the rock. The paddle snagged, held for a second, then snapped like a twig. We spun around and glanced against the cliff face, the raft shuddering beneath us. I flung myself sideways. Grabbing a jutting rock, I clung on grimly until somehow, miraculously, the raft managed to wedge one corner of itself into a crevice.

"Well done," said Simon weakly, raising himself to his knees. I turned around and stared in horror. The firewood cave was hidden from view, but far behind us, on the other side of the Chasm, lay the smoking ruins of the castle. The bombs had finished the job Napoleon had begun on the curtain walls. The gatehouse was missing its roof and leaned precariously into the courtyard. The top of the library tower had disappeared. I thought of the little black cat, the nanny goat I'd left tethered by the cucumber frames, the hens, Spartacus. I closed my eyes, overwhelmed with grief.

Then there was a splash beside me and Carlos slopped his heavy paws onto the raft.

"Oh, Carlos!" I sobbed, hugging his sleek head. "You made it!"

"We almost didn't," Simon said, pointing over my shoulder. Another ten yards and we would have been at the open mouth of the Chasm and headed out into the deep blue waters.

"Now what?" I said, wiping my face with my sleeve. It seemed that any sudden movement would send us back into the maelstrom. But the cliff was craggier here, with sharp rocks to loop our rope over or cling to with our fingertips, and slowly, painfully, we made our way around the curve of the cliff, Carlos bobbing beside us. At last we reached a spot where it was possible to clamber onto the rocks. We hauled the raft above the high-tide mark in case we needed it later (although I had no intention of setting so much as a toe on it ever again), and we crawled and crawled until we reached the top. I collapsed in the prickly grass while Carlos shook himself vigorously. Turning over onto my back, I was amazed to discover that my journal had survived the trip, thanks to the leather cover. It was a bit damp and the ink had blurred at the edges, but it was still legible, mostly. I was less surprised to see that my fingernails were shredded and my palms scored with gashes, although I felt no pain, my hands, and indeed most of the rest of me, being numb with cold.

"We'd better get on," said Simon. The sun was close to the horizon, sending out streaks of red and orange through the clouds. Alarmed at how dark it had grown in the past few minutes, I let him tug me to my feet, and together we stumbled off towards the village. It looked more abandoned than ever, with only a few cottages still intact. The wharf was undamaged, but the gig was at the bottom of the bay. The *Queen Clementine*, though, had fortuitously been pulled up behind a boulder. We even found a spare set of oars.

"We'd better have a look in the cottages, see if we can salvage anything," said Simon. Alice's cottage was lopsided, one wall battered and the roof fallen in at one end, but we managed to find matches, candles, and a flask. We filled the flask from the water tank, having a deep drink ourselves first, then turned to retrace our path to the boat.

Night had fallen by that stage. There was a sprinkling of stars and a curve of white moon, but the cloud cover was thick and the breeze kept snuffing out the candle that Simon had lit. We stumbled along, pitching into rabbit holes and tripping over rocks, guided largely by Carlos. Finally we reached the rowboat and tugged it down to the water's edge.

Relieved that at least it wasn't raining, I grasped the oars, wincing as the splinters cut into my grazed palms. Simon offered his handkerchief to bind them, but certain his hands were in even worse shape, I refused. We pushed off, Carlos at the prow, Simon and I each with a pair of oars, and started back the way we had come. But the tide had reached its height and the currents were against us. Worse, in the darkness we had to rely on the sound of the waves against the rocks to navigate. If we were to drift too close to the cliff, we'd gouge a hole in our hull; too far away and we'd risk being swept off into the open sea. And after each stroke of the oars, I stiffened, straining my ears for the faint drone of an aeroplane, Anthony or the Germans, either one. I heard nothing, though—nothing but the crash of the waves and the increasing whine of the wind. Then we reached the churning mouth of the Chasm and I had to give up on listening for aeroplanes because I needed to put every bit of energy into heaving at the oars. A red pain flared in my shoulders and burnt down my spine; my thighs ached; my hands felt rubbed raw.

"Where *are* we?" muttered Simon.

After ten minutes of rowing, we seemed to have made little progress; indeed, we'd been whirled about so thoroughly I wouldn't have been surprised to find we were now heading back where we'd come from. The darkness was even denser now that we were surrounded by tall cliffs that shut out the stars and the moon. I peered ahead, hoping to catch sight of the ruined drawbridge, but saw nothing I recognized.

Simon cupped his hands around his mouth. "Mother! Veronica!" he shouted. We waited, shaking with tension and cold. "Did you hear something?" he asked.

I nudged Carlos with my foot. "Woof!" he said.

"Wait, was that . . . ?"

"Woof! Woof!"

"Soph?" came a faint cry.

"Quiet, Carlos!" I said. "Veronica!"

"Keep shouting!" yelled Simon. The voice seemed to be coming from behind us, to the left. We wrenched hard on the oars and hauled the boat around. Before long we were passing under the dangling remnants of the drawbridge (I wasn't sure how we'd missed it the first time) and the firewood cave emerged in the gloom. It was already knee-deep in water; Veronica and Rebecca had climbed onto a rock ledge, but were soaked. There was nowhere for us to tie up, but we managed to get close enough for the two of them to clamber in.

"Worried you wouldn't make it back . . . till daylight," murmured Veronica. She was clutching her satchel and her eyes were closed. Rebecca had quickly crawled to the furthest point of the rowboat from Veronica and was now an unmoving, blanket-swaddled lump.

"Mother?" said Simon, but Rebecca stayed obstinately silent. Neither of them had expressed any gratitude for their rescue, marveled at our bravery, or offered to take over the oars. I felt a bit put out. Simon must have felt the same way. He sighed heavily. "Well, come on, then," he said to me.

And we rowed back to the cove, a far easier task now that we were moving with the current. I gave Veronica a brief account of our adventures, but she seemed to have fallen asleep and I was too busy with the oars to shake her awake. I felt more and more disgruntled. It wasn't terribly late, after all, and sitting in a cave for an hour or so shouldn't have been all that tiring for her. We finally reached the cove, and Simon leapt overboard to pull us in.

"Veronica, wake up," I snapped, dropping my oars with a clunk. The cloud had peeled away from the moon and a faint silvery light now reflected off the water. Veronica was revealed as a pale figure slumped against the side of the boat. "Veronica?" I said, grasping her shoulder.

She murmured something. I bent over and touched her cheek. Her skin was icy. "What . . . ?" I started, and then I saw that her jersey was damp with something darker than water.

"Simon!" I screamed. "*Simon!* Rebecca, what happened? What did you do to her?"

I pulled Veronica upright and she winced, cradling her right arm. I reached for it, shoving aside the ripped sleeve. Blood pulsed from a gash along her wrist. There were more cuts crossing her palm.

"Simon!" I shrieked again, but he was already splashing over, taking in the scene in an instant. He tore at his shirttails as I sloshed handfuls of seawater over the wound—I had the idea that it was antiseptic—and together we wrapped a makeshift bandage around her arm as tight as it would go.

"Let's get her out of here," said Simon, and we pulled Veronica free of the boat, onto the rocks. Rebecca had wandered off towards the cottages and I felt a surge of rage—*she* was responsible for this, I knew. I had no energy to waste on her, though, not just then. I propped Veronica up, held the flask to her blue lips, and made her swallow some water. Then I tried to rub some warmth into her other limbs while Simon secured the boat and retrieved the satchel.

"How's she doing?" he said, dropping down beside me a few minutes later.

"Fine," said Veronica weakly.

He snorted. Together, we dragged her up and staggered off to the remains of Alice's cottage, which seemed like the best shelter we'd find tonight. Rebecca was already there, crouched by the door and poking through the clutter. I snatched her damp blanket away, tucked it round Veronica, and settled us both in the corner furthest from the damaged wall. Carlos curled himself around her and whined.

"What happened?" I snarled over my shoulder at Rebecca. "How long has she been like this?"

"Mother?" said Simon. But she was ignoring him, too. "Look," he said to me quietly, "we'll sort it out in the morning, I'm sure it was just some sort of accident."

"No," mumbled Veronica; "came at me . . ."

"Does she have a knife?" I whispered urgently.

Veronica shook her head. "Ax . . . threw it . . . in the water." The bandage had already soaked through, and she was shivering violently. I tried to remember the best treatment for blood loss, but beef tea and a warm bed were all that came to mind.

"Light a fire," I told Simon, but the fireplace had been destroyed, there was no dry wood, and the wind whistling through the broken wall would have snuffed a fire out in an instant.

Simon muttered something about the next morning and pass-ing ships.

"What passing ships?" I shouted. "There aren't any, not any-more! And we need help *now*! Your crazy mother's ready to mur-der us in our sleep—that's if we don't die of cold first or the Germans don't come back to finish us off!" And I broke into jagged sobs then, unable to voice my worst fear—that Veron-ica's life was trickling away as I watched. Carlos leaned over her and started licking my face.

"Look, there's nothing else I can do!" said Simon, clutching at his hair. "Nothing!" At that, Rebecca rose to her feet and staggered off outside. "Oh, for God's sake!" he burst out, and he turned on his heel and went after her.

I sniffled, pushed Carlos away, and wiped my face. Dragging the satchel nearer, I saw that Veronica had stashed the Bible in it. I would gladly have used it to light a fire, but even it was damp. Beneath that were more useless objects—my parents' wedding photograph, some handkerchiefs that were too small to serve as proper bandages, a comb. At the bottom were some peppermints left over from the Christmas hamper. I tried to feed them to Veronica, but she lolled against my shoulder, impossi-ble to rouse. I choked back another sob and fumbled at her neck for her pulse. It was slow and weak.

Then Simon crashed back into the cottage.

"Ship!" he panted. "About a mile off!"

My heart clenched. "The Germans!" I said. "They've come back to see what their bombs did!"

"No, no," said Simon impatiently, jerking at my arm, "Come and see!"

"But . . . oh, all right! Carlos, *stay*." And with a backwards look at Veronica, I stumbled off after Simon, who still had a bruising grip on my elbow. The moon was higher and brighter, tracing a broken path across the rough sea and illuminating a small black ship. The outline was vaguely familiar and I was sure Henry could have identified it at a glance. But was it Otto Rahn's ship, its blue swastika flapping like a skull and crossbones? Or something else—one of the fishing trawlers that used to pass by regularly, an American cabin cruiser, a cargo steamer?

"She's coming closer," said Simon. The captain seemed to have some idea of what he was about—he was steering clear of the treacherous shoal a half mile off South Head. "She's definitely heading towards us."

Was it a friend or an enemy? We had no choice—we had to take a chance. We turned and ran back to the cottage. Simon hoisted Veronica over his shoulder while I grabbed the satchel and Carlos.

"Mother?" called Simon. As far as I was concerned, Rebecca could stay on the island and rot, but it turned out she had wandered off towards the rowboat. She even helped Simon drag it into the water and, at his urging, took up a pair of oars.

"Hurry," I moaned, cradling Veronica's head in my lap. The rest of her lay crumpled on the floor of the boat, covered in the blanket. Carlos scrambled over us to take up his favorite position at the prow and we heaved off. If it came to the worst, I thought savagely, if the ship turned out to be full of Nazis, at least he'd manage to take a few bloody chunks out of them before they shot us. Meanwhile, Simon and Rebecca were battling the waves. Beyond the cove, they rose like white-tipped mountains, whipped into enormous peaks by the increasing gale. The boat felt as flimsy as paper as we slammed down into a trough and then were tossed into the air. One of Simon's oars was torn from his grasp.

"It's no use!" he cried. "We'll never make it!"

It was terrible. It was as bad as the day we'd buried George.

It was the stuff of nightmares.

I leaned over the side of the boat, as I'd done so many times before in my dreams, but I wasn't scared this time. I was furious.

"Damn you!" I screamed into the wind and the water. "Don't you *dare* try to stop us!" A wave reached up and slapped me in the face. "Isabella!" I shouted, leaning over further. "Don't let them!"

And perhaps it was my imagination, but the wave that surged up behind us at that moment seemed to push us closer to the ship. I peered down into the depths and saw a pale shape glide beneath us.

"Isabella!" I screamed. "Help us! Help *her*!" Veronica stirred in my lap. I was vaguely aware of Rebecca starting to flail at me, of Simon twisting in his seat trying to restrain her, but I ignored them, focusing on the damp wood under my fingernails and the black, swirling waters. The boat had shifted sideways now, and wave after wave was urging us on. I stared down into the sea.

"Thank you," I whispered.

The pale shape sank lower and lower, and then it was gone. I glanced up, swiping impatiently at my wet face. The lights of the ship were brighter than ever. I could hear the thrum of an engine idling down to a stutter, men shouting in a language I couldn't understand, the clatter of chains against a metal hull. A wave swamped us, then another, but we were almost there. A rope landed with a wet thud at Simon's feet. He threaded it through the metal loop at the prow, cursing his frozen fingers, and then we were being hauled on, faster and faster. The moon was blotted out as blackness rose above us, as we bumped gently against the towering hull. I could smell rust and oil and engine fuel.

"Let go," said Simon, trying to peel Veronica away from me, but I only clung to her harder, and in the end they hauled us both up together in a canvas sling. We were lowered onto the deck, into a huddle of men.

"Please," I said, grasping the nearest sleeve. "She needs a doctor, her arm . . ."

A bearded face pushed itself forward. I peered up at the man and I almost sobbed with relief.

It was the Basque captain.

14th? January 1937

I never would have imagined that motorcars were so noisy. They're quite cold, too, even though Aunt Charlotte's chauffeur has given Veronica and me enormous furs to wrap around ourselves and Carlos is stretched out on the floor, acting as a very heavy foot warmer. Simon and Rebecca are sitting in the front of the car, yards away, separated by a set of windows with velvet curtains. I wonder if it's warmer where they are. It's such an exhilarating experience, though, driving along in a car! I don't think I've ever traveled so fast and so smoothly. Even with my head bent over my journal, I'm not feeling the slightest bit seasick—I mean, roadsick. Landsick. Whatever it's called.

The car's not the only exhilarating experience, though. There are electric streetlights each time we drive through a town, and rows of very tall trees, and once a passenger train running on tracks alongside the road. The windows were lit up and there were hundreds of people sitting inside. It was quite overwhelming—until that moment, I'd only ever seen a dozen people at a time in one place. I wish Veronica were awake so I could point out things and exclaim over them with her. There was a moment when we halted abruptly at some traffic lights and she was jolted awake. She glanced around, bewildered. Then she caught sight of me, said, "Oh, Sophie, *you're* here," and slumped back against me. So although it makes me very sleepy just watching her, I am determined to stay awake. Someone needs to be in charge, in case anything happens. It's about time it was me.

Veronica still looks unnaturally pale, but her pulse is good and there is no fever at all. We have the Basque captain's first mate to thank for that. He cleaned her arm, stitched it together neatly, and kept checking on her bandages. He even fixed my own hands (there were a few grazes and torn fingernails from all that adventuring Simon and I did). Then Captain Zuleta himself gave up his cabin for us, and insisted on making a detour so he could deliver us to the nearest English port. I always did say he was a nice man, and it's lovely to be proved right.

It was Anthony who sent him to our rescue. It turns out his aeroplane made it back to England but only just (the Dratted Engine, again), and none of the pilots he knew wanted to risk a flight to Montmaray with the storms that were forecast. So Anthony telephoned Julia from the airstrip and Julia contacted her uncle, who knew someone high up in the navy, who put out a signal that was picked up by the Basque captain, whose ship happened to be the closest to Montmaray.

But why had he chosen to sail through waters so treacherous when there were safer routes northward? I like to think

Isabella had some part to play in that. I think she was watching out for Veronica. And I wonder if it was mere coincidence that Rebecca lost her footing as she started to climb the ladder up to the ship's deck? It was only Simon's quick reflexes that saved her from slipping beneath the hull. It's interesting, that's all I'm saying, given how surefooted she was along the cliff ledge. I think I'll share my thoughts on the matter with Veronica after she wakes up, when she's feeling more herself. Of course, once she's feeling more herself, she'll probably scoff at the idea that we were saved by her dead mother. But then I'll say, "There are more things in heaven and earth, Veronica, than are dreamt of in your philosophy." After all, I was there; I saw it, I felt it. And one can't really argue with Shakespeare.

On the subject of arguments, I was all for calling the police and having Rebecca arrested the moment we set foot on land, but Simon managed to talk me out of it. He said it was pointless until Veronica was feeling better and could make a formal statement; besides, he was sure that it had been an accident. I suppose I can't expect him to say anything else. People can be very stubborn when it comes to their mothers. At least Captain Zuleta took me seriously, for all my difficulties making myself understood in English—he had Rebecca placed under some sort of Captain's Arrest and locked in a cabin far away from ours once he realized how Veronica had been injured. I think Henry's claims about his being in love with Veronica may have had some truth to them—he kept making excuses to hover around Veronica, even though she wasn't doing anything but sleeping.

The rest of the crew fell in love with Carlos. They chatted away to him in their various languages and kept feeding him bits of their meals. No one fell in love with me, thank heavens. I think I've had enough of love for the moment, it causes such problems. I'll wait and see what I feel for Simon in the weeks to come, but I hope I'll be more Sensible about him from now on. Living with Aunt Charlotte should make it easier—she'll probably lock me in my bedroom for the rest of my life if she suspects anything unseemly. Besides, I'll probably be meeting lots of other, more suitable, young gentlemen now . . .

Oh dear, the road's grown bumpy, which makes writing rather difficult. We've turned in past a pair of gateposts with some strange stone creatures curled up on top . . . Good heavens, they're sea monsters! Are we here at last?

Veronica is stirring now. This gravel drive seems to go on for miles and miles, but now the trees beside us are thinning, and oh, there's the most *enormous* white rectangle of a house, with hundreds of windows blazing at us in the early morning sun. The car is curving around a fountain (yet another sea monster, this one erupting from the pool) and we're crunching to a stop in front of a long colonnade.

And the front doors have burst open and Henry, looking most peculiar in a kilt, is rushing towards us, followed more slowly by Toby on crutches and a very tall blond man dressed in black, who I think might be the butler. A couple of women in black frocks and starched white aprons have also appeared to help Veronica out of the car. Henry is rolling around on the manicured lawn with Carlos, who is emitting little yelps of joy. Toby is leaning on his crutches and trying to hug Veronica, and Simon is issuing orders to the butler, and Rebecca has wandered off down the drive . . .

Well. Here I sit in a beautiful drawing room, my journal balanced on my knee, as I wait for the doctor to come downstairs. Above me dangles an electric chandelier, brighter than a thousand candles. The footman has just put another log on the roaring fire, and a maid has set a steaming teacup on the table. There are thick windows that keep out the drafts, heavy brocade curtains, a soft woolen rug underfoot—so why am I shivering? Is it that this feels like a dream, that I'm frightened I'll wake and find everything has disappeared? Or is it that this is all *too* real? For so long, I've imagined being here—and now it feels wrong. I wanted to come here, but not like *this*. Not as a refugee, cast out into an exile that may last forever . . .

For does Montmaray even exist anymore? Each tick of the exquisite ormolu clock beside me seems to nudge Montmaray a little further into the past. Already it seems an eternity ago that I ran down the cliff path towards the village, the tall purple grass scratching my bare legs, George looking up from his fishing nets to wave at me. Isabella is there, too, in that vanished Eden. She's laughing and batting down her long skirt as it swirls in the sea breeze, and Uncle John is standing by the rocks, gazing at her. And there's my mother, touching my father's cheek as he leans into her embrace, and she glances over and smiles at me and how could I *ever* have imagined I'd forgotten her? Because there she is, each time I catch sight of myself in the looking glass—the same wide blue eyes, the same quiet smile. She's been there all along, and Montmaray will be, too, no matter what happens to it. For we carry what we love inside us, always.

And if, by chance, I was ever to start to forget, here is my journal—somewhat sea-stained, it's true, but still readable. And very nearly complete, because I've just turned to the final page. One last sheet of parchment, waiting for my pen-and-ink wisdom . . . but now the doctor is in the hall and I can hear Aunt Charlotte's imperious tones. Henry has run in and is tugging at my elbow and shouting the doctor's report in my ear. Veronica will be fine, Henry says.

". . . and, Sophie, you *have* to come upstairs at once and look at where Aunt Charlotte has put you, right across from my room, and oh, *wait* till you see Toby's dressing room, it's got a *safe* hidden behind a portrait and a—"

"Now, Henry," says Toby, appearing in the doorway. "Give Sophie a moment. She's *writing*."

Toby's correct; it's very important I finish this final page of my own brief history of Montmaray. History, I've learnt, can take many forms. I flash a reassuring smile at Henry and she's off again, dashing back into the hall. Toby rolls his eyes at me and grins, and there's another reminder of what I've lost and what remains, because Toby's the very image of our father. Just as Aunt Charlotte has Uncle John's flashing eyes and imposing height. I am just a *tiny* bit shy about going into the hall to join her . . . No, I'm not, that would be silly. I mean, after all, she's *family*.

Here I go, then.

I take a deep breath, scenting not salt and sand, but hot-house roses and velvet upholstery and lemon furniture polish. And now I will close up my book and stand, my chin as high as Queen Matilda's, and I will step bravely into my terrifying, exciting future.

Author's Note

This novel is a blend of historical fact and imaginative fiction. Real people and groups mentioned include King Henry VIII, Catherine Howard, Queen Elizabeth I, Fabergé, the Romanovs, the Bolsheviks, Salazar, Franco, King Alfonso XIII, William of Normandy, Napoleon, Henry St. John, the Marquis de Torcy, Hitler, Mussolini, Marx, Stalin, von Ribbentrop, the Mitford girls, King Edward VIII, Wallis Simpson, Churchill, Oswald Mosley, the British Union of Fascists, Freud, Mrs. Beeton, Otto Rahn, the Deutsches Ahnenerbe, Wolfram Sievers, Himmler, the SS, the Cathars, the Druids, Wagner, the Salian Franks, King Edward III, and Oscar Wilde. However, the FitzOsbornes and any other characters who appear in the story are figments of my imagination.

Similarly, although Montmaray does not exist, many of the events mentioned in the novel did occur. These include the Battle of Hastings, Catherine Howard's beheading, the defeat of the Spanish Armada, the War of the Spanish Succession, the Battle of Malplaquet, the Treaty of Utrecht, Napoleon's invasion of the Peninsula, the Great War of 1914–1918, the influenza epidemic of 1918, the stock market crash of 1929, the burning of the Reichstag, the Spanish Civil War, and the abdication of King Edward VIII.

The incident of the Communist protesters getting lost on the way to Downing Street and having to ask a policeman for directions comes from Jessica Mitford's memoir, *Hons and Rebels*. The libel case involving Gef the Talking Mongoose is described in *The Long*

Week-end: A Social History of Great Britain 1918–1939, by Robert Graves and Alan Hodge.

Other information about life in the 1930s came from several books by Anne de Courcy, including *1939: The Last Season* and *Society's Queen: The Life of Edith, Marchioness of Londonderry*, and from biographies of the Mitfords, including *Life in a Cold Climate* by Laura Thompson and *The House of Mitford* by Jonathan Guinness with Catherine Guinness. *The Story of Cornwall*, by A. K. Hamilton Jenkin, provided useful information about Cornish customs, including the engraving on the hurling ball. *The National Trust Book of British Castles* by Paul Johnson, *Geraldene Holt's Complete Book of Herbs*, and "Homing Pigeons" by E. S. Starr (an article published in the magazine *The Century* in July 1886) were also invaluable sources.

Quotes from the following poems and plays were used:

"The Bell-Buoy" by Rudyard Kipling (p. 21)

Hamlet by William Shakespeare (p. 52 and p. 290)

The Tempest by William Shakespeare (p. 121)

"Lady Clara Vere de Vere" by Alfred, Lord Tennyson (p. 127)

"The Holy Grail" by Alfred, Lord Tennyson (p. 161)

"The Passing of Arthur" by Alfred, Lord Tennyson (p. 172)

"The Jumblies" by Edward Lear (p. 276)

I'd also like to thank Zoe Walton, Zoë Sadokierski, and the rest of the team at Random House Australia; Nancy Siscoe and the team at Knopf; and Rachel Skinner, Rick Raftos, and Catherine Drayton.